THE TWENTY-FIRST MAN

THE TWENTY-FIRST MAN

Eric Manasse

iUniverse, Inc.
New York Lincoln Shanghai

The Twenty-First Man

Copyright © 2006 by Eric Manasse

All rights reserved. No part of this book may be used or reproduced by any means, graphic, electronic, or mechanical, including photocopying, recording, taping or by any information storage retrieval system without the written permission of the publisher except in the case of brief quotations embodied in critical articles and reviews.

iUniverse books may be ordered through booksellers or by contacting:

iUniverse
2021 Pine Lake Road, Suite 100
Lincoln, NE 68512
www.iuniverse.com
1-800-Authors (1-800-288-4677)

ISBN-13: 978-0-595-39128-8 (pbk)
ISBN-13: 978-0-595-83514-0 (ebk)
ISBN-10: 0-595-39128-1 (pbk)
ISBN-10: 0-595-83514-7 (ebk)

Printed in the United States of America

"A nation can survive its fools, and even the ambitious. But it cannot survive treason from within."

—Marcus Tullius Cicero, 42 B.C.

CHAPTER 1

Kabul, Afghanistan, December 15, 2001.

The driver of the black Ford SUV dodged the last escaping Taliban fighters in the chaotic streets of Kabul. Overhead the drone of unmanned U.S. predator planes and Apache helicopters lit up the dark night sky of the Afghan capital. Inside the speeding SUV, the nervous passengers were still incredulous that their forces had collapsed so astonishingly fast. The army of deceased anti-Taliban resistance leader, Ahmad Shah Massoud, combined with the Americans Rangers, had overwhelmed the Taliban fighters across the entire front line. The collapse was complete and American soldiers and their allied warlord forces were already within the walls of the ancient Afghan city.

"*Jahllah, bibi, jhallah* (faster, faster)," Mullah Mohammed Omar, former leader of the collapsing Taliban army, said to the driver. They were heading to the only remaining road open that led to the mountains outside of Kabul.

Inside the same SUV, Osama bin Laden, Dr. Ayman al-Zawahiri, and Sheik Omar bin Bakri Mohammed, leader of Hizb Al-Tahrir, prayed silently that they would make it out of Kabul alive.

"This was supposed to be a ten-year war," said Al-Zawahiri. "How could the infidel Americans defeat us in two months on our own ground?"

"We were betrayed by the warlords," said Mullah Omar. "The Americans bought them body and soul. They will burn in hell for generations to come. We must reorganize our Taliban forces in the mountains and counter-attack."

"That's if we get out of here alive," said Al-Zawahiri.

The SUV lurched dramatically to the left and almost tipped over as they avoided a burnt-out Taliban tank. Five hundred feet above them, Captain Derek Wright and his co-pilot, Gunner Charles Ryan, were following the SUV in their AH-64A/D Apache helicopter. An unmanned predator drone had sent images to the CIA center in Langley, Virginia, indicating that some Taliban VIP were traveling in a black SUV heading out of Kabul. With the sudden collapse of the Taliban forces, the CIA was on the lookout for possible Taliban and Al-Queda leaders escaping the capital.

The images had then been sent to the Pentagon and then relayed via satellite to the helicopter command center. Minutes later, Captain Wright had his orders to track and possibly destroy the SUV.

The AH-64A/D Apache helicopter had been the revelation of the Afghan war. Used extensively in Operation Anaconda to squeeze the Taliban forces, the Apache carried sixteen AGM-114 Hellfire missiles with a range of eight to twelve kilometers. They operated in full fire and forget mode, in that they rarely missed their targets once fired. The Apache also had the Advanced Precision Kill Weapon System known as Hydra, using a M230 gun with a fire rate of 625 rounds-per-minute. Gunner Charles Ryan lined up the SUV in his sights. Although it was probably bulletproof, the Hellfire missile would destroy the SUV and all its passengers in seconds. Captain Derek Wright kept his Apache helicopter in line with the SUV, using his pilot night-vision goggles to see the truck in the darkness.

Inside the SUV, the driver saw the lights of the helicopter following them in the night sky. "An American helicopter is following us. We're lost!" He did his best to zigzag in the street but the helicopter was firm on their tail.

"If they fire on us, we're all dead," screamed Mullah Omar in panic. Al-Zawahiri knew they had only seconds to live or die. He pulled out his cell phone and dialed the direct number to Prince Abdullah in Saudi Arabia.

Answer your phone, Al-Zawahiri frantically thought.

"Yes, it's me," answered Prince Abdullah. "It must be important for you to call me at night like this."

"Kabul has fallen. We are escaping on the mountain road but an American helicopter is about to blow us to smithereens. All of us, understand? Your cousin, too."

"How could this have happened so fast?" asked the prince. "We planned for the war to last for years."

"Only Allah knows," said Al-Zawahiri. "I estimate that we have maybe a minute to live before the helicopter fires. Call our friend in Washington immediately."

"I will do it now," said Prince Abdullah. He hung up, immediately dialed the number in Washington, and explained the dramatic and urgent situation that they were facing. The receiver understood perfectly the gravity of the situation. He promised he would take care of it. Prince Abdullah felt better. If his cousin and his terrorist friends were killed, all links to him and the attacks would disappear. If the terrorists managed to escape, the master plan could continue. He was safe in both cases. Prince Abdullah turned out his night-light and went to sleep.

Hovering 500 feet from the ground, the Apache Gunner Charles Ryan initiated the firing sequence. "Armed and ready to fire," he told Captain Wright.

Captain Derek Wright called into his headquarters for his final instructions.

"We have the bandits in our sights and are ready to eliminate target. Expecting final okay." He maneuvered the Apache through some flack that was coming from the ground, never losing sight of the SUV.

Wright expected to receive an immediate affirmative and his hand was about to squeeze the trigger button, launching the deadly Hellfire missile to dispatch the SUV and all its inhabitants to the hell they deserved.

But there was no answer from HQ.

"I repeat: requesting permission to fire and destroy target," said Captain Wright.

Still no answer.

Finally a confused voice replied, "Negative. Abort mission. I repeat: abort mission."

"Are you sure?" asked Captain Wright.

"Comes straight from the Pentagon," said the operator from HQ.

"Shit," said Captain Wright. "They are dead meat. Okay, we're pulling out." He pulled back the throttle stick and lifted up from behind the SUV and headed back to base camp.

The astonished driver looked up into the sky to see the helicopter turning away from them.

"They're leaving," screamed the driver of the SUV in jubilation. "I can't believe it. We're going to make it out of here alive. *Anikak!* ("Fuck you!")" he screamed to the helicopter in the sky.

"Allah be praised," said Osama bin Laden. "We live to fight again."

"It pays to have good allies," said Al-Zawahiri. The group congratulated itself on its miraculous survival as the black Ford SUV headed out for the mountain range of Tora Bora.

CHAPTER 2

Life was not turning out as planned for Sandra Carter in Portland, Oregon. Sandra had moved to Portland from New York with her ten-year-old boy, Adam, to marry Gregory Carter, a twice-divorced therapist. Her widowed sister, Susan, had begged her not to go. "I don't like the guy, Sandra," Susan told her. "He's just too smooth for a guy who's been divorced twice." Sandra didn't listen. She was in love with Gregory and had put the objections down to her older sister just being too protective of her, as usual.

Sandra and Susan Baines had been the two most beautiful girls of the Delmont preparatory school in New York City. Two years apart, Susan had married first, to David Stillati (a cop of all things), cute but definitely in a dangerous line of work. *I liked Dave*, thought Sandra. *In many ways, Dave and I were soul mates. Pity it didn't work out.* Sandra married a year later to the captain of their football team but that hadn't worked either. Susan and Sandra had divorced in the same year. A year later, Susan married a hedge fund manager who would later work on the 105th floor of the World Trade Center. He died there on September 11, 2001, and left Susan a widow with two children. Sandra's football husband had ripped his ACL, was waived by his NFL team, and quickly determined that a young child and a wife hampered his future television-acting career. He left her alone with a young son, Adam, in a one bedroom apartment on East 65th Street.

A few years later, Sandra met Gregory Carter at a seminar on single parents. He was a guest lecturer. A short courtship followed and he had proposed to both her and Adam at the Daniel Restaurant with a three-carat diamond and a violinist. It was very romantic. Adam had run out of the room and hid in the men's toilet. He wasn't as fond of Gregory Carter as his mother was. Adam was a loner and really wasn't fond of many people save his grandparents, his Aunt Susan, and his aunt's first husband, Dave. Nevertheless, Sandra accepted the proposal gratefully and Sandra and Adam moved to Portland to begin their life in Oregon.

Things had not turned out as Sandra had dreamed. The four years in Portland had been as difficult as anything Sandra had ever experienced. Gregory Carter was a possessive, cheap man who had neither a clue about how to raise a boy, nor the time or interest. Adam hated him and showed it by spending as much of the day on his computer as humanly possible. Gregory Carter went to conventions on a weekly basis and was rarely home. When he was at home, he constantly fought with Sandra about Adam. Finally, Gregory insisted that Adam be sent to a boarding school. Susan refused. Many more arguments followed and, near the end, Sandra rarely saw her husband anymore. He was always traveling on conventions. Finally, she received two lawsuits in the mail from former patients with whom Gregory had had intercourse. That was the last straw. She filed for divorce the following day.

The divorce had been as quick and painless as these things could be. She wanted nothing from Carter and moved out into a small apartment in the outskirts of Portland. Sandra got a job as a receptionist at the ACLU headquarters and enjoyed her newfound independence. Adam was thrilled by the move. He preferred living with his mom alone, without other men around. Still, the house they lived in was small and dingy. The roof leaked when it rained. Her sister Susan and her parents begged her to come back to New York, but Sandra though it best that Adam finish his junior high school. He had been held back one year for poor grades. Not that he was stupid or anything, but he greatly preferred playing Mortal Kombat or high speed auto chase on his ancient computer than studying.

That morning it was raining in Portland. *As usual*, thought Sandra. She was in her yellow kitchen reading the morning classifieds and saw an ad that caught her attention:

> DEM TWO GALS, sell out warehouse inventory. Everything must go. Airport lost and found, laptops, computers, glasses, books, briefcases, money clips, tickets, gone…gone…gone…at the lowest prices. Sale on Saturday, November 1, 2005. Lowest prices.

Sandra had been at one of these tag sales before. Dem Two Gals were two seventy-year-old spinsters who organized all the tag sales for houses and businesses in Portland. Their ability in selling everything cheap was legendary. They did a thriving business and sold everything at dirt cheap prices. She cut out the classified ad.

Now, if I could get a good deal on finding Adam a laptop, that would be something, she thought. *Then he wouldn't be locked in his room all the time. At least he could play on that thing while I cook or watch TV or work around the house. Things could still be good here. I could still turn it around.*

Susan reminded herself to go to the tag sale that Saturday. She took scissors and cut the classified ad out of the paper and put it in her pocketbook. Maybe it would prove to be her lucky day.

CHAPTER 3

Washington, D.C., Thursday, August 20, 1998.

Michael Cherry was sitting in his luxurious office overlooking the busy street in Georgetown, the fashionable area of Washington, D.C. As chairman of the Holliwell Corporation, the fifth largest military contractor to the Pentagon, he had become accustomed to taking calculated risks for greater returns. Twelve years of the Reagan and George Bush administrations had made him a wealthy man and given Holliwell a position as a major player in arms and oil deals around the world. Holliwell had more than 100,000 employees and subsidiaries in over thirty-five countries in Africa, the Middle East, Russia, and Europe. His company supplied the U.S. Army and other forces with everything from oil and weapons, to the tents in which the men slept, the food they ate, the trays they used to eat the food, and the trucks they drove. Michael Cherry was a man of huge influence with several generals and admirals on his direct (or indirect) payroll, and yet he was also a man on the brink of desperate trouble.

Holliwell had overextended its reach in the 1990s, expecting military expenditures to continue forever. The collapse of the Soviet empire had instead made many in the U.S. government question the ever-growing military budget of the United States. Peacetime dividends were now expected. To make matters worse, Bill Clinton had defeated George Bush in an unexpectedly contested electoral campaign. Michael Cherry had contributed more than $50 million of the Holliwells' money to win that campaign but it hadn't helped. Despite winning the Gulf War, Bush's economic programs hadn't worked, and the voters had turned to the Democrats.

"Voters," scoffed Cherry to himself. "Those idiots."

The first thing Clinton did in office was try to balance the federal budget and slash the government debt. That was seriously bad news for Cherry and Holliwell. A cut in expenditures meant fewer government contracts, fewer orders, a process of competitive bidding, and the end to several guaranteed army contracts that allowed him and his associates' deep pockets to buy even more influence in the military apparatus.

In order to stem the flow of red ink, Cherry, as chairman of Holliwell, had altered the company's year-end books in an Enron-type manner so he could put future accrued profits and sales in the current fiscal year. The accounting change had worked for Enron, even though there were rumors of potential problems. Trouble was, Cherry knew there were no immediate future sales on the horizon, not for Holliwell. Not with the Clinton Administration in charge. The Democrats had awarded the few new contracts to their best donors and left him and Holliwell out in the cold. Despite every attempt to impeach Bill "Teflon" Clinton, the president had survived and Vice President Al Gore looked like a shoe-in for the next election, ensuring four more years of bad news for all Holliwell operations. The Holliwell shareholders were not happy. They were demanding better performances and a higher stock price. Many were starting to question Michael Cherry's ability to lead the company through troubled times.

Cherry knew that if Holliwell went belly up and filed for bankruptcy, all of the inner workings of the company would be examined. Bribes had been paid, accounting books falsified, crimes committed—all under his leadership. The Democrats and the liberal press would have a field day attacking him and the senators that had favored him with generous, no-bid contracts in a myriad of countries spanning the globe. Michael also knew he would probably be indicted and go to jail. The huge 8,000-square-foot house in Bethesda, Maryland, the cars, the trust accounts, his friends, the respect of his wife Helen and their two daughters would be gone as well. They would be ostracized.

No, I cannot let that happen, thought Michael, wiping the sweat from his wide bald head and removing his glasses. *I am a fighter, and will do everything I have to do to survive.* He made his decision and picked up his 200-pound frame from the leather chair as if to underline his call to action.

He lifted the "clean" phone line, which he'd had installed and dialed the private number to the Saudi Minister of Defense, Prince Bin Abdullah. They had met each other at Harvard and had dealt with each other on fighter and arms sales to the Kingdom of Saudi Arabia. Both had been bitterly disappointed by the election of Bill Clinton and the subsequent reductions in government spending in oil and weapons. It had been Prince Abdullah, after all, who had frantically called Michael Cherry after Saddam Hussein's invasion of Kuwait. Michael had helped him convince President Bush, Sr., to intervene and launch the first Gulf War. That had saved the Kuwaitis and the Saudis from Saddam Hussein and the Iraqi army. Now Michael needed help himself.

After a few minutes, Michael Cherry had the defense minister on the direct line.

"*Salaam aleichem*, Mr. Minister," said Michael Cherry.

"*Aleichem salaam*. How is my old and trusted friend?"

"Well, Mr. Minister, my family is fine, and I trust yours as well?"

"We get older, but not wiser."

"That is certainly true here in Washington as well."

"How can I be of assistance to you?" asked the minister.

"It's a *quid pro quo*, Mr. Minister. Maybe we can be of assistance to one another, as always."

"That is our favorite approach to business."

"We have mentioned one of your compatriots before, the one who lives under the Taliban regime."

"Ah, yes, an unfortunate relative of mine given to radical causes."

"He has launched two deadly attacks on our embassies in Africa. Our government plans to retaliate, tonight."

There was quiet on the line, as the minister understood suddenly that Michael Cherry was upping the ante in a very steep way.

"And how do you know this?" asked the minister.

"Our influence in the Pentagon is still very strong, Mr. Minister. Tonight, your friend and cousin will be visiting his guerilla-training base in Khost, Afghanistan. A massive Tomahawk missile attack will obliterate him and his men, this very Thursday night."

"But that would represent the violation of an independent Arab state. Even Clinton wouldn't dare go so far."

"He would and he has. The attack has already been approved," replied Michael. "My sources in the Pentagon are of the highest order."

"I see," said the minister. "I am grateful to you as always for having given me this important information and saving the life of my dearest cousin. He is a radical idealist who lost his father at an early age, but a good man. He doesn't deserve to die. How can I ever repay you? If this is true, I will be in your debt forever."

Michael Cherry prepared himself to launch his pitch.

"If the information I have given you turns out to be true, and I am sure it will, I wish to have a meeting with your cousin and his associates in Afghanistan within the next month, face to face. There is a very important matter I must discuss with him," said Michael Cherry. "Matters of the utmost importance to both you and me, as well."

"What you say is difficult, as he lives under the Taliban's protection and is subject to many assassination attempts. But I am sure that if your information is correct, and you have saved his life, he will be open to a meeting. I will be glad to set it up then for you."

"Thank you, Mr. Minister."

"No, thank you, Mr. Cherry. Allah thanks you as well for your service to our Muslim brother."

The conversation ended on that note. Michael Cherry wiped his brow with his handkerchief and removed his glasses. *Decisions like these are not easy, but that's what differentiates the true leader from the rest*, he thought to himself.

"I must do what has to be done, regardless of the consequences," he said to himself convinced of his actions. With that thought, Michael Cherry walked out of his office, confident that he had initiated something important that would save him and his company, and perhaps change the world. The fact that he had just betrayed his country never entered his mind.

CHAPTER 4

❀

I was freezing cold. So cold, in fact, that I could no longer feel my nose, my ears, my feet, my hands, or my two ass cheeks frozen to the grey, weathered stands of the Metropolitan Oval in Queens, New York. Winter in January in Queens makes Antarctica look like a place for wimp scientists who run around the ice dressed in sleeping bags. I have no doubt that anybody who has played or watched a sporting event anywhere in the northeast United States in January could easily cross the North Pole, without a shirt, screaming "Go Giants!" to the television cameras.

What was I doing there? Scouting a soccer game, of course. I wish I had taken my mother's advice and finished that internal plumbing course. Anybody who thinks all sports agents live a life of luxury, cute girls, and easy cash needs to come scout an amateur soccer game in the Metropolitan Oval in the middle of January. At least that's how I have to make a living. It's not a pretty sight.

The Metropolitan Oval is a legendary soccer field stuck in the middle of the biggest cemetery in Queens, New York. Anybody who has played semi-pro soccer in New York would know it. The field used to have a dusty dirt field so that the wind would blow up and around the players, creating a scene from the desert storm attack in Lawrence of Arabia. During my long and unpaid career as a semi-pro league soccer player, I had played numerous glorious games at the Oval and remembered it fondly. The deceased always outnumbered the small but vocal number of ethnic followers crazy enough to come watch our games. Now the Soccer Association had replaced the dirt with bright green synthetic turf. There was little more surrealistic in the world than watching soccer players run around on an ice-covered, bright green turf in the middle of a grey cemetery in the 5:00 PM darkness of a New York winter.

And it's a beautiful day, I thought to myself.

"So what do you think, Dave?" asked Angelo Popescu, the Rumanian coach who had dragged me out to watch his protégé number ten play on this dark night.

"I think I should have stayed home and watched the news," I said while trying to stomp some circulation back into my feet.

"Come on, Dave. What do you think of my boy?"

"I think he has talent, but his body is out of proportion."

"What do you mean, 'out of proportion'?"

"His head is too big for the rest of his body," I said.

Angelo looked at me quizzically.

"Angelo, he scored a goal and went around congratulating himself to the fans. There are no fans here, Angelo—just you and me. Plus, he is playing against mailmen and taxi drivers. What happens when I bring him out to play against people that train seven days a week?"

"But he has talent, no?" said Angelo.

"He has some talent, but it's hard to play well when carrying that big head around on his shoulders."

Just then a defender slide tackled the player in question, who went down grabbing his leg. Then he got up and kicked the defender in the back, and that player went down as well. More players got into the mix and everybody was pushing and kicking and shoving at each other. The referee (who was about eighty years old) and had seen it all before came over to talk to me.

"Hey, Dave. What are you doing out here in the cold?"

"Hi, Bill. Angelo brought me here to look at some players."

"Hey, Angelo," said the ref. "You been eating too much goulash. There are no players out here—only shoemakers."

"Shouldn't you be breaking this fight up?" I asked the old and wise ref who I had known for years.

"They are just keeping warm," said the ref, downing a small bottle of Italian grappa he kept in his pocket. Finally, he blew the whistle ending the game and broke them up.

"But there's twenty minutes left in the game?" said Angelo.

"You call this a game? It's over," I said. "Tell your player to come see me next week in the office. Bring the defender along as well, the big tall guy."

"That's his younger brother."

"Younger but smarter. Look at him sitting there looking at the fight, staying far away from it. He knows soccer's about discipline, not just fighting, plus he didn't miss a tackle all game. Bring him along as well."

"Thanks, Dave," said Angelo. "You won't regret it."

"I already am." I got up and walked quickly to my car while I still had active blood circulating in my veins. For those of you fortunate to be unfamiliar with me, my name is Dave Stillati, and I am an ex–New York City cop who now runs a small sports agency. Many years ago, my partner was gunned downed in the Bronx, my wife divorced me, and, truly disgusted with the quality of felons in the area, I turned in my badge in search of a different line of work. I chose sports as I had been a soccer player myself back in the day. The sports agency covered most of my work day. However, every now and then some truly desperate people were referred to me by the police department—people who had no place to go, whose cases had been closed years ago; people for whom justice was not only blind, but deaf and dumb as well.

The police knew I was a soft touch and that, sometimes, just to do a favor (or make some extra cash), I would try my best and look deeper into a case than they had the manpower to do. Cheryl Ickes had been just such a case. A talented figure skater whose stepfather had killed her mother and stolen her inheritance, Cheryl had nowhere to go and no one turn to except for me. As a result, I now had two ugly scars in my shoulder and thigh that served as a weather vane.

I should work on the Weather Channel, I thought. *That would be a hoot. The scar on my right thigh tells me that a strong weather system is approaching with variable winds.*

Cheryl had reclaimed her inheritance and her life. She still sent me letters from Yale. I also got monthly letters from Naomi Wyatt, the gorgeous and volatile figure skater who was serving her sentence up in Danbury Federal Prison for her part in that case. Her letters were full of interesting suggestions, the memory of which could keep me warm in the coldest of winters. We might have a future, Naomi and me. But you never know how these things work out. I was just imagining that when her publicized release took place in the glare of the television spotlights. The memory of Dave Stillati, life-saving sports agent, could become just that: a photo-obliterated memory in the life of a superstar athlete turned convict turned model. The probability was high that such a thing could happen.

I got into my car and fumbled with my keys. There was always the remote possibility that I would freeze to death in my old blue Mustang before I could turn on the ignition. The headline in the sports section of the *New York Post* would read: "Sports Agent Found Dead in Queens. Block of Ice Thawed by Firemen with Flame-Throwers. Car Towed for Non-Payment of Tickets."

Luckily for me, the car started immediately, and I headed for the Van Wyck Expressway while pressing my hands to the heat vents in the dashboard. The radio played an old song by Marvin Gaye ("What's Going On?") and I looked forward to reaching the Triboro Bridge and calling Petra Temesvari.

Whenever the weather dropped below freezing, I thought about Petra Temesvari. She was a talented, shapely blonde tennis player from Hungary, whom I had represented at her first and last U.S. Open. She had lost 6–0, 6–1 in the first round at center court, but her remarkable figure had earned her a three-year contract with the Maidenform "Cross Your Heart" Bra campaign. She quit tennis and became a kindergarten teacher.

Lucky kids, I thought.

Petra was a girl of generous spirit who never forgot that I was the one who helped her get her first money and the chance to stay in the United States. I rarely took advantage of her generosity, but tonight was just too cold for me to go home to an empty apartment and a glass of bourbon. I dialed her number on my cell phone.

"Dave, is that you?" she said in that Eastern European accent.

"Yes, Petra. How are you?"

"Alone, grading pictures my children made for me."

"Can I come over to see them? I'm in the neighborhood." I could have been in Spain, and I would still have been in the neighborhood.

"Dave, why do you ask? You know you are always welcome here."

Indeed, why did I ask? God bless you, Petra Temesvari. "I'll be right over," I said, hanging up my cell phone.

It was still negative ten degrees outside of my speedy Mustang as I headed for the Triboro Bridge, but inside the car, things were beginning to warm up considerably.

CHAPTER 5

Sandra Carter headed toward the Portland Metropolitan Exposition Center, located at the juncture of Routes 84 and 5. Dem Two Gals were having their weekend flea market sale outside of the Exposition Hyatt, and Sandra could see the cars lined up already.

Damn, I'm late, thought Sandra. *There won't be anything left.* Sure enough, cars were packed all around the hotel as buyers from around Portland drove miles to scoop up items selling for a tenth of their original value. Dem Two Gals always sold out everything they offered, because their prices were just so low. This time they were offering items from the lost and found departments of the Portland Transit Authority. These included all the items not claimed at airports, train stations, bus terminals, ferries, and taxis in Portland over the last five years.

Sandra parked her car and looked at the tables covered with mountains of eyeglasses, phones, bags, valises, laptop computers, toys, cameras—all of it had been left behind by somebody, somewhere, somehow in Portland.

"Jesus," she whispered to herself.

People of all natures and kinds were sizing up the different items, opening them, plugging laptops into outlets, trying on glasses, listening to radios. A line of people had already picked out their favorite items and were waiting to pay for them. One of the Two Gals was at the cash register in the front, counting bills as people came in and goods went out.

"Two Armani glasses, $20; laptop computer, $150; Nikon camera, $25; total $195. Cash only. No checks, please. Thank you."

Sandra could see why the women were so well known. Prices were indeed a tenth of what they would normally be in a store.

Sure, the things are used, she thought. *But beggars can't be choosers.* She desperately wanted to buy Adam a laptop; she had not been able to get him anything in the longest time. *Poor Adam,* she thought to herself. *I brought him here, gave him a lousy stepfather, and put him through a divorce. What he needs is a new mother.*

As she walked around the stands, she came to a long table where two beat up computer laptops sat open. A small sign next to one of them read, "Sony Vaio, thinnest model, fully functioning, $350." The other sign read, "Dell Laptop, some circuit work necessary, $100." That was her choice.

"The laptops go the quickest," said a man standing next to her.

"Do you think this can work?" Sandra asked him.

The man plugged in the laptop and turned it on. A green screen lit up, with the words "Dell Computer" on it. Then the screen went blank.

"It needs to be reconfigured, and then there must be a new password for it," said the man. "Is it for you?"

"No, it's for my son," said Sandra.

"How old is he?"

"He's fourteen. He's in his last year of junior high."

"Well," said the man, "if he's like most fourteen-year-olds today, he'll figure it out in a jiff. We're the stupid ones. You should buy it for him."

Sandra thanked the man and picked up the computer. It looked worn and some of the plastic on the side had been broken off. *I wish I could get him a new one,* thought Sandra. *He deserves that, but we don't have the money. The man said it still worked and Adam would get a big kick out of it, so what the hell?*

She pulled out five twenty-dollar bills and headed to the line that was moving at a rapid pace.

"Good deal," said one of the old Dem Gals waiting on customers. "Can't beat it."

"I hope my son likes it," said Sandra paying her the money.

"If he doesn't, he can always sell it in our next sale. Our motto around here is: Here Everything Goes. Remember: Here Everything Goes."

CHAPTER 6

Monday morning, I made my way to the corner Starbucks to get my tall skim latte on my way to my office on 42nd and 11th Avenue. Manhattan has more than 2.5 million souls that run around the city every day in pursuit of gainful employment. Most of these people drink their coffee regular with milk. Others like espresso. Still more like lattes with a twist, or a soy latte with decaf coffee, or maybe a double shot of espresso with non-foam milk. Then, there are those that only like tea. That is to say, of the 2.5 million people that inhabit New York, everybody has likes and preferences that differentiate themselves from the norm and render this microcosm of the universe fascinating.

I walked into my office just shy of 10:00. My personal assistant, Kelly Claire, was waiting for me with her usual caustic wit.

"My, oh my. Look what the cat dragged in," said Kelly. "Did you have a good weekend, or should I ask?"

"Two words," I replied. "Petra Temesvari."

"Twin Peaks?" asked Kelly in mock fear.

"The very one."

"The Teutonic Mountain chain?"

"None other."

"I thought she was teaching kindergarten now."

"She took a break for the weekend."

"Last time she took a break, an avalanche broke out."

"Very funny, Kelly. Petra is a very nice girl."

"I'm sure she is," said Kelly. "What were you doing out with her?"

"I was trying to keep warm after seeing the game at the Metropolitan Oval. Anybody call?"

Kelly was my faithful assistant and secretary. Years ago she had married my best friend and, for reasons unbeknownst to anybody with a brain, she continued to work for me and indeed save my ass time and again.

"Fernando called and said that he wants to leave the team in Greece."

"Any particular reason?" I asked.

"They haven't paid him in two months."

"Good reason."

"He says if he had a good agent, he wouldn't be in this situation."

"Tell him that if he was a great player, he would have a better agent," I said.

"Lucas Moyano called from Bergamo and says the coach in the Italian team hates him."

"Why?" I asked.

"Because he puts him in the game only in the second half."

"He must only hate him halfway. Tell him I will speak to the coach."

"Angelo called and said you made an appointment for him. He said he would be in next week. Oh, and Susan called."

I made a mental note to call my ex-wife back that morning.

"Okay. Anything else?"

"Eddie called," said Kelly referring to "Magical" Eddie Carpenter, the ex-boxing middleweight contender who now worked for me doing investigations and muscle work.

"Oh yeah? What'd he say?"

"He wants you arrange a comeback for him."

"He's forty-eight-years old."

"He says that after the way he handled that Jamaican punk at the hospital, he understood he could still fight."

"That was fifteen seconds with a psychopath. Tell Eddie he's lucky I pay him a regular salary."

"Will do."

"Anything else?" I asked, expecting bad news.

"No," said Kelly, smiling.

"No?" I asked, surprised. "No collection agencies? Credit cards, American Express, Visa? No landlords or telephone companies calling to get paid?"

"Nope. I paid them all," said Kelly. "I even had your sign fixed. Did you notice?" I looked at the door. The sign now read: Dave Stillati, Sports Agent. Before it read: Spot Agent. Things were looking up.

My case for Cheryl Ickes had resulted in an unexpected payment of $100,000 that I had given to Kelly to pay bills that were outstanding since the First World War.

"So, Kelly, you paid everybody? What are you, crazy?"

"It was either that or open an office in Sing Sing."

"So, how much have we got left now?"

"$835.19"

"We were that in debt?"

"More. They took pity on us. Even the landlord's all paid up."

There is something to be said for being in the black, I thought to myself. *A feeling of pride, of being a man of property...*

"Stop daydreaming," said Kelly.

"I was thinking of what yacht I was going to buy."

"You can take the Staten Island Ferry 800 times," said Kelly. "Best view of the Statue of Liberty."

I went over to my office and turned on my Apple computer. It was only Monday and I had more than forty-nine e-mails from players around the world looking for teams. I also had the standard Nigerian scam letter promising to send you $20US million if you gave them your bank account number. Those I got every day.

Before I answered them, I called Susan. She had probably just dropped the boys off at school. Susan and I had divorced because I was a cop and it was too much for her to handle, thinking I wouldn't come home one day. She had married a hedge fund manager who worked on the 105th floor of the World Trade Center. There was nothing I could say to her about her decision or about him except it left a hole in my heart as big as the Lincoln Tunnel. He was a good reliable man who gave her two sons. On September 11, 2001, he didn't come home. I dialed her number.

"Susan, it's me."

"Dave, I left Kelly a message."

"I know."

"The boys are going to be playing soccer with their travel team on Friday. I thought it would be fun for you to come out."

"It would be," I said. "Thanks for asking."

"The boys wanted you there," she said. "They are only twelve and fourteen and they are planning to go pro already."

"I don't doubt it. They are great kids and good players."

"Well, they think of you as their uncle."

"It's an honor for me that they say that."
"So, we'll see you on Friday?"
"Okay."

I hung up. Somewhere in my heart I knew that Susan would always be the girl with whom I was meant to grow old. But things had taken a different turn and now we were friends—real friends. So that was as fine as things were ever going to be between us, and that was just fine with me, too.

If I had to say I had a philosophy in life, or a political orientation, I would say I was a Marxist—as in Groucho. It was always hard for me to take life too seriously or respect people in positions of authority, and that made my decision to leave the police force and open my own sports agency easier. It was also why I didn't have a seven-figure bank account, enjoy spectacular year-end bonuses, or plan to retire any time soon. You paid a price for being an independent wise guy. The most important things are not to do harm, and to try to help who you can. As Casey Stengel once said, "If you help the person to your left, and help the person to your right, you're doing pretty good." Also, if somebody threatens one of those people with a submachine gun and you take him out, that's good, too.

"Gus is on the phone," said Kelly.

Gus was the coach of a team in Scotland called Hibernian.

"Gus, you miserable son of a bitch. What can I do for you?"

"Top of the morning to you, too, Dave. I need a centerforward for the January transfer window. What've you got? Must have a European passport. Must be tall as well, good header."

I reached over to my curriculum books to have a look at the young Argentine players I represented and said, "I think I got just what you need. Nineteen, played at Boca Juniors, 1.90 m, Italian and Argentine passports, free agent. Sound good to you?"

"Send me a tape."

"Will do."

After my trials and tribulations in Jamaica on the Ickes case, I was glad to just be alive and working in my office, nice and calm. I need to have a few weeks of steady work and no hassles. Monday was starting off on the right foot

CHAPTER 7

Adam sat in the last seat in the back row as the algebra teacher droned on and on in a monotone voice. He was thinking about the latest video game he had downloaded on the Internet. As a fourteen year old in the eighth grade of the Portland Central Junior High School, Adam felt very self-conscious that he was both the oldest and smallest member of his class. In fact, Adam disliked his school and had very few friends. He did his best to remain as invisible as possible in both the classroom and the hallways—and also on the soccer team. It was a talent he had developed; he could actually be so quiet as to be practically invisible. In class, he was rarely called upon to answer any questions. In the crowded hallways, he could slip in and out without offending any of the local bullies who often preyed on the smaller kids. On the soccer team, he sat on the bench without saying a word, hardly ever noticed by the coach who played the bigger, more vocal and ambitious players. That suited Adam just fine as well.

The move to Portland had been a shock to his life. Growing up in New Jersey with only his mom and without a dad had been bad enough. He had enjoyed the elementary school in New Jersey that was minutes from his house. They lived close to his grandparents and his Aunt Susan. His aunt's husband, Dave, had been his coach on his travel soccer team and had taught him a lot, playing him at forward and encouraging him to participate on the team and to make friends.

Surprising everybody (including himself), he had become the top scorer on his travel soccer team. Then his mom had met "the jerk" as Adam liked to think of him. Adam thought the courtship was bad enough, and then they got married and he had to move to Portland where he was the small, scrawny new kid in the school. It was like moving to hell.

A new school, new bullies, new teams. Carter, his new stepfather, hated him and constantly corrected everything he did. Adam's only outlet was his ancient computer and he spent every minute on it, playing games and writing the friends he had in New Jersey. After a couple of years, they got tired of writing him back.

The good news came with the divorce. The jerk kicked them out of his home. They took their things and left with dignity, and they rented a lousy apartment in a building just outside of Portland. However, Adam appreciated the fact that he didn't have to deal with Carter anymore. He felt a little sorry for his mom. She loved him but was always falling for the wrong type of guys. *I wish we could move back to Jersey*, thought Adam. *Maybe when I finish this stupid junior high school.*

"Adam Baines?" said a voice from in front of the room.

Adam adjusted his glasses to see who was calling him.

"Adam Baines," repeated the teacher's voice.

Adam realized that the teacher was calling his name and in the surprise adjusted the chair he was leaning on against the wall and fell down with a bang. The whole room burst out laughing. Some laughed at his fall; others laughed at him. Most thought he was just a geek, with short black hair and glasses.

"Wake up, Baines," said one of the boys in the front row.

The class laughed some more.

"Did I wake you up, Adam?" asked the teacher.

"No, it's fine," said Adam, composing himself. "What can I help you with?"

"You can help me by participating in the algebra classroom and not falling asleep, young man," said the teacher.

"He needs a pillow," said another boy.

"I wasn't asleep," said Adam.

"Come up here and finish this equation."

Adam's heart was pounding as he went up to the front of the room. He hadn't read the book, much less done any of the homework assigned to him. He was too busy playing his computer games and didn't care much for schoolwork in any form. The teacher gave him some chalk.

"It's a simple equation, Adam. You don't need to be a genius to answer it."

"He doesn't have a clue," yelled the bully in the second row.

Adam adjusted his glasses and looked at the room. They were all waiting for him to fail. His heart began beating more and more.

"The blackboard. Look at the blackboard," laughed the teacher.

Adam looked at the blackboard and could hardly see the equation to solve. He wished he could turn completely invisible and disappear. Then again, that didn't look likely either. He tried to focus on the figures. It was an equation X, Y, where you were to identify the variables. He began to analyze it on the blackboard running down the possibilities. It wasn't hard, like figuring out a password, or a hidden clue in a video game. Soon he was writing out the possible answers. As the bell rang, he wrote what he thought X and Y were supposed to be. The kids were too much in a rush to get out of the classroom. The bully smacked him on the back of his head on his way out. "Failed again, moron."

Adam went back to his chair to get his books. The teacher looked at the equation.

"Hey, Adam," he said. "You got it right."

"I did?" said Adam in surprise.

"I bet you didn't even study the chapter, and you still got it right."

"But I did study," Adam lied.

"Adam, you're smart. Smarter than the boys in this class. Why don't you apply yourself?"

"I don't know. Probably I'm lazy," said Adam.

"Probably," said the teacher. "But you know, Edison said genius is one percent inspiration, ninety-nine percent perspiration, don't you?"

"I think I heard that somewhere."

"Get to work, boy. And perspire a little."

"I will, Mr. Mittleburger. I promise I will."

"Somehow I doubt it," said the teacher. "Go along, boy."

Adam left the classroom. He wasn't altogether surprised that he had solved the problem. In his games he had had to solve much harder clues and answers. He just hoped the teacher wouldn't call on him again and embarrass him. He walked down the hallway hoping to be as invisible as the school would allow him to be.

CHAPTER 8

Kabul, Afghanistan, September 11, 1998.

The private jet bearing the Holliwell insignia landed on the tattered airstrip of the Kabul airport with a thud. The runway was still in disrepair from the bombings the Russians had inflicted during their ten-year war Afghan war. Michael Cherry looked out of his plane window to see the dreary conditions of the Afghan landscape. Accompanying him was his personal bodyguard, Szabo Tanovich, a six-foot-five-inch former Serbian militia leader under Arkan. There was also another man, Fawazy Ferhab, the envoy of the Saudi Defense Minister who was to act as his safe-conduct in Afghanistan. Officially, the meeting was to develop ties with the Taliban government for possible oil development between Holliwell and Afghanistan. Unofficially, Cherry was there to meet a radical group of ruthless Islamic terrorists.

What the hell am I doing here? Michael Cherry thought to himself. *I must be really up ass creek to have to do this.* Indeed over the last month, the situation at Holliwell had grown considerably worse. His friend, Kenneth Lay, had been indicted over fraudulent transactions at Enron. That company was self-destructing. Cherry knew that once the prosecutors were made aware of the dealings in Enron, all energy companies would come under scrutiny. The very same accounting "misrepresentations of future profits" in which Enron had engaged, Holliwell had done by a factor of twenty. Plus there was the question of Iraq. Due to the Clinton Administration's boycott of Iraq, Holliwell had been shut out of its promised oil-for-food deals with Saddam Hussein. The French, Germans, and Russians had stepped in to fill the void. *The fucking Germans, French, and Russians were taking all my deals, for Christ's sake*, thought

Cherry. *My competitors are just laughing at us, at our naïve American incompetence.*

All the investments that Cherry had made in Iraq through Holliwell's subsidiary, Bear and Well, were going down the drain. More than $200 million in bribes, oil contracts, and payoffs to Saddam Hussein, all for naught. An investigation would look into that, too. For the first time in his life, Michael Cherry was looking at a black void that was hard to comprehend: financial ruin, social suicide, jail time. *I have no choice*, said Michael to himself. *I have to do what I have to do to save myself and my company.*

A Taliban official clad in an ominous black caftan waited for them outside of the plane.

"Welcome to Afghanistan," said the Taliban official. "I am Mirwad, official interpreter for the foreign ministry."

"Pleasure to meet you," said Michael Cherry as he set foot on the tarmac. "This is Fawaz Ferhab from the Defense Ministry of Saudi Arabia."

"It is always good to meet an Arab brother. *Tahreeb, Akh, ukwam*," said the Taliban with a traditional greeting of welcome.

"*Sa'eed yahbiT Afghaanistaan*," answered the Saudi, telling his host how glad he was to be in Afghanistan. "Prince Abdullah sends his best regards."

Szabo Tanovich grunted a salute as he looked down upon the shorter Taliban greeter. Szabo hated most people, but he hated Muslims in particular and had filled the graves of Srbenica with their tortured bodies. As the right hand man of the Serbian militia leader Arkan, Szabo's sheer size and ruthlessness had made him a poster boy for the evils of the Serbian civil war. Even his loyal Serbian soldiers had been shocked by his passion for raping and murdering women and children. For Szabo, it was just part of being at war and putting his personal brand of fear into his enemies.

A black Skoda car left over from the Russians stay in Afghanistan escorted them out of the airport. On their way to the city, they passed the soccer stadium that was now used for public executions.

"More than 500 people have been hung there in the last year," said Michael Cherry. "It's their killing field."

"Reminds me of home," said Szabo.

Afghanistan had become a grim, hopelessly retrograde Islamic nation during the years of Taliban rule. Sports such as soccer were outlawed. Hobbies such as kite flying were prohibited as was any kind of western clothes and music. Long beards were encouraged for the Islamic faithful. Poppy production, the mainstay of the Afghan drug trade, was run by the Taliban. Women's rights were abolished and they were forced to wear the black burkas, covering them from head to toe.

It's like living in the Middle Ages, thought Cherry, driving through the ravaged city. *The Taliban want to set back the clock forever.*

The driver took a left turn and headed for the mountains.

"It will be a three-hour drive," said the driver. "Hello, my name is Ali Mahalati and I used to drive a taxi in New York City."

"*Samt!*" The Taliban representative quickly told the driver to shut up. "Excuse our primitive driver. He doesn't know his place."

Michael Cherry just nodded. They were going to the Northwest province, site of the new terrorist camp. After the U.S. Tomahawk attack that had caused so much damage, the terrorists had relocated their headquarters into the mountains. Cherry observed the ruins of tanks and military equipment, much of it Russian, that still lined the roads of Kabul and pointed them out to Szabo.

Cherry had first heard about the huge Serb after Serbian President Slobodan Milosovic had been arrested. When his militia boss, Arkan, was murdered, Szabo had gone into hiding. He was wanted for war crimes against humanity: Muslim, Bosnian, and Croatian. There wasn't a group in former Jugoslavia that didn't want to hang him. The head of a Holliwell subsidiary company in Rumania had recommended the huge Serbian to Cherry, saying that he was a remarkable killing machine, totally ruthless and loyal to his boss. Cherry felt he could use a man of those qualities within his firm. Using his contacts in Serbia, he had sought Szabo out and had him flown to their office in Kuwait. From there it had taken all of Holliwell's influence and money to clear up his name and get him to their branch in Washington with a new history and identity. Cherry had made him chief security consultant at Holliwell, and his personal bodyguard. He taught him English, cleaned up his manners and gave him a six-figure bank account. Szabo knew that Cherry has saved his life. He was a dead man in Serbia. For that he would repay the American with undying loyalty in any service he might need. Szabo was a ruthless assassin who could kill a man with any kind of weapon—including a newspaper. Cherry never left the U.S. without the imposing Serbian by his side for protection.

Michael Cherry did not have a military history. He had never been in a war. During Vietnam, he had been the leader of his college ROTC inspiring others to enlist. He had claimed to have a hearing impediment that sadly prevented him from serving his country as he wanted. In truth, his father was the vice president at Dow Chemical (which produced napalm bombs, among other weapons). His father and had convinced a senator to give his son a student deferment. Cherry had no desire to put himself at risk. He had other priorities. In college he had seen a pretty co-ed who was dating the football captain at Harvard. It hadn't taken him long to convince the young man to do his duty and enlist, despite his girlfriend's many objections. Cherry was a very effective speaker and he filled the boy's head with patriotic indignation that the Vietnamese communists could defeat a power of might and truth like the United States. The football captain had enlisted in the Marines and gone off to war. He was killed at Khe Sanh and came back in a wooden box. Cherry had consoled the young beauty to such an extent that they became engaged a few months later. She was the ideal girl of his dreams and he got what he wanted. *It was the right move to make*, Michael reminisced. *Sometimes you must befriend the enemy to defeat him.*

Cherry saw himself in those days as a representative of morality and virtue in a sea of war protesters and pot-smoking debauchers. He led the Young Republicans and the ROTC and made himself friends in high places. *Now the hippies are in power and I'm going out of business*, he thought ruefully.

"You must put this on now." The Taliban guide handed Michael Cherry a black hood. "There was an attack. It's a precaution."

Szabo looked at him for an indication of what he should do. Had Michael Cherry said so, he would have quickly killed the driver and the Taliban official with his bare hands. But Cherry just nodded and put on the black hood over his head so he would not know where the terrorists' camp was located. The Saudi emissary did the same. The Serb followed suit.

Amateurs, thought Cherry dismissively. *They don't want me to know where they are, as if satellites aren't tracking them already.*

The car continued driving through the steep Afghanistan hills. Winter was coming and the air felt cold in the unheated car. Michael Cherry closed his eyes under the hood and tried to get some sleep so he would be refreshed by the time he got to the camp. He had a crucial pitch to make, and he knew it would undoubtedly be the most important sale of his lifetime.

CHAPTER 9

❀

Adam came home from school that Friday and found his mother in the small yellow kitchen preparing spaghetti and meatballs for dinner. The dingy kitchen had one of those four burner stoves that looked like it had come out of the Korean War. Susan tried her best to make him warm meals there and give him a semblance of a comfortable home life.

"Hi, sweetheart. What happened in school today?" asked Susan.

"Nothing," said Adam.

"Nothing? Why do you always say nothing? Something must have happened. It's a big school, more than 300 kids. What happened?"

"I got up, got on the bus, went there, and came back," said Adam grabbing a Coke from the old fridge.

"Sounds real exciting. Did you play soccer today?"

"Yeah. We had a game but I sat on the bench for the whole game."

"What was the score?"

"We lost 3–0."

"Why doesn't the coach play you more often?"

"I don't know. I don't think he likes me," said Adam sitting down at the kitchen table.

"Why wouldn't he like you?"

"He says I'm too small, that I'm not fast enough for the team."

"Uncle Dave said you were a good player, and he's a sports agent so he should know," said Susan. "He was a pro player once."

"I know, but he's in New York. He's not here. I've got to deal with these assholes."

"Adam, don't use bad language."

"Sorry, Mom, I just don't want to talk about it."

Adam knew his mom didn't like when he swore, which wasn't often.

"I have a present for you," said Susan.

Adam looked up. It had been a while since his mother had bought him a present. She took out the black laptop and laid it on the table.

"You know I don't know anything about computers, but this laptop was in a garage sale and they told me it could be restarted or cleaned up or something to work like new."

Adam could not believe his eyes. Here was something that he really wanted and needed, a laptop to replace his ancient computer. Something he could carry around with him to play games or send e-mails, go to wireless cafés and look at the girls.

"Mom, this is really great!" he said enthusiastically.

Adam took the laptop into his hands, plugged in the electric cord and felt the computer stir to life.

"It's a bit banged up, but we can put electric tape on its side," said his mom.

Adam waited till the screen came to life and then saw the Dell image, and a request for a password.

"What's happening now?" asked his mom.

"It has a password to stop people from accessing information. The previous owner must have put it there."

"So you can't use it?"

"No, of course I can. I can get some software to reconfigure the hard drive, and then some other hardware to retrieve the previous files. Tomorrow, I'll go down to Radio Shack to get that. Where did you get it? Was it expensive? Can we afford it?"

"Of course, we can. I got a good deal in this huge garage sale. It was turned in at the Portland airport. Some executive must have lost it in the scanning machine. It has the tag on the side and it's been in storage for over four years. That's why I didn't know if it would work or not."

Adam looked at the tag that said "Turned in on 11/12/01, item number 10901."

"The airport turns in all their lost-and-founds every few years to be sold to raise money. Does it work?" asked Susan.

"Yeah, Mom. It works, it works," said Adam happily. He went over and gave her a hug. "I'm going in my room to go plug it in, okay? Thanks a bunch."

"That's fine," Susan said, overjoyed that something she had done for Adam seemed to be really making him happy. He had had such a tough time of it, and

Susan felt terrible at how he had suffered during her marriage to Carter. *Maybe I can start putting things away now*, she thought optimistically.

Adam went down the hallway to his room and shut the door. He then pulled the air conditioning screen off the wall near the base of his bed. Adam kept all his favorite things behind a green metal vent screen. His Swiss knife was there, as were his favorite video games, pictures of his grandparents, and the one picture he had of his father. He kept his things in the vent, so that if somebody broke in they wouldn't find his stuff. Security was terrible at the apartment complex and the neighbors had been broken into twice already. The vent was just big enough for him to crawl through and it led down and out to the back of the house, near the large and perennially broken air conditioning unit. Adam could climb in and out of the apartment without anybody noticing him, including his mother, but he rarely had anywhere to go. He put the laptop next to his video games and to his wallet that contained fifty-five dollars he had saved babysitting the kid downstairs.

Tomorrow I will go and get the software to get this thing up and running, he thought. He replaced the vent screen and went to his desk computer to play Grand Theft Auto. True, he had homework to do, but that could always wait.

"Adam, are you really studying?" called his Mom from the kitchen.

"Sure thing, Mom," answered Adam. "Of course I am."

CHAPTER 10

❦

My ex-wife Susan's two kids were running up and down the field like bees after honey. Mathew, the older one, had better ball control, but Charles was quicker. Both kids were the best players on their Bergen Kickers travel team. As I watched them play from the stands, I controlled my impulses to yell instructions out onto the field. Susan had asked me to come see them play and I had taken my ice-blue Mustang over the Washington Bridge to New Jersey after work. Few things gave me greater pleasure than to watch kids enjoying themselves playing a soccer game. Time itself became suspended in the innocence of youth pursuing athletic excellence for their own pleasure. No contracts, money disputes, pay-offs, salary arbitrations, or voracious owners, just youth and talent, a ball and a goal. Call me a sports romantic but as realistic as the decision had to be, when the Olympics went pro something was lost for me, forever.

"Come on, Mathew, Go!" screamed Susan two inches from my left ear. Mathew got the ball, faked to the left, passed off the ball to his brother Charles on the right, who took it down to the sideline and chipped it in. Mathew leaped over the defender and headed the ball down into the net. "Goal!" The kids all piled down on to congratulate him and they raced back to the midfield line for the kickoff. The game lasted ten more minutes and the Bergen Kickers travel team won 2–0 continuing their unbeaten streak.

"They're going to be playing for the state championship," said Susan, hugging the two boys after the game.

"Uncle Dave, wasn't that great?" said Charles. "Matt scored a great goal."

"Yeah, but you set him up. I liked that more."

"You're always complimenting him," said Matt.

"'Cause you get too many compliments already, Mr. Superstar."

We walked off the field together. After their father had died on 9/11, Susan had done a fantastic job raising the boys on her own. They were as happy and healthy kids as you could find and I admired her for that. Her husband had left her a sizable inheritance (and the 9/11 fund was going to pay for the kids' college), but Susan still went to work every day as vice president of Tuttle Advertising. She still had time to do that and take care of her kids. She liked inviting me out to see them play.

"So how are your Jamaican war wounds, Dave?" Susan asked. "Kelly told me all about your adventure in Jamaica. It must have been terrible."

"My shoulder hurts in the bad weather. My thigh's okay," I said. "It was touch and go for a while."

"Always the hero," said Susan.

"I must have left my white horse somewhere in the parking lot."

"I thought you were just going to concentrate on sports now."

"I am. This was a story of a figure skater, Naomi Wyatt."

"I read about her in *People* magazine, I bet it didn't hurt that she was beautiful."

"She was? I never noticed. Nobody will ever be as beautiful as you, Susan."

"Aw, that's sweet. But you know, I'm going to be thirty-nine this year. I'm an old lady with two kids and a job. Nothing glamorous here."

"You look better now then ever," I said, which was true.

"How come you weren't this nice when we were married, Dave?"

"I was young, and stupid, and thought being a cop was the best thing in the world. I should have dedicated more time to you."

"That you should have. But we were both too young and stupid. Sometimes the best things just go wrong for no reason," said Susan, smiling at me. We kept walking toward her Tudor style house that was not far from the field.

"Have you heard from your sister Sandra?" I asked. "And her kid, Adam?"

"She called me last night. She's working at the ACLU there. You know she finalized the divorce at last. Carter is finally out of her life. They will be staying in Portland until Adam finishes junior high school. Then I think she will be coming back here."

"Adam's a great kid. Is he playing soccer out there?"

"He's on the team, but they won't play him. The coach doesn't like him, apparently. Says he's too small."

These kinds of things just make me want to take out my Beretta nine-millimeter revolver and start shooting, but I didn't say anything to Susan about it and contained my irrational reaction to myself.

"Well, if he comes back here, I can help him," I said.

"I'm sure you can. You helped the boys."

"It's more fun for me than for them."

"Dave, I want to thank you for being there for me, and for them after John died. Many guys wouldn't have done that. They would have stayed mad at me."

"Susan," I said, "it's a privilege for me to be part of your lives."

She touched my hand. We kissed on the cheek and I said good-bye to Mathew and Charles who were disappointed to see their Uncle Dave leave.

"Come back for the finals," said Matt. "I'll score two more goals!"

Ah, the mindless confidence of youth, I thought.

"Call me, okay?" said Susan. "And take care of yourself?"

"Okay, I will."

I got in my car and drove away as Susan walked into her house. Looking in the rear view mirror at my worn face, I thought, *I know, I know. I messed up a long time ago. She was the girl of my heart and I let her walk out on me, and no other girl could ever take her place and I am going to die alone in an old age home dribbling spit from my mouth.* With that optimistic perspective, I pointed the car toward the New Jersey Turnpike.

CHAPTER 11

❀

Khost, Afghanistan, 1998.

After driving almost an hour on winding roads and steep hills, the car came to a complete halt. The doors opened and Michael Cherry and the others passengers were led out of the car and their hoods removed. Michael Cherry's eyes adjusted to the bright light of the mountain camp. He was in a primitive military encampment at the foothills of the Afghan mountains. The air was cold but refreshing. Cherry looked around to see Szabo and the Saudi assistant behind him. Soldiers in green guerrilla outfits were performing exercises in the camp with makeshift guns in their hands. Cherry could see the black, burned out shells of what used to be cars that had been detonated as car bombs.

The men leading them took them into a cave that was lined with ammunition and military equipment. Inside the cave was a white tent from which voices of prayer were coming. The men ordered them to wait. After about ten minutes they were bodily searched and then allowed into the tent.

A spectacled older man in a white gown was waiting for them inside. Next to him a taller, younger man with a long beard was reading the Koran.

"*Salaam aleichem*, Doctor," said the Saudi envoy.

"*Aleichem salaam*, my brother," said the man. "I am Dr. Ayman al-Zawahiri."

Michael Cherry looked up at one of the most wanted terrorists in the world, Ayman al-Zawahiri, leader of the Sadat murder in Egypt and more than twenty-five bombing attacks—including the two U.S. embassy bombings in Africa.

"Your fame precedes you," said the envoy. "I bring you the greetings and support of your friend Prince Abdullah in the defense ministry."

"We are always grateful for the support and help our generous friend continues to give us."

"This is Michael Cherry, chairman of Holliwell International. He comes with the blessings and protection of our minister who recommends this meeting."

"Although we are at war with the American administration, we are not at war with all Americans," said Al-Zawahiri. "Any person under the protection of Prince Abdullah is welcome here."

He offered Michael Cherry, Szabo, and the envoy a seat in the tent. The man praying did not move and continued to read his Koran.

"I believe we owe Mr. Cherry a note of thanks," said Al-Zawahiri. "Had he not informed us of his government's Tomahawk attack, we would probably be with Allah now. Many of our soldiers were injured and killed." The envoy translated and Michael nodded his appreciation of Al-Zawahiri.

"But that leads me to a question. Why would an American want to help someone that is at war with his country?"

The envoy translated the words to Michael and he started to respond to the envoy but then changed his mind.

"Is it all right if I speak English?" he asked Al-Zawahiri.

"It is all right. I was educated in an English school."

"First, I would like to thank you for this meeting," said Michael. "I know that you are at war with the current administration of my country and they are at war with you. You have blown up the embassies in Africa. They have sent Tomahawk missiles to kill you."

"Their arrogance knows no bounds," said Al-Zawahiri.

"You would like to become a world-renowned force to rid the lands of the Middle East of all influence. Is that not correct?"

"In theory, we want to all Arab militants to join us in fighting the Americans, like we did to the Russians here in Afghanistan."

"But the Americans are not here. You are bombing their embassies in Africa."

"We will kill them anywhere we can," said Al-Zawahiri.

"But wouldn't it be better if you could entice them here to fight them in this country, with this terrain, on your home turf, for years to come?"

"That would be our goal. In coming here, they would be defeated like the Russians were," said Al-Zawahiri.

"And you would be the first Islamic force to defeat the two world super powers," said Michael Cherry.

The tall man stopped reading his Koran.

"And how do you propose for this to happen, Mr. Cherry?"

The envoy introduced the men to Osama bin Laden. They exchanged deferential greetings. Michael Cherry knew that Osama bin Laden was the spiritual leader of the terrorists while Al-Zawahiri was the day-to-day strategist.

"What I propose, gentlemen, is for you to launch the first large-scale terrorist strike against the most important targets in the United States. To strike at the very heart of the financial, military, and legislative branches of the American government."

The two terrorists looked at each other and at the American.

"And how, when, and why do you propose we do this, Mr. Cherry? We have many men, and some resources—none of which are in the United States. How can we achieve this miracle you are talking about? And why would you want that?"

Michael knew he now had their complete attention.

"We have a common enemy. The Clinton administration has sent missiles to destroy you. The Clinton Administration has gone out of its way to destroy my company, Holliwell. They have cut the military budget and put my company on the brink of bankruptcy. From the number-two position we have gone to number ten and are sinking fast. Worse than that, they have put my country on a path of moral and spiritual decadence. Abortion, divorce, adultery, pornography, all condoned and encouraged with the support of the government. We have descended into a morass of degeneration. Eight years of Democratic leadership have been bad enough. Four more years with Vice President Gore becoming president will destroy me, my company, and our country irreversibly. I cannot allow that to happen. That's why I am here."

"Interesting reasoning. Go on," said Al-Zawahiri.

"The reason that you have not been able to strike within the United States is that the CIA, FBI, anti-terrorist units, and the military are focused on your activities. You have vast forces arrayed against you. I can change that."

"How?" asked Osama bin Laden.

"We live in the age of satellite information. Holliwell is a company of immense influence. Half of the Pentagon is on our payroll. Key men in the CIA and FBI are being paid by us as well. You have seen how easy it was for me to gain information about the Tomahawk strike against you. I could do the same to protect you if we were planning a strike in the United States."

"But how could we get sufficient weapons into the U.S. to launch a massive attack?" asked Dr. Al-Zawahiri.

"You wouldn't have to. If you have dedicated suicide squads ready to give their lives for you, and we know you do, they could hijack commercial planes full of fuel and use them to strike targets in the United States. You had already planned to do this in France against the Eiffel tower."

"What targets in the United States?" said Bin Laden.

"Targets of sufficient importance to affect the most important elements of American life," Cherry said. "For example, the World Trade Center in Manhattan to affect the financial world, the Pentagon to affect the military establishment, and the Capitol Building to affect the legislative branch of government."

"A strike of this magnitude would be seen and heard around the world," said Al-Zawahiri.

"You would have the attention of the world. If you made it a public statement against America and claimed responsibility, then the U.S. government would have to send troops here to find you."

"We could fight them in the mountains for years, just like we did with the Soviets. The Taliban forces would fight with us," said Bin Laden.

"Islamic soldiers from around the world would join us in the battle," said Al-Zawahiri. "From here we could extend the battlegrounds to Pakistan, Iraq, Iran, as those countries would help us in our fight against the American infidels."

"An endless war, and I would be there to protect you from possible defeat and capture," said Cherry.

"Like in the novel by Orwell, *1984*," said Bin Laden. "The guerrilla leader who is almost caught but never really is. I studied that during my college days in the United States."

"And when would you want this strike to take place?" asked Al-Zawahiri.

"We need two years to prepare this strike," said Michael Cherry. "That would make it two months before the next American election, September 11, 2000. An attack at that time would show the voters how weak Clinton and his gang had made the United States. The voters would throw them out of office and elect a Republican president to lead the war against terror. My company would benefit greatly from the resulting war in forms of sales, contracts, and supplies. We are talking many billions here."

"And what would we get for this?" asked Osama bin Laden.

"You would get international fame, the protection of my company and information on the conduct of the war, and ten percent of our sales—equal to about $350 million in the next five years. Enough for you to launch strikes throughout the world."

Ayman al-Zawahiri and Osama bin Laden exchanged words in Arabic.

"Yours is an interesting proposal, Mr. Cherry. Perhaps enemies can help each other after all. We will consider it and let you know."

"I am grateful to you for your consideration," said Michael Cherry.

"So are we," said Al-Zawahiri. "Now come join us and see our military installation. As you know, we just moved here. But you will find our soldiers are not without courage or training."

The men stood up and headed outside of the tent.

Michael Cherry felt the sweat cling to his armpits. He had made his pitch. Inside, he felt they would go for it. That or they would cut off his head and put it on a stick. But the way things had gone up to now, that wasn't going to happen. He had shown them the effectiveness of his plan and the importance of what he was offering. They needed him. He needed them. It was as simple as that. Together they could rewrite the history of the Middle East and even affect the next election of the new American president. Alone, Al Queda would always be a little known fanatical splinter group destined to die, and he would soon be bankrupt and in jail. Not a good alternative for either of them.

He stepped out into the terrorist camp with Szabo by his side and felt better about his future prospects than he had felt in a very long time. A short distance away, Ali Mahalati, the car driver, was writing down the time and place of the meeting and the description of the two westerners visiting the terrorist camps. Rahid worked secretly for his idol, Ahmed Shah Massoud, the leader of the Afghan resistance movement against the Taliban. Massoud would be grateful for the information. Ali had lived in the U.S. and hated the repressive Taliban regime. He wanted a free Afghanistan for his children and wife to live in. Today he was getting paid by the Taliban Ministry and doing a good deed for Massoud. He felt it would be a double payday for him.

CHAPTER 12

❀

Adam was at home, after school, playing his favorite video game—The Prince of Persia. In the game, the prince had to defeat his enemies and rescue the princess. The game took place in a mythical Arab city called Babylon and there were castles, dungeons, and deserts to conquer.

Die, you bastard, die, Adam said to himself as he cut the video guard with his knife. The guard disappeared in puff of smoke. The prince was getting close to liberating his beautiful princess when—bam!—a hidden guard had killed him with a lance.

Damn, Adam said to himself, *I died again*. He turned off his desk computer and went to the air conditioner vent by his bed and pulled out the laptop that his mother had given him. He would load the game onto the laptop so he could play at school. That would make his school life more interesting for sure. He took out the software he bought on his way home. Opening the black and grey computer, he installed the reconfiguration software and waited patiently for it to load. The software would circumvent any passwords the previous owner had put on the laptop. Once this was accomplished, Adam turned the computer back on and was thankful to see it boot up to life. Despite its age, the laptop computer had a ton of memory capacity and could load DVDs and offered high-speed Internet access. It was way more advanced than the old desktop he worked on every day. Adam then loaded a memory software program to retrieve the files made by the previous owner. Adam wanted to do this to see if the computer had any old games he could use. He waited patiently for the files to appear on his desktop. One file appeared on the right side of his screen.

"Adheem Harb" was the name of the file, with Arabic writing next to it.

Great, Adam thought. *A new video game.*

When he clicked on the file, information began to flood the screen. First there were the names of four people: Mohammed Atta, Waleed Alshehri, Abdulaziz Alomari, and Staam La Suqami. There were details of flight schools, hotel reservations, and bank accounts in their names. Then there was the flight number (Flight 11) leaving from Portland and a date: September 11, 2001.

Next there were flight coordinates of the city of New York and a three dimensional detail of a target: the World Trade Center towers, with a specific altitude and range at which the jet was to hit one of the towers.

Well, it's not a video game, Adam thought to himself. *It's just a description of the World Trade Center attacks.* Adam had been only ten when the attacks had taken place, but he was living in New Jersey then and his Aunt Susan had lost her husband in the attacks. Also two players on his travel soccer team had lost their fathers who commuted to work at the towers every day. He had seen the attacks on TV and couldn't believe the towers had fallen as quickly as they had. It had all happened live on TV.

Nothing seemed terribly out of the ordinary until Adam looked at the date the file was downloaded: September 11, 2000.

That is weird, Adam thought. *This was downloaded a full year before the attacks ever happened.* Whoever had made the file and sent it from this laptop had done it two full years before the attack of 9/11. Adam looked again to make sure. The file was e-mailed by a Pharbor@aol.com It looked like the computer file was made as an instruction manual to be read by the owner or recipient of the laptop. Adam kept looking at the different pages of data that appeared on the screen.

Didn't Mom say that she had bought the laptop from an airport sale? thought Adam. *Didn't one group of terrorists leave from the Portland airport for New York?* Adam got on the Internet just to make sure. Sure enough, Mohammed Atta had left the Portland airport in the early morning of 9/11 to catch a connection to New York. The laptop Adam was holding in his lap could possibly have been the terrorist's computer, which he left at the Portland airport.

Holy shit, Adam said to himself. He stepped away from the laptop, understanding the significance of what he might be holding in his hands. *This can't be possible, man. Fucking awesome,* he thought to himself. *I have to show this shit to Mom when she gets back from work.*

Adam turned off the laptop and put it away behind the vent next to his bed. Then he reached up on the shelf and pulled out his algebra book. He opened the book for the first time in weeks and started to do his homework. *I don't want to look stupid in front of the class again,* he thought to himself. *My teacher will kill me if I do.*

CHAPTER 13

I was sitting in my office, behind my worn mahogany desk talking to the parent of a soccer player I had scouted. It was a fairly typical conversation. Most parents think their kids are much better than they really are. Some parents don't have a clue or are not interested at all in the kids' career or their lives. Then there are the parents that put a lot of pressure on their offspring to work harder, train harder, and essentially be better than they were. This advice usually comes from fathers who are usually forty to fifty pounds overweight and smoke a pack of cigarettes per day. This one on the phone with me was the first kind of parent. The one who overestimated his son's soccer ability by a million percent.

"So your son is playing in your local high school and he is the top scorer in Westchester," I said, "but you would rather that he play for Manchester United or Chelsea?…Yes…I can understand that…I would have liked to play for them, too…But chances are that won't happen."

I continued speaking against his objections that I was being too negative about his son's chances to pursue a professional career.

"Why not?" I said. "Because for a non-European to play soccer in England you need to have played on seventy-five percent of the national team games for the last two years or have a European passport. You didn't know that, did you? They would never give him a work permit even if he did make the team." The father kept asking me more questions as he understood some of the realities I was telling him.

"Well, it's my job to give you all the information you need to make the right choice for your boy. He is a good player. I think you should be realistic and find him the right college to play ball in and get a college degree in the meantime."

"Realistic" is not the right word that fathers want to hear applied to their sons or daughters in sports. Great potential, talent, innate ability, European scouts, are all the key words that agents use to snare a scribble on a piece of paper that could mean nothing or maybe hundreds of thousands of dollars. One in 300,000 players has the potential to be a professional. Of that only one in 1,000 actually makes real money, so to make money you have to be good—really good.

That's why if a player is only just good, the security of a college degree is my first advice to a player living in the United States. Maybe I was conditioned by the fact that I made only a few dollars playing soccer in my career, or that I saw way too many of my soccer teammates having to scramble for temporary jobs late in their lives. Whatever it was, I decided long ago to give the honest advice I believed in to the players I represented so that they could deal with it. I guess that's why my bank account was just barely in the positive—and even so for the first time in many months.

"Well, send me a tape then of your son and his CV and I will keep it on file," I said. "Any tape will do, but preferably a whole game." Highlights tapes can be cut so well as to show my grandmother as the best scorer in soccer history.

"Someone's on the phone," interrupted Kelly, sticking her head in the door.

"Who? David Beckham?" I asked optimistically.

"Your prison pen pal, Naomi Wyatt. Calling collect."

I concluded the call I was on with the player's father. Then I accepted Naomi's collect call. I thought about the very last time I had seen her in her orange prison jump suit up at Danbury Federal Prison. She was starting her sentence for being an accomplice in the murder of Charles Ickes III, the stepfather of a skater I represented. We had sworn undying affection and some sort of love, at least long-distance undying love.

"Dave!" she said. "Is that really you? You sound so close."

"Naomi, how are you doing in there?"

"I'm getting out, Dave. Next week! Can you believe it?"

"What?" I exclaimed happily. "But you have three more years to go."

"The Governor of Connecticut commuted my sentence for good behavior after he saw the show about me on *60 Minutes*. The state couldn't handle all the fan mail the prison was receiving. He commuted my sentence today. My publicist is picking me up and we are having a press conference here outside the prison next week. Isn't it just grand?"

"I'm so happy for you, and I will be there when you get out."

"Hold on, Dave. That's why I called. My publicist doesn't think that's a good idea."

"Why the hell not?" I asked indignantly.

"He says it would remind everybody of the case, how you saved my life, blah, blah, blah. He says I need a new image. After the press conference, we are flying to L.A. for my book tour, *Black Beauty Behind Bars*. The orders are piling in. The book will be a bestseller for sure."

"But Naomi, I thought we said we would be together when you got out."

"We will, baby," Naomi said. "But after all of this. I've been stuck in this hole for so long, I need to breathe a little. You understand, baby, don't you?"

"I guess," I said.

"Dave, you're not sore, are you? You know I owe it all to you. You saved my life."

"Yeah, that and fifty cents will buy me a *New York Post*."

"They want me to hang up now, baby. One love!"

"Blessed," I said, hanging up.

Kelly walked in my office and said, "She dumped you."

"We're taking a break," I said.

"But she's been in prison for two years. How much more of a break do you want?" Kelly insisted, twisting the knife in my ribs.

"I guess it's hard falling in love with a convict. Ever happen to you?"

"No," said Kelly. "I always looked for a higher class of people to dump me, but I can't say I didn't see it coming down the road."

"Why me?" I asked stupidly.

"You broke the cardinal law of the sports agent," said Kelly. "Never fall in love with a former Olympic skater that is serving a sentence of five to fifteen years in federal prison."

"Sounds like a good law," I said. "I'll remember that."

"You do that, Dave. I'm just trying to keep you honest and focused on what's good for you," said Kelly.

"Kelly, dear, I'm as focused as a fucking laser on a blinking cornea."

CHAPTER 14

❈

Khost, Afghanistan, September 11, 1998.

Michael Cherry, Szabo Tanovich, and the terrorist Al-Zawahiri walked around together visiting the terrorist training camp. Future terrorists in camouflage outfits were doing push-ups, firing AK-47s, practicing with explosives, and generally looking busy for their guests. It was very rare for the Arab fighters to see Westerners in Afghanistan under the Taliban regime.

"That was an interesting proposal," said Al-Zawahiri.

"I hope it was effective," said Michael Cherry.

"Don't you feel that you are betraying your country with what you proposed to us?"

"No, Mr. Al-Zawahiri. Did you feel you were betraying Egypt when you killed your president, Anwar Sadat?"

"He betrayed our country by negotiating a peace with Israel."

"Clinton has betrayed my country, and my company as well. We all have our own reasons for our actions."

"If we were to accept, how would the details be handled?"

"I would fly to Saudi Arabia to discuss passport visas into the United States with our common friend, Defense Minister Prince Abdullah. He has already agreed, provided we fly out all of his immediate Saudi relatives right after the attack. That includes all of Bin Laden's relatives in the United States as well. I will have the FBI do that. You must contact me as soon as you have the right potential candidates to launch the attacks. I will have their visas to the U.S. prepared and issued in their names at the U.S. embassy in Riyadh. Upon their arrival into the United States, they will be given instructions, cash, and a laptop computer. I will feed instructions via the Internet into their laptops. All information concerning flight schools, apartments, flight instructions will be given to them both in English and in Arabic. I suggest there should be five full teams with four hijackers in each team. In that way at least one will get through to the target."

"What about detection in the United States?" asked Al-Zawahiri.

"After the bombing in Oklahoma, we have pointed most of our anti-terrorist activities towards right-wing militias in the United States. This has been done purposefully by me and my friends to allow a major attack by a terrorist group. I will personally be monitoring any FBI or CIA detection of the men entering the United States and counter any anti-terrorist activities."

"You are sure you can actually do this, Mr. Cherry?"

"I am betting my life on it," said Michael Cherry.

"Should anything go wrong, should you betray us in any way, we will kill you and all of your family," said Ayman al-Zawahiri, looking at him through his spectacles.

Szabo Tanovich smiled when he heard the threat. This was the kind of language he was used to uttering himself.

"I would expect nothing less of you," said Michael Cherry.

"You think the Americans will then invade Afghanistan?" said Al-Zawahiri.

"Yes, I am sure they will want to retaliate to get you. That is our plan."

"We will kill them like we did the Russian dogs. All Islam will hail us as heroes. The glorious religious war will last decades."

"That is our plan," said Michael Cherry.

"If so, then we have a deal," said Al-Zawahiri.

"Don't you want to ask Osama bin Laden?" asked Michael.

"He is our spiritual leader and was our initial guidance," said Al-Zawahiri. "I make all the political and military decisions."

"Then we have a deal," said Michael Cherry.

They shook hands.

"Now, I must show you something," said Al-Zawahiri.

He brought Cherry and the giant Serb into a small dirt square with a single block of wood standing in the middle. Al-Zawahiri clapped his hands. A massive militant carrying a long wooden axe walked into the square with two other militants that were dragging a crying young boy, a terrified older man, and a woman.

"The young boy was caught playing soccer with his friends, instead of saying his prayers," said Al-Zawahiri. "That is against our Islamic law."

The giant militant grabbed the boy by his foot and placed his ankle on the block of wood. The two other guards held the screaming boy down in the dirt ground. The bearded militant giant lifted up the ax over his head and swung it down upon the block of wood, severing the boy's foot from his leg.

"He won't play soccer again," said Al-Zawahiri as the moaning boy was led away.

Next the old man was made to kneel before the militant giant and he took the man's head and placed it on the wood block. "This old man was working as a spy for Massoud."

The bearded militant raised the ax over his head and smashed it down on the wood block. With one blow he severed the man's head from his neck. The man's eyes blinked at Michael Cherry as the head rolled around in the dirt floor. One of the guards retrieved the head, and then they dragged the old man's body away.

"Executions are our Sunday pastime," said Al-Zawahiri.

Next a crying woman was dragged into the pit by the militants and they chained her to the bloody wood block, still wet from the blood of the boy and the old man.

"This woman has committed adultery," said Al-Zawahiri. "She betrayed a loyal fighter with a man from the village."

The huge militant picked up a huge rock and smashed it on the woman's head. She screamed the first time as blood flowed down her face. He repeated this time and time again until she no longer moved and pieces of her skull and brain covered the wood block.

"We want an absolute state governed by Islamic law in our country, in all Arab countries," Al-Zawahiri said. "Mr. Cherry, make no mistake about it. This is how we impose our law on our own Arabs. Imagine what we will do to infidels like the Americans or the Jews that dare to occupy or invade our land."

"That man, he is as big as me," said Szabo. "Can he fight, or can he just kill women, old men, and children?"

"He came from Syria to Afghanistan just to join us. He is one of our best fighters," said Al-Zawahiri, surprised to hear the huge Serbian speak. "Care to challenge him?"

Al-Zawahiri called the militant giant over and explained to him what Szabo had said. The Syrian just grinned and held on to his bloodied axe. Michael Cherry and Al-Zawahiri moved away.

"He accepts your challenge. Do you want a weapon?" said Al-Zawahiri.

"That wouldn't be fair," said Michael Cherry, who had seen the Serb in action and knew what he was capable of.

The bearded Syrian began to swing the long axe over his head while Szabo barely moved at all. He narrowly missed the big Serb by inches with his first thrust and repeated the gesture three more times. Each time he got closer. The huge Serb hardly had a reaction.

"Doesn't seem like your man likes to fight," said Al-Zawahiri.

The Syrian giant made another lunge at the Szabo but this time his axe came crashing down near the Serb's foot. The Serb kicked at the axe and punched the militant in the face; he then doubled up with a roundhouse kick to the man's chest. The Syrian backed away, wiping away the blood from his face. He pulled out another knife with his left hand while retrieving the axe with his right hand. The other Islamic militants were cheering him on as if they were at a soccer game. The Syrian lunged at Szabo with his knife and kept swinging the axe over his head. He even smiled to his friends in the crowd giving them a look at his great strength and confidence.

"*Boos teezi* (kiss my ass)," he said in Arabic to the Serb. Szabo began to attack him with a rapid series of kicks and punches. The Syrian responded by swinging his axe at Szabo's head, but the Serb ducked and then followed the axe in its swing and held it down with his foot. The Syrian then thrust his knife with his left hand, and the Serb grabbed his wrist. As both giants wrestled against each other, it wasn't clear at first who was going to win. Then Szabo used his great strength to slowly turn the knife toward the Syrian's chest. The Syrian made one great effort to push it away, but Szabo was too strong. He stuck the knife into the Syrian's chest. The Syrian screamed and staggered back, releasing the axe. Szabo picked it up and swung at the Syrian's right knee, cutting his leg in two. The bearded Syrian fell to the floor in his own blood.

Michael Cherry and Al-Zawahiri both watched impassively as the other militants went silent. Szabo dragged the huge man onto the wood block where just minutes before, the Syrian had cut the boy's foot off, executed the old man, and stoned the helpless woman. Szabo lifted his right hand and made a three finger sign over the man's body using his thumb, index and middle finger of his right hand. Michael Cherry knew it was the sign of the Holy Trinity that the Serbian paramilitary groups flashed before they killed Muslims, Croats, and Bosnian men and women during the civil war.

Szabo lifted the long axe above his head, swung it around a few times, and landed it deep into the Syrian's neck with a thump. The man's head quickly toppled off the wood block onto the ground. Then the giant Serb turned the head around and with the man's own knife cut out the right eye of the Syrian.

"*Boj te Jebo* ("May God fuck you")," Szabo said.

"*Quaser* ("Disgusting")," said Al-Zawahiri. "What did he do that for?"

"Souvenir," said Michael Cherry. "It's a tradition where he comes from."

Szabo Tanovich started to walk away from the scene of the terrible fight. Two of the guerrilla soldiers raised their weapons, looking to Al-Zawahiri for instructions to shoot him dead. Michael Cherry looked at Al-Zawahiri as well.

"Let him go," said the terrorist. "We can learn much from this man. He is *shirir* (evil). We must be more like him."

Szabo walked toward them, placing the bloody eye of the Syrian in his shirt pocket.

"That was fun," he said to Cherry and Al-Zawahiri.

"Well, Mr. Cherry, looks like we are all going to be working together to start the conflict in the Middle East," said Al-Zawahiri.

"Yes, my friend," said Michael Cherry. "Together, we're going to set this world on fire."

CHAPTER 15

❀

I was moving around the ring, shooting out a combination of jabs, hooks, and uppercuts and sweating like the Iguasu waterfalls in Brazil. Trouble was, I was only hitting air. Despite being fifteen years older and thirty pounds lighter, "Marvelous" Eddie Carpenter was staying well away from my longer reach showing how he had amassed a professional record of fifty-three wins and five losses while keeping his brains intact.

"Stay still for once," I said to him through my mouthpiece.

"Cut off the ring on me," he answered landing a sharp jab to my face. Despite the headgear I was wearing, I felt pain.

Once a week, Marvelous Eddie and I went down to Gleason's gym to work out. He went there to keep his weight down. I went there to sharpen my limited boxing skills and in the hope of learning something from him. I had met Marvelous Eddie in Rome, Italy, when his previous manager had run off, leaving him penniless and without a return ticket to the United States. He was standing in the lobby of the Hassler Hotel in Rome arguing about his bill. I had paid his hotel bill, and bought his airline ticket home. Then I was able to arrange his last two televised boxing fights that allowed him to buy the house in Brooklyn where he now lived with his family. A good friendship was born and after his retirement, Marvelous Eddie came to work for me full time at my agency doing odd jobs.

Of all the sports in the world, nothing can get you into better shape than boxing. Try getting into a ring for one round of three minutes of competitive boxing and the sweat will be pouring off of you and your heart will be beating like a locomotive going west. "Pace yourself, man," said Eddie, cornering me and peppering my body with some low uppercuts. "Move, react, get out of trouble."

I moved to his right and actually hit him with a left hook. It didn't bother him in the least. Professional boxers are fighting machines that can inflict incredible injury to their opponents. Yet they are some of the kindest and nicest people I have ever met. It's almost as if they don't like hurting you but their profession forces them to do so. It's a trade they do and they do it with respect. That's why I will never support the abolition of professional boxing. It teaches training, hard work, and discipline. Eddie and I continued sparring in silence for the remainder of the round and I thought I got in some good shots while he was distracted. The three-minute bell rang and the training session was over.

"You did good, Dave," he said to me, coming over to my corner to help me take off my gloves.

"Don't put me on," I replied.

"No, really. You did okay. You move well, but you drop your left guard when you throw your right out. I could have popped you on the chin plenty of times."

"I thought you popped me enough, but thanks for not hitting my shoulder," I said.

"No problem, you're a big guy, hard to miss. I'm smaller and quicker, I dodge and weave, that kind of stuff. I'm hard to hit."

"You're a pro, and I'm an amateur," I said.

"You're a good amateur; don't be too hard on yourself. You could take out most guys," said Eddie.

"But not pros," I said.

"Pros do this for a living every day. They do it to earn their food and pay their rent. It's like picking up a knife and a fork. They learn how to hurt other fighters and not get hurt at the same time."

That made a lot of sense to me. We walked over to the locker room to get some water.

"I saw that girl got out of jail," Eddie said.

"Who?" I asked, feigning ignorance.

"You know, the colored skater, Naomi Wyatt, the one you liked that I saved in the hospital."

"Oh, really? When did she get out?" I asked.

"Kelly told me about it. Told me now things were kind of over between you two."

"What is it? Kelly put it on the eleven o'clock news?"

"We just worry about you. You okay, Dave?"

"Yeah, big mon. I'm okay. Just another hole in my heart," I said to him.

"Flirty-flirty girl like that, with looks like that, hard for her just to settle down one day with a regular guy," said Eddie.

"Yeah, I know. It was stupid for me to think so."

"You got to get yourself a good girl, like my missus," Eddie said.

"Trouble is, good girls don't go for guys like me—only the nasty ones," I said.

"Trouble you have is that you only go for the nasty good-looking ones."

"It's a personal and professional flaw I have."

We toweled off and walked out of the gym together. The good thing about knowing a guy like Marvelous Eddie and having him work for you is that you know you are working with and talking to a pro. Not just a pro in the ring, but a pro in life. I had once helped Eddie in his sports career, and he was always there for me, time and time again.

"See you on Monday," I said to Eddie.

"See you, Dave." He walked away with that quiet dignity and pride that is hardly around today in an age of instant celebrities who would sell their own mothers just to be on television. We live in an age of moronic make-believe where actual reality is something everybody tries to avoid at all costs. Credit card offerings, state-run gambling, and reality and gruesome television shows fill our daily lives—all make-believe things that are offered on a daily basis to distract us from the fact that our lives are getting emptier and less important every day. These were my very important philosophical thoughts as I was using my Metrocard to get on the number three Lenox line subway to my one-bedroom apartment. It's easy to have depressing philosophical thoughts like that when you are have just been dumped by your girlfriend and are single, unattached, and living in a city like New York.

CHAPTER 16

❃

Adam and Susan were sitting down at the table in their cramped kitchen and Adam was showing his mom the information he had discovered on the laptop.

"So what does this all mean?" Sandra asked Adam, who was rapidly becoming exasperated with his technologically disabled mom.

"After you gave me the laptop yesterday, I went out and bought some software to reconfigure it," said Adam.

"You didn't like its shape?" asked Sandra.

"Not its shape, Mom. Its hard drive."

"Its memory?"

"Something like that, all its inner workings," said Adam.

"And then?"

"Then I got some more software so I could see if the previous owner had kept any games I might use," said Adam.

"And did he?" asked Sandra, wondering how she had given birth to somebody so computer literate.

"No, no video games as such," said Adam. "But he left this behind."

Adam turned the laptop to Sandra and showed her all the information in Arabic, plus the images, coordinates, flight instructions, departure airports, and gate numbers to be used in the hijacking attacks.

"This is a recreation of September 11," said Sandra.

"That's what I thought at first. But no, it's not," said Adam. "This information was e-mailed and downloaded by the user on September 11, 2000—one full year before the attacks."

"How do you know that?" said Sandra, starting to understand the relevance of what Adam was telling her.

"Because it has a date on when the information was received and who sent it."

He pulled up the information to show Sandra, and it read, "09/11/2000, Pharbor@aol.com."

"So somebody sent this person instructions on how to make the attacks take place before 9/11," said Sandra.

"Exactly, Mom. Somebody was telling somebody else how to do it. I can't read Arabic, but these look like instructions."

Sandra looked at the English and Arabic writings on the laptop. She became truly alarmed by what Adam had found. The attacks of 9/11 had a very personal meaning to her as her brother-in-law had been killed in the World Trade Center, leaving her sister a widow.

"Where did you get this laptop, Mom?" asked Adam.

"I bought it at a sale of lost-and-found items from the airport."

"What date did they find this?"

"There was a tag on the computer dated September 12, 2001," said Sandra.

"That means that it was found a day after the hijackers left the Portland airport for New York. Maybe one of them left it there and it took a day for somebody to find it," said Adam.

"Well, it wasn't like they were planning on coming back," said Sandra. "Do you really think it belongs to one of those terrorists?"

"I think so," said Adam, relieved that at last his mother finally understood what he had uncovered.

"Then we should tell somebody about this. This could be useful information for the FBI or somebody like that to use," said Sandra. "I saw a pamphlet at work telling people to call the National Security Agency, 1-800-Freedom."

"Maybe we can get a reward," said Adam.

"I wouldn't count on it," said Sandra. "We're just doing the right thing. I hope they don't come and confiscate the computer. It did cost me $100 after all."

"Maybe the FBI will buy us a new one," said Adam.

Sandra took out her cell phone and dialed the number. She was put on hold for about ten minutes until a friendly Midwestern voiced guy named Vince Patten took down all the information.

"So, you say you found this computer at the airport?" asked Vince.

"No. I bought it at a sale outside of the airport. Somebody left it there."

"And you say it has information regarding the 9/11 attacks?"

"Yes, but made one full year before the attacks happened. Is that significant?"

"Here at the National Security Agency, we take everything seriously."

"So what happens now?" asked Sandra, nodding to Adam who was listening in on the conversation.

"We will refer all the information to our central switchboard and they will contact you in two to three weeks," said Vince.

"Will they call us here?" asked Sandra.

"Well, I have taken down all your home information so I am sure an agent will. We want to thank you for calling us here at 1-800-Freedom. America's security is our business."

"Okay, bye," said Sandra and she hung up.

Adam was more excited now at the prospect of being personally involved in a clue on the worst terrorist attack made against the U.S.

"You see, I told you," he said to his mom. "It was important after all and now even people at the National Security Agency will know who we are."

"Yes, I guess that's good," said Sandra, but a deep feeling of foreboding went through her at the thought of being somehow connected to such a vile and deadly attack.

Thousands of miles away, in the city of Bangalore, Vince played back the recording of the conversation he had just had with Sandra Carter. Vince's real name was Vijay Singh and he was an Indian Muslim who worked for the Feedback Data Corporation. The National Security Agency had outsourced the information line to a company in India at considerable savings. After all, they received an average of 10,000 calls per day. Along with the other telephone operators, Vince had practiced faking his Midwestern accent and using a made up western name to make the American callers think he was just next door. It made them more comfortable and more apt to confide in him. All the operators had the same instructions and used the same methods. Sandra Carter had thought she was talking to a middle-aged Midwestern operator named Vince Patten in Washington, D.C. Instead, she was talking to a young Indian male in Bangalore. Of all the hundreds of conversations that Vijay had had with American clients, this was the first one that might be relevant. Vijay Singh wasn't only working for the Feedback Data Corporation. That was his day job. His night job was as an operator of Al Queda in India identifying potential terrorist targets. Every now and then, he even had some information in the U.S. to relay to the relevant people in charge. They would know what to make of this lost computer story. He wrote down Sandra Carter's phone and address and put the tape of the conversation they had had in an envelope to be carried by messenger to the mountains. After work he would drop it off at the predetermined grocery store. He sealed the envelope with some tape and put it on his desk, then he picked up his headphones again, ready for the next call. "NSA Information Center, Vince Patten here, 1-800 Freedom. Can I help you?"

CHAPTER 17

Szabo Tanovich was eating a toasted bagel and drinking black coffee sitting in the New Wave coffee shop in Washington, D.C. *Jew food served by Greeks*, Szabo thought to himself. *Only in America*. His cell phone rang and he picked it up.

"Szabo here," the big Serb said into the phone.

"It's me," said Michael Cherry.

"Hey, chief," Szabo grunted.

"We have a small problem that has just come up," said Michael.

"What is it?"

"I got a call from our friend in the Middle East. A really strange loose end that has to be quickly tied into a knot," said Michael. "You have to fly out to Portland, Oregon."

"When?" asked Szabo.

"Today at 4:00 PM. There's a reservation waiting for you at Reagan Airport."

"What do I have to do once I get there?"

"Some lady bought a laptop for her kid with some old information on it regarding the 9/11 attacks. The same kind of laptops you delivered to the groups that came over in 2000. Remember, Szabo? I think it might have been Atta's. Can't believe he would be so careless with it."

"Don't think he had a use for it where he was going," said Szabo sardonically.

"I don't either. Go find this woman. Her name is Sandra Carter and she lives at 372 Sycamore with her son."

"And what do I do once I find her?" asked Szabo, dipping a piece of his bagel into the black coffee.

"Eliminate everything and bring back the computer. Make it look accidental. Be careful and thorough."

"Okay. The kid, too?" asked Szabo.

"Everybody involved or who knew about this computer. Then call me back from there and confirm that it was done."

"Okay, boss," said Szabo Tanovich. He finished eating his bagel calmly and asked for the check. He never questioned Michael Cherry's orders and enjoyed doing the grunt work for him. Without Cherry, Szabo and his family would have been dead or in prison in Serbia a long time ago. Instead they lived in an expensive home in McLean, Virginia, and his kids went to school with the wealthiest Americans. But even more than that, Cherry had given Szabo Tanovich real power in his adopted country. As a federal agent with the National Security Agency, the Serb had almost unlimited powers to arrest individuals, to eavesdrop, and even to kill if he had to. It was better than being in Serbia during the war.

It's better than working for Arkan, Szabo thought as he got up from the table. He looked at the blonde waitress and called out to her. The pretty waitress walked toward his table without looking at him.

"Check, please," he said smiling grotesquely at her.

She wrote up his check, hoping that he would pay and leave in a hurry.

"Hey," he said. "I'm going on a trip. When I come back, you and me go out?"

"I don't think so," said the waitress.

"Don't be so difficult," said the huge Serb. "When I come back, I come here again."

"I hope not," said the waitress.

"You say that, but you change your mind. You see," said Szabo. "*Kurva* (whore)."

"Have a nice trip," said the waitress, ironically. Szabo left her the money to cover the check and a quarter tip.

"Big spender," the waitress muttered to herself.

American bitch, kucka, thought Szabo to himself, *I'll take care of her when I get back.*

In the NSA offices in Washington, facing the Capitol, Michael Cherry was reading the *Wall Street Journal* at his mahogany desk. *Things at Holliwell are going exceedingly well,* thought Michael to himself. *The stock is at a record high.* The war in Iraq was in its third year. Pentagon orders for oil, weapons, materiel, and machinery were escalating like never before. America was spending billions of dollars in Iraq. Orders from the U.S. Army in Afghanistan had exceeded the allotted Pentagon budget. Government military spending in Iraq and Afghanistan was giving Holliwell its most profitable year in business to date. Cherry was the largest shareholder in the company with an estimated stock value of $350 million. He was no longer the chairman of the firm. Cherry had had to step down from his post in 2000 to assist the campaign for the presidency of George Branch. The Holliwell board, acting on his recommendation, had selected Colonel Bob Forrester as his replacement for chairman. It wasn't an accident that Bob Forrester was his ally and liaison at the Pentagon.

With the election of President Branch, and the return of the Republican Party to the executive office, Cherry had been appointed to the FBI as deputy commissioner. After 9/11, he had been relocated as deputy commissioner to the newly-formed National Security Agency where he became the most powerful man in America with almost unlimited powers of espionage and information gathering.

Things have certainly turned around since 1998, thought Michael Cherry. *I was almost ruined back then. Now Holliwell is the number-one military supplier to the armed forces and I'm rich as a result of this. I am also one of the most powerful men in America. I made it all happen by myself.*

The telephone call he had received from Prince Abdullah regarding the laptop had unnerved him just a tad, but not too much. It was a small loose end of the 9/11 attacks. There had been others he'd had to suppress, first at the FBI and then at the NSA. In this case, Prince Abdullah had given him the information that the center in Bangalore had received. The terrorists were in direct contact with Prince Abdullah. They had received a tape of the phone call from their operative in Bangalore by mule.

Cherry would take care of it much like having a cavity filled, quick and painless. He had handled much more complex problems in the past preparing for the attacks and making sure the terrorists were not discovered. There had been some real close calls like the arrest of Moussaoui by the FBI agent, Kara Murphy, in Minneapolis. Fortunately his position at the FBI had allowed him to keep the information sealed until after the attacks. Now this problem with some woman in Portland buying a laptop full of old information would have to be taken care of personally by the big Serb.

You could always count on Szabo, thought Cherry, *He was a real pro*. The Serb would get rid of the woman, her son, and the laptop. Then it would all be over once and for all. Michael's involvement in the 9/11 attacks would be hidden forever. Like it had never happened. No one would ever know or even suspect that he had been the prime instigator of the worst terrorist attack against the United States.

Michael Cherry got up from his black leather chair and looked down at the Washington Mall from his window as he mentally justified his actions to himself. *The country is on the right track now*, he thought, *With a solid Republican majority after the dark years of Democratic decay, we are now spreading American values and smiting our enemies across the globe.* Cherry himself was doing even better—enriched by Holliwell, the war, and now courted by every politician and lobbyist in Washington for campaign donations and political support.

Things have turned out so much better than I thought they would, he thought to himself, *beyond my wildest dreams.*

CHAPTER 18

❀

Adam waited impatiently for the school bus to come get him at his apartment on the corner of Sycamore Street. He had put his new laptop in his backpack and was looking forward to playing his video game on the bus. Adam had loaded the *Prince of Persia* onto the laptop and could hardly contain his joy at being able to play his favorite game whenever he wanted to, even on his school bus. Of all the presents his mother had ever given him, this was certainly the best. Plus, there was all that cool stuff about the terrorists in the hard drive, and he thought there was even a chance they could get a reward for their discovery. Finally, the yellow bus came and Adam got in.

"Good morning, Adam," said the grey-haired African-American lady who had been driving the same bus for fifteen years.

"Good morning, Ms. Barry."

"You're such a polite young man," said Ms. Barry, who had seen her share of obnoxious junior high students during her bus-driving career.

He walked toward the middle of the bus and sat down in the tenth seat on the right, near the window. Adam opened his backpack and took out the laptop that had a battery use of almost three hours. *Plenty of juice for me to play with until I get to school*, Adam thought to himself. The bus stopped again and two older boys got on. They walked down the aisle past Adam and then stopped suddenly.

"Hey, dickhead," the boy said to Adam. "What's that you got there?"

Phil and Mike Sheridan were two brothers who bullied everybody in their school. They played football and were bigger than the rest of the Junior High students.

"It's a laptop," said Adam. "My mom got it for me."

"His mom got it for him," said Phil Sheridan. "Pass it over here."

"No, I'm playing a game on it," said Adam.

Mike ran over to Adam and ripped the laptop from his hands.

"Give it back," said Adam. "Give it back!"

"Give it back, give it back, shuddup," said Phil.

They started to look at the game and Adam ran up to them trying to grab it back. Mike pushed him into one of the seats. The other kids started screaming, "Give it back! Give it back!"

"You guys want to get some, too?" asked Phil Sheridan menacingly.

"It's just a shitty little laptop," said Mike. "I'm going to throw it out the window. My father has one much better than this piece of shit. This is an old one."

Mike stuck the laptop outside of the top window and dangled it outside of the bus.

"I'm going to drop it," he said, taunting Adam.

"No, please don't," Adam begged.

"What'll you pay me for it?" he said to Adam.

"Don't!" yelled Adam.

"I'm going to drop it in a million pieces," said Mike.

"I'll give you all the money I've got," said Adam.

"How much is that?" said Phil Sheridan. "If it's not enough kiss your laptop goodbye."

"I have five bucks to buy my lunch," said Adam.

"That's it?" said Mike, dangling the computer outside of the bus.

Adam could just imagine his computer crashing into the street, and being run over by the other cars.

"Give me the five bucks," said Mike.

Adam forked over the Jackson.

"Give it to him," said Mike Sheridan to his brother Phil.

Phil pulled the laptop from outside the bus and gave it back to Adam.

"I wasn't going to drop it, pussy," he said.

"What's going on back there?" asked Ms. Barry.

"Adam's having a girly tizzy fit," said Phil.

The other kids laughed.

Adam went back to his seat embarrassed by what the brothers had done to him, but at least he had his laptop back. He wouldn't be able to eat but he would be able to play and that was all that counted to him. *I hate bullies*, he said to himself. *If Uncle Dave was here he would have taken care of them. He has a gun and was a cop.* He missed his adopted uncle and his whole family in New

Jersey, but he was in Portland now and his mom said he had to make the best of it.

He opened the laptop and turned on the game, hoping to lose himself in it for a while and forget all about the Sheridan brothers.

CHAPTER 19

❀

Prince Abdullah sat in the backseat of the Maybach Mercedes as his driver drove him to the Royal Palace in Riyadh. They passed the long lots of used and new cars that lined the capital city of Saudi Arabia.

Oil and cars, thought Prince Abdullah to himself. *The lifeblood of modern civilization.* As Minister of Defense it was the prince's duty to protect the interests of the last real monarchy on earth. Few people realized that Saudi Arabia was run by the whim of the king and his various family members. They had power of life and death over all the subjects in the kingdom and showed it in the occasional beheadings in Chop Chop Square, as it was called.

Democracy, indeed, thought Prince Abdullah to himself. *Do the Americans think that we will just give all this power and wealth away to whoever wins a stupid election?* In his mind, his collaboration with the American Michael Cherry had had positive results for the both of them, and for the Kingdom of Saudi Arabia as well.

Most of the Al Queda hijackers had received their visas to the United States from the American consulate in Riyadh. They had received clearance from his ministry in Riyadh. All it had taken was an organization consisting of four teams of five terrorists each to subvert the known order in the Middle Eastern world. At their arrival in the United States, Michael Cherry had supplied the groups with five laptops full of instructions for the team leaders. The terrorists also received monies and detailed instructions by e-mail directly to their computers once they landed inside the United States. From early 1999 to 2000, the terrorists had enrolled in prearranged flight schools across America learning how to fly. There had been close calls and reports made to government agencies from the flight schools about Arab men wanting to learn how to fly planes.

Cherry had had to quash that information or misdirect it away from the various security and investigation services. This had taken a lot of money and influence to which Prince Abdullah had contributed in a significant manner. He had also given a check for $20 million to the 2000 presidential election campaign of Florida Governor Jim Branch. At the outset, nobody had thought that Branch could defeat the incumbent Democratic Vice President Al Dour, not even Cherry who had planned the attacks for November 2000, two months before the election. But Jim Branch proved personable and persuasive and won by the narrowest of margins putting a Republican back into the White House. Cherry had changed the dates of the attacks several times awaiting the results of the election. He was sure his financial contributions would give him the choice of any job in the new administration.

However, at the outset of his new term, President Branch appeared completely uninterested in foreign policy or in thanking Michael Cherry for his support. He ignored what Cherry had done for him by giving him the funds to buy the presidency. Branch's chief of staff called Cherry to offer him a job as deputy director at the FBI as a consolation prize.

"Cherry called me to complain bitterly," remembered the prince. "He said that without U.S. intervention, Holliwell was going to go bankrupt. He called Branch an ungrateful idiot. Couldn't he see what was happening in the world? Oil prices were at an all-time low, and Saddam Hussein was threatening to rearm, something Saudi Arabia could not afford. By then we both, Cherry and I, didn't care which U.S. administration got attacked as long as it happened quickly."

Allah Akbar, thought Prince Abdullah to himself. *Things had turned out in their favor after all.* America had been attacked. Thousands had died. Al Queda took responsibility for the attacks goading the Americans to come and get them in Afghanistan. The U.S. sent troops to Afghanistan and worked with their allies there. The war in Afghanistan had lasted for a much shorter time than anybody had predicted. America was a rich country. The army supplied the anti-Taliban forces with food, money, and equipment—something they hadn't seen in years. Army Rangers helped them plan the campaign. Faced with a choice of freedom with America or repression with the Taliban, the Afghans chose the former. Superior air and manpower from the U.S. forces and the help of the warlords had ensured the route of the Taliban forces.

Prince Abdullah had received two frantic calls from his cousin, Osama bin Laden—once on the road escaping from Kabul when a U.S. Apache helicopter had spotted him escaping in an SUV, and once from the cave hideout of Tora

Bora. At that time, the end was near and Osama and Al-Zawahiri were completely surrounded by the U.S. Rangers. Only a timely call from Prince Abdullah to Cherry and his Pentagon liaison had allowed his cousin to escape. Both Michael Cherry and Prince Abdullah needed the Islamic radical to be kept alive and eventually Osama and the Al Queda leadership had fled to the mountains of northern Pakistan.

Further link-ups between the terrorists and Iraq were falsely established to encourage an American invasion there. Key information about the presence of weapons of mass destruction was fed to an inexperienced and naïve President Branch. The subsequent invasion of Iraq had completed their grand business plan and made all their dreams and aspirations come true.

Never mind that 40,000 Iraqis and 2,300 American soldiers had to die, thought Prince Abdullah to himself. Oil was at $75-per-barrel, higher than ever before. Saudi Arabia had never been richer, and now had direct access to the oil in Iraq as well. Holliwell had been awarded all the reconstruction contracts in Iraq and Afghanistan. Even better, Islamic fanatics were leaving the kingdom to fight the Americans in Iraq, thus weakening opposition to the monarchy within Saudi Arabia. Michael Cherry had become the number-two man at the National Security Agency making him an even greater asset. Abdullah's cousin Osama was still at large, with his infinite numbers of religious suicide bombers at his complete disposal for any mission Prince Abdullah might need.

And now the old king is dying, thought Prince Abdullah as the Maybach limousine passed through the Royal Gate of the King's Palace. *And I am third in the line of succession. That will put me at a heartbeat from becoming the new king and one of the most important men in the world.* He sighed thinking that he was already sixty-five and that this great power and opportunity had only come to him late in life.

Better late than never, he said to himself. *Thanks be to Allah and his miraculous ways.*

CHAPTER 20

❦

It was a late Thursday night in Portland and Sandra Baines was working on a case for her boss at the ACLU from her living room. The case involved an African-American girl that had been expelled from the prestigious Portland Music Academy. The girl's mother had filed a discrimination suit with the help of the ACLU. It was up to Sandra to investigate all aspects of the case and recommend a suggestion to her boss, as to whether they should pursue the case or not. Sandra's son Adam was in his room playing on his computer as usual, and in the kitchen the old dishwasher was making as much noise as a cement mixer at a construction site.

Suddenly Sandra heard the downstairs doorbell buzz.

Who could it be at this late hour? thought Sandra. Recently her ex-husband Gregory Carter had been harassing her with late-night phone calls and sob stories. He wanted them to get back together. He claimed she was the only woman he ever loved.

Not a chance in hell of that, she thought to herself. She walked back into Adam's room.

"Adam," she said, "I think Carter is downstairs and wants me to buzz him up."

"Don't let that asshole in," said Adam, not looking up at his mom.

"I have to or he will just keep ringing," said Sandra. "I'll get rid of him in a minute, but don't come out of your room."

"That's fine with me. I don't want to see him," said Adam. "I hate him."

"Well, I don't like him, either. So stay in here or, better still, go to your hiding place behind the vent," Sandra said, surprising her son.

Adam stopped playing. "You know about the vent?" he said, truly surprised.

"It's a mom's job to know how her son gets in and out of the house without going through the front door."

"I just do it for fun," said Adam.

"I know," said Sandra. "Don't worry about it. I'll get rid of Carter in a few minutes. Don't come out whatever you hear."

She left closing the door. Adam decided to go sit inside the vent and keep playing his game. This way if Gregory even thought about coming into his room, no one would appear to be there. Adam crunched himself into the small space and closed the metal screen behind him.

Sandra went back into the living room and heard a strong knock on the front door of the apartment. She walked to the door and opened it. Sandra was very surprised to see that it wasn't Gregory Carter at all. A giant man with a blonde crew cut and a red tie and a blue jacket was standing in the doorway.

"Can I help you?" asked Sandra. "We have no money to buy anything."

"Are you Sandra Baines? Sandra Carter Baines?" Szabo asked.

"Yes. Yes, I am," said Sandra.

"I am Szabo Tanovich from the National Security Agency."

He pulled out his badge and showed it to her.

"I believe you filed a phone report about a laptop computer with some information on it?" Szabo said in his heavily accented English.

"Yes, I did," Sandra said. "I didn't think you would get here so soon. I only did that a few days ago."

"The NSA takes all these reports very seriously," Szabo said. "We try to track as many of these reports as we can. I was in the Portland area so they asked me to come by."

"Please come in and sit down, excuse the mess."

Szabo looked around the apartment. It was scarcely furnished but clean and in good taste.

Two bedrooms, one kitchen, only one entrance to get in or out. Perfect layout for a killing, he thought to himself.

"So when did you find this computer?" asked Szabo sitting on the couch.

"It was a laptop," said Sandra. "I bought it in a flea market sale for my fourteen-year-old son, Adam. He is kind of a computer geek. The sale featured items that had been forgotten at the Portland airport and brought to the lost and found. I bought it for $100."

"Cheap," said Szabo eying Sandra up and down.

The woman is attractive, too, he thought to himself looking at her long, brown hair and delicately chiseled features.

"That's what I thought," said Sandra. "I gave it to Adam and he was really happy. Then the next day he showed me some information he had retrieved on the computer and I was, like, in shock."

"What had he found?" asked Szabo.

"It was a set of instructions in English and Arabic on how to attack the World Trade Center. Adam said it was dated one year before the attacks," Sandra said.

"Did you find this unusual?" said Szabo.

"Yes, very," said Sandra. "Don't you?"

"It could just be hackers or bloggers trying to make themselves interesting," said Szabo. "Do you have the computer here?"

"My son has it in his room. Should I call him?"

"No, that's okay," said Szabo smiling at her. "We can call him later. Could you be so kind as to get me a glass of water? I got awfully thirsty on my long drive here."

"No problem," said Sandra, then felt a bit uneasy sitting there alone with this massive giant sitting in her living room. She got up and went to the refrigerator to open it, looking inside for a fresh bottle of Evian water. As she leaned into the refrigerator to grab the bottle, a massive hand came behind her and covered her mouth as the Serb's other hand physically lifted her up off the ground from her crotch. Szabo Tanovich had quickly followed her to the fridge without making a sound. He was amazingly fast and quiet for his large size. It was a skill he had mastered in the Serb militias in the former Jugoslavia. Sandra was lifted straight off the ground and into the air. She tried hard to yell but her mouth was covered by his hand. Sandra kicked back, her heel ferociously catching the giant in the shin but he never loosened his grip. He carried her over to the couch and threw her down on her stomach and face. Sandra tried again to scream but his hand pushed her head down into one of the couch pillows. She felt the man grab her wrists and put them behind her back. Then he tied them with some tape and she felt powerless as his great strength completely overwhelmed her. Once he was done tying her wrists, he turned her around and slapped her across the face twice stunning her into silence. Szabo took out a piece of masking tape and covered her mouth. The whole action had taken two seconds at the most.

"Now, let's go see where this boy of yours is," said Szabo. Sandra's eyes went wide with fright and she tried to move herself off the couch to no avail. Szabo walked into the hallway and opened the door to Adam's bedroom expecting to see a young boy at work. However, the room was completely empty. Inside the air-conditioning vent Adam was holding his breath looking at the huge man who was walking around his room.

Who the fuck is this guy? thought Adam to himself.

Szabo looked in all the closets and under the bed, and was visibly upset that Adam wasn't in the room. He proceeded to smash everything he could find sending books and DVDs crashing into the walls. Adam cowered further away from the screen deep inside the air-conditioning tunnel.

"She lied to me, the little bitch," Szabo said to himself and stormed out of Adam's room and back into the living room.

"Where's your son?" Szabo yelled at Sandra.

He turned her around and ripped off the tape from her mouth.

"Who the hell are you?" Sandra screamed at him. "What do you want from me?"

He hit her again hard and threw her back on the couch on her stomach. Then he punched her hard in the back. Sandra felt all the air leave her lungs. She gasped hard trying to breathe in some air but none was coming. She felt herself unable to breathe.

"Where is he, *pizda* (cunt)? Tell me or I will keep hitting you again and again."

Finally Sandra was able to breathe some air and answer back.

"He's at a friend's house," Sandra managed to say. "He'll come back tomorrow."

"What friend?" asked Szabo.

Sandra tried to think quickly, but only one name came to her. "Dave. He's at Dave Stillati's house," she said. Sandra didn't know why she had said that but it was the first name that came into her head.

"Why did you lie to me?" Szabo asked her. "Why did you say he was in the house?"

"I don't know. Maybe I was embarrassed that my son was not at home so late, that you'd think I was a bad mother."

"You are a bad mother and a whore or you'd have a man in the house. *Kurva*," said Szabo spitting out the words at her.

"Leave me alone," Sandra cried. "Take whatever you want."

"You don't understand," said Szabo. "I'm not a thief. I don't want your useless shit. I am here to kill you and your little boy and take his computer away forever."

"No!" yelled Sandra and she managed to throw a back kick that caught the Serb in the groin area. He flinched slightly but then recovered enough to punch Sandra again in the back and cover her mouth again with the black masking tape.

"Well, all this action has gotten me excited," Szabo said to Sandra. "As long as I'm here, we might as well have some fun."

He pulled out his seven-inch serrated fishing knife and cut off the back of her jeans from the bottom leg up. After slicing the jeans all the way to her crotch he ripped them off. Sandra was struggling to keep her dignity, rocking back and forth on the couch in her black underwear.

"Very pretty," Szabo said to her. "Did you put those on for me? The women in Croatia were not as accommodating. *Yebem te pichku* (I'll fuck you in the cunt)."

He proceeded to rip off her black panties, and then took off his own pants and underwear. Then he mounted Sandra from behind grabbing her throat with his two huge hands. Sandra felt herself being violated and strangled at the same time. She tried to mentally put herself in another place, but it was useless. The pain was just too strong. As she felt her neck squeezed tighter and tighter, she realized that Szabo was going to kill her.

I pray at least Adam got away, she thought to herself. *Please, God. Let it be that he got away.*

Szabo continued jabbing himself into her as he squeezed her neck until he felt her body go limp. He then pulled his penis out of her and released his semen on the floor. He cleaned up after himself making sure she was dead. He knew enough not to leave any DNA traces that might be linked back to him. After using Windex and paper towels to clean the area, he lifted up his right hand and made the three-finger sign of the Holy Trinity with his thumb, middle, and index finger over the lifeless body of Sandra Carter Baines. He still had one more thing left to do.

CHAPTER 21

There are days that you just know things are not going to go your way. It's like if a little genie wakes up and says, "Dave Stillati, today you are going to have a really shitty day." It can be something as stupid as not being able to find your favorite pair of matching socks, or you miss the bus and get to work late, or you wake up in the morning with a Glock pistol pointing at your forehead. Today was one of those days. I woke up with a beautiful girl sitting on my chest pressing a Glock revolver against my forehead. Normally that might even be a kinky way of waking up, except that the gal was Samantha Eggers, Olympic Silver medalist in skeet shooting from the Sydney Olympics.

"Samantha, what are you doing?" I asked her.

"Why don't you ever return my calls?" asked Samantha straddling me on my bed.

"How'd you get in here?" I asked her.

"I still have the key, remember?"

"Can you put that thing down? It might go off. You are married now, remember?"

"What's that got to do with it?" she asked indignantly.

"I don't sleep with married women."

"Yeah, right." She kept poking me with the gun.

"No, I mean it. Why aren't you in bed with your husband?"

"Him?" she said. "He's at the Australian Open."

Samantha had gotten married to Robert Case, one of the best tennis players in the world. The marriage had been in most of the gossip magazines, and they appeared blissfully happy.

"Marriage bores me," she said, getting off my chest.

"I wouldn't know," I replied. "Haven't been married in years."

"I had more fun with you," she said. "You were my agent and my lover."

"It was a big mistake," I said. "Couldn't get you to train right without wanting to jump on top of you."

"I didn't complain," Samantha said.

"Robert is a great athlete and a better guy than me," I said.

"That might be true, but you're no fun," she said standing up.

I looked at her tight ass and long tanned legs with some longing but kept firm on my decision to resist temptation that would only lead to disaster.

"Tell you what," I said as I got out of bed. "If you wait a second, I'll buy you breakfast at Jimmy's Cafe downstairs."

"Okay, you're on," she said. "But I get to see you get dressed."

"If that's how you get your jollies," I replied.

I threw on a pair of jeans and took Samantha out for some eggs over easy and some Canadian bacon. I had done some sponsor work for her after the Olympics and things had gotten hot and heavy for a while. My commitment level wasn't really there and she went on to meet a great athlete who made tons of money and loved her for her craziness, and they had gotten married within a week. As crazy as she was, I think he still got the better deal. We finished our breakfast and parted company with pecks on both cheeks. My personal motto was: Better a good friend than a pissed off lover.

I headed to my office, which was about a ten-minute walk away, and noticed how resilient New York was. Despite a massive terrorist attack, traffic, and terrible weather, people still flocked to visit and live in the city in droves. Real estate prices just kept climbing and climbing. It made permanent inhabitants of Gotham feel a little bit more unique and vintage. As I arrived on 11th Avenue and 42nd Street, I noticed my ex-wife Susan's green Mercedes station wagon double-parked outside. The emergency lights were flashing and she had left the keys in the idle car.

Trouble, I immediately thought to myself while rushing up the steps of the townhouse.

Inside my office, Kelly was hugging Susan as tears streamed down her face.

"What happened," I said, anxiety gripping my stomach. "Are the kids okay?"

"She's dead," Susan cried "She's dead!"

"Who's dead?" I asked her.

"Sandra," Kelly said. "Susan's sister. They found her dead in her apartment this morning. She was strangled."

"But wasn't she living in Portland?" I asked taking my ex-wife's hand in mine.

"I just spoke to her on the phone yesterday. She was doing fine and planning to come back here after the school year. I can't believe this. Not again. Not again."

Susan had lost her second husband in the 9/11 attacks. Now her sister was dead, too. It was too awful to contemplate the odds of that happening to one person.

"Who called you?" I asked.

"The Portland Police called me. They want me to fly our there to identify the body. I can't, Dave. I just can't do it. I can't see my sister lying in the morgue."

"What about Adam," I asked. "Where is he?"

Susan just burst out crying again.

"They don't know. He's gone, disappeared, maybe kidnapped," said Kelly who had met Sandra and Adam when they had lived in New York City.

"Dave, you got to go there, for me, now," Susan implored. "I can't go there, you understand? I can't. I can't leave the boys here."

"Susan, don't worry about it," I replied. "I will leave for Portland this afternoon. We'll have you sign a power of attorney for me to identify the body. Then I will go and find Adam, I promise."

"Please, Dave. Please…" Susan cried in Kelly's arms.

"Susan, you're in shock now," I said. "Kelly will get you some pills to help you through this. I'll take care of the rest. Don't worry." It's always easy to say "Don't worry" to other people when you're not the one taking the hit. We tried to console Susan but to no avail. Finally I told Kelly to get her bag and coat and take her home.

"Kelly will drive you back to New Jersey," I said to Susan.

"Let's get your stuff together," said Kelly.

"Stay there with her till I call you," I said.

Susan just nodded. She was too crushed to speak. My heart felt her pain and I felt powerless to stop her pain or to really help her.

"I've got her," said Kelly heading outside.

I walked them outside of my office and into Susan's car. I wanted Susan to get back to her familiar surroundings in New Jersey. I knew that and her sons would give her comfort. After they left, I went back inside and proceeded to book myself a flight to Portland for late in the afternoon. I didn't kid myself that I would be able to solve anything. The Portland Police had a lot more manpower than I did. Even so, many crimes are never solved or, if they are, it's by an accidental clue or just plain luck. The best I could do was to go there, identify the body, and look for Adam. After all, Susan had been my wife, and Sandra was her sister.

Sandra had been my friend and sister-in-law as well. I had coached Adam on the travel soccer team in Clinton, New Jersey. He was a good kid and had a father who abandoned him and a stupid stepfather to follow that act. Sandra and Adam were part of my extended family. It was my duty and obligation to do everything I could do to find Adam first and foremost and then see the killer of Sandra brought to justice. I took my Beretta 92 semi-automatic, nine-millimeter revolver and some shells from my desk to put in my overnight bag.

The Beretta 92 was the weapon of choice of the Los Angeles Police Department and the United States Army, so it was good enough for me. It could fire fifteen consecutive shots and weighed slightly less than a kilo. I had been using it for a year and felt proficient that I could hit a bull's eye at twenty feet nine out of ten times. I took $200 from the petty cash box in Kelly's desk. I picked up my overnight bag and walked outside to hail a cab for LaGuardia Airport.

CHAPTER 22

❀

Michael Cherry was listening to Bach on his sleek Bang and Olufson stereo in the mahogany-paneled library of his mansion in McLean, Virginia. His wife had left him some swatches of material to choose from for the new drapes the decorator was going to have installed. Michael enjoyed the sensuous feeling of the rich, black felt material in his hand when his private cell phone rang. Michael looked at the caller I.D. and saw it was Szabo Tanovich.

"Hey, Szabo," he said into the phone. "Did you take care of it?"

"Partly," said Szabo, "I'm still in Portland. I took care of the woman but the son was at a friend's house."

"And the computer?"

"The kid has it. I am waiting outside of the house for him to come home. It wasn't in the house when I was there," said Szabo.

"That's not like you, leaving things unfinished," said Michael Cherry, slightly annoyed.

"It's a minor detail that I will take care of today," said Szabo. "I'm going to go to his school to get his friend's address. The kid's friend is called Dave Stillati. I got it from the Baines Carter woman. After that, I will liquidate him, get the computer, and come back home."

"And the police?"

"They're at the house now looking into it. They think it was a random murder or robbery kind of thing."

"Well, take care of it quickly. I don't want this thing going on and on."

"Not a problem," said Szabo hanging up. He was anxious to finish up this job and get back to Washington, and he didn't like disappointing his boss.

Cherry hung up the phone in time for his wife and daughters to walk into the studio.

"Daddy," said his older daughter, Barbara. "Look at all this stuff we bought at Nordstrom's."

Michael gave them an approving nod. Both his blonde daughters were in college at Georgetown now and had grown up as beautiful as their mother.

"We spent a bundle of money," said his wife.

"That's what it's there for," said Michael kissing his wife on the forehead. Michael cared for his family and didn't mind spending money on them now that Holliwell was having another record year. The National Security Agency also paid him a salary that he considered as his petty cash fund. Michael's stock in Holliwell was now worth upward of $300 million. He had handpicked Colonel Forrester, former member of Oped Pentagon intelligence to succeed him at Holliwell. The colonel had been his main supplier of information at the Pentagon and he had been pleased to put him at Holliwell. In return, the colonel had given him a $100 million bonus in stock for each year Holliwell remained profitable. The deal had greatly enriched both men.

"Well, I've got to go back to work now," said Michael to his daughters.

"But it's Saturday, Daddy," said his younger daughter, Cynthia.

"Daddy has to work so he can pay for all the stuff you just bought and the stuff you will buy next week," Michael said.

The girls left the room chit-chatting among themselves. They were very proud of their rich and successful father who had left the profitable private sector as chairman of Holliwell to dedicate himself to the security of his country as deputy commissioner of the National Security Agency. Rumor had it that Michael Cherry was even being considered as the possible Vice-Presidential candidate for the election of 2008 with Senator Stevens a Republican from Ohio. The girls were looking forward to seeing themselves on the cover of Time magazine someday.

Michael went back to reading the NSA papers that were on his table. *What would they think if they knew what I'd done?* thought Michael Cherry. *Would they think I'm a monster teaming up with terrorists and killers? They probably would. But it's too late now and they will never find out anyway. The girls do like their amenities, that's for sure.*

Michael felt sure that long ago he had made a Faustian deal with the world and now he was truly enjoying all the fruits of his endeavors. *There is no good and bad, evil or goodness*, thought Michael. *Only what needs to be done, and who has the guts to do it.* He felt sure he was safe from all possible retribution from his acts and that he had covered all the loose ends. *After all,* thought Michael Cherry to himself. *The terrorists would never reveal my participation in their attack. They would lose credibility with their fanatical supporters if it was known that an American had set up their attacks. Plus, they still needed my help to save their asses again and again. I did it in the Tomahawk attack on their compound, during their escape from Kabul, and especially when Bin Laden was surrounded by the Rangers in Tora Bora. I pulled some real strings to make that happen.*

Cherry had to coordinate that rescue with Colonel Forrester at Intelligence at the Pentagon. He had key satellite coordinates changed allowing the terrorists to use a small corridor of freedom to escape from the Rangers. *Colonel Forrester had served his purpose well at the Pentagon and had been adequately rewarded,* thought Cherry. *There was nothing left to tie me to the hijacking attacks. Nineteen of the hijackers were dead, and the one left in prison wasn't bright enough to know anything of importance.*

Michael compared the various fabrics his wife had left him. He liked the black one the best. *The discovery of this one remaining laptop was a nuisance the Serb would take care of,* thought Cherry. *Szabo would find the boy and his laptop, kill the boy in Portland, and return the laptop to me. Szabo is a killing machine and has never failed me so far.*

Michael Cherry felt as safe and secure as a young boy in a candy store. He definitely selected the black felt swatch and put it aside for his wife, as the scales of Bach's music filled the air of his library study.

CHAPTER 23

❀

Adam kept looking out on his house from behind a parked truck. He had been sleeping in the public park behind the apartment complex, covering himself with leaves for the last two nights. During the horrible night on which his mother was murdered, Adam had escaped through the air conditioning duct with his laptop computer and fifty-five dollars in change. He had used the money to eat at McDonald's but was growing weary of sleeping outside in the park. There were other older homeless men there and it was cold and rainy. In the early morning, he had returned to the apartment complex to see what was happening. He knew he couldn't go back inside.

The police had two squad cars parked outside the apartment building and there was yellow tape outside of the downstairs entrance. Adam had tried to circle back to the apartment on the night of the attack, but the police had already sealed off the area. Adam would have gone right up to speak to the police had he not seen the giant man who had come into his room talking to them in front of his house. He could tell it was the same man who had come into their house from his size and crew cut blonde hair. On the night of the murder, Adam had to watch in shock as his mother was taken out of the apartment on a stretcher with a blanket over her body. He knew she was dead and reacted in horror as a wave of nausea and fear went through him. He ran back to spend the night in the park alone.

Standing in front of his apartment, not knowing what to do, Adam missed his mother terribly. He had never been so alone in the world. Adam was still in shock from the terrible events that had happened and could not admit to himself that his mom was really dead. He had cried himself to sleep in the park at night and stayed close to the house during the day without exposing himself. Adam didn't know what else to do.

"Maybe I should take the bus and travel all the way to Aunt Susan's in New Jersey, or Uncle Dave Stillati in New York." He didn't know if he had enough money to get there by Greyhound bus. He resolved that he would try and call his Aunt Susan collect later that night. *Dave was a cop once*, thought Adam. *He must be able to help me.* Later at night, Adam returned once again to spy on his old apartment. The giant was sitting in a car below his old apartment.

Why did he kill Mom? Adam asked himself. *Does he want to kill me, too?* These were all questions that he asked himself in fear and guilt at still being alive. *I should have come out of inside the vent and fought him like a man*, Adam said to himself. *I should have defended Mom and saved her.* He thought about it in shame. More tears came to his eyes as he thought about the absurdity of what he was thinking. *Mom told me not to come out*, he thought. *I would be dead if I had not called. She saved me.*

Adam decided to go back to his school. At least there he could get lunch and see some of his friends. It would take him an hour to walk there, but that was okay. He went through the dense park area toward the junior high school. In his pocket, he still had forty-two dollars and he carried his laptop computer with him. *At least I still have my laptop and my game*, he thought to himself. *That's not a lot, but it's all I got left in this world.*

CHAPTER 24

❈

Most people lose their cool in emergency situations. That's not my case. I don't know why that is, but I was always more comfortable in emergencies than in the tedium of everyday life. That's what I was like in soccer; when I played, sweeper and attackers came down on me again and again. I didn't panic and just tried to stop their attacks one at a time. I see a particular problem in slow motion and I try to figure out how to fix it in a limited amount of time. I then can put my priorities in order in a hurry, choosing the most promising solution. My brain is just made that way, I guess.

In this particular situation there was very little I could do to help Susan immediately. Watching her cry her blue eyes out with her face contorted by grief only made me want to protect her more. I wished desperately that I could have prevented her sister Sandra's death, but that was not an option I had been given. What she had asked me to do was save her nephew Adam and find out who killed her sister. As I prepared to get on my flight, I geared myself up to do this in the best possible way. I walked from the airline terminal onto my flight to Portland and found myself placed in a miniature couch seat, between a lady who had a farm in Texas, and a vitamin salesman. There were only two inches of space on either side of my seat and three inches of space to the table in front of me. Thirty years ago, flights were an exciting mix of adventure and service. Today they are as uncomfortable as riding the subway in New York. That's progress for you. I always thought there should be a special tribunal assembled for people who commit ordinary crimes against humanity and in that docket, to be judged by their peers, I would put airplane interior designers, airline food chefs, telemarketers, telephone operators for credit cards, all collection agencies, celebrities who advertise sex pills for seniors on national television, divorce lawyers, people who flaunt their sexual orientation and people who judge other people for the same orientation.

As a man six feet, three inches tall, I found my legs to be a complete liability on any standard coach airline flight. If I could have checked my legs as luggage, I would have—only they probably would have gotten misplaced on a plane to Nepal. Today, a passenger is imprisoned for fifteen hours in a pretzel-like formation and unable to move an inch in any direction. I am sure the conditions are a violation of the Geneva Convention. Upon our departure, a female representative of the AARP offered me a watered-down Bloody Mary for $5.50.

Since when was it required that stewardesses have to be over fifty-five? I thought to myself. When trying to attract business clients, it would help if airlines hired attractive younger help, both female and male. Just to punish me for my dirty thoughts, the octogenarian stewardess threw me a pair of headphones that hit me in the ear. I passed on the opportunity of watching a ridiculous program of another ridiculous person playing practical jokes on innocent people so we could all laugh at them together. People had been imprisoned for much less. I tried to use the time on hand to make sense out of the case instead.

Sandra Carter had been murdered. Why did someone murder her? What method did he use? Was there a reason for the murder? Robbery? Sex? Was the murderer working alone? Did he have an accomplice? Those are the questions I posed to myself as I sat prisoner in my tiny airline seat. Sandra was just an innocent mother with no affiliations to crime or drugs, murdered in a peaceful city like Portland, Oregon.

Was it a robbery gone bad or a crystal meth addict looking for stuff to sell? And Adam? Where was he? Was he involved? I would have to speak to the local police detective handling the case and check out the scene of the crime for any clues or fingerprints. In my previous career as a cop, I found that even the smallest clues could lead to something, but it took a lot of work, dedication, and consistency. This was personal, after all. Susan was my ex-wife and Sandra was her sister, which was as close to family as I had since my father died. My mother lived with her sister in Brooklyn and routinely called me up to harass me every weekend. She warmed my heart with her constant laments.

"So why are you going to Portland?" asked the nice lady two inches away from me on my right.

"Rainfall convention," I said. "We're studying levels of rainfall in the West."

"Global warming nonsense," said the salesman, two inches from my left. "Just some leftist radicals making noise."

"Couldn't agree more," I said. "Those people in Indonesia certainly had it coming, you know. The tsunami and all that. Imagine living so close to the beach, absolutely ridiculous!"

He nodded vigorously, eyes darting left and right as if on a mission to tell me his political opinions.

"Well, I live on a farm," said the nice lady, and proceeded to tell me a story that would have taken up more than the five hours necessary for us to reach Portland. The only polite way for me to end the conversation would have been for me to commit *seppuku* or *hari-kari* right there in my seat, inserting two knives in my abdomen. But since that was not possible, I had to nod politely until the movie started and then beg forgiveness for my incredible desire to see the lowest grossing movie of the month, *Lost on Planet Pluto*, on a three-inch screen five feet away.

Traveling in steerage on ocean liners in the nineteenth century must have been golden compared to how passengers on airlines are treated today. To avoid blood clots forming in your limbs, the airlines now give exercise guidance—although no one in the airline business has ever considered expanding your personal space. In any case, as soon as we landed on the tarmac in Portland, people bolted for their belongings, smashing overweight carry-ons against each other in a frenzy for immediate liberation. I headed for the Hertz Rent-A-Car counter at the airport, steeling myself for the drive into Portland. A visit to the morgue to identify Sandra Baines Carter's lifeless body was not something I was really looking forward to doing.

CHAPTER 25

❦

After parking my rental car in the municipal parking lot, I walked into the Portland city morgue. The smell of antiseptic filled my nostrils in the ice-cold room.

"You the next-of-kin?" said the sandy-haired pathologist, Angelos Papalos, without getting up from his desk.

"Brother-in-law." I showed him the power-of-attorney Susan had signed for me. "Her sister didn't feel up to making the trip."

"Can't blame her," said Papalos, signing the papers and giving them back to me.

County Sheriff Walter Winneker walked into the morgue at that time. We had agreed to meet there to make sure I properly identified Sandra's body. My old sergeant from the New York City 39th Precinct had given him a call regarding my trip up there.

"It's always cold as hell in here," he said. "Gives me the creeps."

We walked over to the metal drawers containing various bodies, and Angelos Papalos pulled out the middle one marked number 34. He slid open the large metal drawer. In the drawer, lying perfectly still and naked, covered only in a sheet, lay Susan's sister, Sandra Baines Carter. I recognized her immediately. She looked angelic, untouched and could have been sleeping except that one of her eyelids that was sewn shut and there were bruise marks on both sides of her neck.

"Why is her eye sewn shut?" I asked the pathologist.

"Whoever killed her cut it out," he said.

"Is that her?" asked Sheriff Winneker.

"Yes," I said. "That's Sandra Baines, sister of my ex-wife Susan Baines."

"Sign here then," said the pathologist.

I proceeded to sign the recognition papers.

"How was she killed?" I asked.

"She was strangled from behind while she was being raped. It seems to have happened at the same time. There were contusions on her neck and force abrasions in her vagina," said the pathologist as calmly as if he was commenting on the weather.

The murder of a close relative is shocking enough without adding sexual assault and mutilation. I was glad nobody had told Susan about what had happened to her sister.

"Did she suffer much?" I asked.

"The whole thing probably took two to three minutes at most. It wasn't pleasant, that's for sure," said the pathologist.

"Any clues? Semen?" I asked.

"No," said the pathologist. "There was forced penetration but no semen. The guy probably got off on the suffocation part."

"Any forced entry?" I asked.

"I'll say there was," joked the sheriff.

"In the apartment," I replied giving him a disapproving look.

"No, all the locks were in good condition. Whoever did this, it seems she let him in herself."

"Did you speak to the former husband, Gregory Carter?"

"Yes. Believe it or not, we actually know how to investigate crimes here in Portland, Mr. Stillati. He has been at a Nutso convention giving a speech."

"I didn't mean to imply anything," I said. "This just hits close to home."

"No offense taken," the sheriff said.

"Any other suspects?"

"We know from the hand bruises on her neck that it was a big guy. He probably surprised her in the house and attacked her. Then he went through the house, probably looking for jewelry and valuables, and tore up the place," said Sheriff Winneker.

"Did the neighbors hear anything?"

"Nothing, really. There's been a spate of robberies in that apartment complex recently. Might be connected to that?"

"What about her son, Adam?"

"We think he was in the house but escaped through a vent in his room. Seems he had a hiding place there. We've put out an APB on him, but nobody has seen him so far."

"Thank you," I said to the pathologist.

Life is so precious, so quick to end from one moment to another. One day you are running around worrying about the seemingly important problems of your life and the next you are lying on a cold slab, dead, and without a care in the world. *Makes you want to become a Buddhist*, I thought to myself, *so you can be aware of every second of every minute while you are on earth.*

The sheriff and I proceeded to walk out of the morgue together. I asked him, "Has there been a rapist or murderer running around Portland? Any serial rapists around?"

"No," he said. "It's been quiet lately. Violent crime has actually been coming down. This is the first murder we've had in the month of January."

"Is there anything else I should know about this case?"

"Well, we'll go visit the apartment where it happened and you can look around there. Stuff was smashed so it seems whoever did this was looking for some jewelry or drugs."

"I don't think Sandra had much money. She worked at the ACLU. It's not exactly a high paying job."

"Yeah, I know," said Sheriff Winneker. "I talked to the NSA guy about that. He was asking the same kind of questions."

"What NSA guy?" I asked as my ears perked up.

"An agent from the National Security Agency came to the scene of the crime and told me he was called by the ACLU to check out the murder. He said he thought it could be related to extremist or terrorist activity in the area."

"Did you have any evidence of that?" I asked the sheriff.

"So far, no. But with all the craziness in this world, you can never be sure. He mentioned that her son might have spread some pro-Arab Islamic literature at his school."

"Adam?" I asked in disbelief.

"Yeah. You never know what kids will get into these days," said Sheriff Winneker.

"Did you get his card?" I asked.

"No," said the sheriff. "He was a huge ass guy with a Russian sounding name. Rakovic, Draskovic, something like that."

I wondered what kind of trouble Adam and Susan could have possibly been in for the National Security Agency to be looking into this case. I followed the sheriff over to Sycamore Street and passed through the various yellow lines of police tape. Inside, the apartment was a mess. Everything had been either ripped up or torn down. Officers were combing the apartment for prints.

"Any luck?" the sheriff asked of some of the forensic inspectors.

"Just the woman and the kid's prints so far. Nothing else," they replied.

I walked around trying to make sense of all of this. *Take nothing for granted*, I thought to myself. *Look at everything and question what doesn't make sense.* My old habits from my police days took over and I looked for details and clues. The living room looked like a tornado had ripped through it. The yellow couch has a red stain in the top of it.

"That's where the victim was raped and murdered," said the sheriff.

I looked at the sad reminder of where Susan's life had ebbed away.

"There is no sense to any of this," I said.

"There rarely is. The boy's room is down the hall," said the sheriff.

I walked down the hallway and into Adam's room. A poster of the Brazilian soccer player Ronaldo was on the wall. I had given him that many years ago. The vent opening next to his bed was open.

"The boy must have escaped through the air-conditioning vent. It leads out to the back of the house," said the sheriff.

"He's a smart boy," I said to Sheriff Winneker.

"Looks that way. He might have seen the perp from behind there."

"So that would put him in trouble, right?"

"It would make him an eye witness," said the sheriff.

"Have you been to his school?"

"They haven't seen him in two days. He's out on the street somewhere or hiding at a friend's house. We'll find him," said the sheriff.

"I hope we find him before the other guy does," I said ominously.

The sheriff nodded in agreement.

"If there's nothing else her for me to see, I think I'll drive over to his school," I said to the sheriff.

"Okay, but keep in touch. I promised your sergeant I would look out for you," said the sheriff. "You're not a policeman anymore, remember? So stay out of trouble. If you find out something, give me a call."

"I'll keep that in mind," I said to him.

Finding Adam alive was now my first priority. If the killer found him first, he would get rid of him immediately. Adam's life was in serious danger. *The clock is ticking now*, I thought, *and there's not a lot of time left*. I got into my rental car and headed for Adam's school.

CHAPTER 26

Prisons and public schools have a few things in common. Their population for the most part is forced to be there against their will. Both institutions usually have the same drab architecture, the same barred windows, the same parking lots. I parked my car behind the red brick school and walked into the office of Principal Antonia Paduano. Walking into any school brings back the horrors of my childhood. The smell and atmosphere filled me with dread. I could not help but remember how I had feared and disliked most of my own education, waiting impatiently for the 3:30 afternoon bell so I could run outside and play soccer. Needless to say, I was not a good student.

The Portland Central Junior High School was housed in a large, red brick building that seemed solid enough to withstand an atomic bomb attack. The halls were clean and the few teachers I saw seemed in a hurry to go home. Ms. Paduano greeted me in her office. She was a full-sized woman, with a large mole on her right cheek. I could see her inspiring terror and fear into the misbehaving students brought before her. I gave her my card and told her why I had come to see her.

"Mr. Stillati, I cannot tell you how sorry we are for what happened to Ms. Baines-Carter. Were you related?" she asked.

"Yes, she was my sister-in-law," I said.

"It's truly horrible. And I understand you are looking for Adam. We have not seen him in three days now. We told the police that."

"I know," I said. "I was wondering if he might have some friends or a teacher he was close with."

"Not that I know of. I spoke to several of his teachers and they told me he was mostly alone. He had no close friends that they knew of. Then again, this is a large school and we wouldn't know everything he did."

"Had Adam ever been in trouble?" I asked her.

"No," Ms. Paduano said. "I would know about that. The bad ones all get sent here to me."

"Was he ever involved in any political affiliations?"

"We're not very political here at Portland Central. The biggest controversy we have is the Xbox vs. PlayStation systems."

I laughed at the little joke.

"I told the federal agent that when he asked me the same question. He didn't laugh," the principal said.

"What federal agent?" I asked.

"It was an agent from the National Security Agency. He showed me his badge. He was a very big man with a Russian accent that came in to see me yesterday and sat where you are sitting," said Ms. Paduano.

"Why did he come here?" I asked.

"He was looking for Adam and for a kid with your name, too. He said Adam and a kid name Dave Stillati were friends."

"He mentioned my name?" I asked surprised.

"Yes, isn't it strange? He asked if he could meet this student. I told him there was no Dave Stillati registered in our school here. Now, today, you show up with the same name. What a coincidence."

"I should say."

We talked another ten minutes with her about Adam and his habits and it was obvious that she had way too many students to remember him well. She was a hardworking, well-meaning woman with way too many students to have to deal with on an everyday basis. I thanked her for her time and walked out of the school.

It was my experience that there weren't many coincidences in the world that didn't have a meaning to them. An NSA agent was at the murder site. Now the same agent had come looking for Adam at the school, and even knew my name. Clearly the NSA was involved in this case somehow. That couldn't happen in an everyday murder case.

Sandra, honey, I thought *Give me a clue as to what this is all about.* I got in the car and started the ignition thinking about the murder and where Adam could be. After a few seconds, I got the fright of my life.

"Uncle Dave?" said a low voice in the backseat of my car.

I almost had a heart attack and hit the brakes. Two cars behind me narrowly avoided hitting me by inches. The drivers gave me the finger as they passed by my car. Adam was lying down in the backseat. At least it looked like some filthy creature of the bog who had taken on his appearance.

"Holy shit," I said. "You almost gave me a coronary. I thought a ghost was talking to me. Where have you been? The police have been looking for you all over Portland."

"I've been in the park sleeping and then here at the school hiding out. I didn't know where to go. Then I saw you drive in. I was so happy to see you here. Mom's dead. She was killed," he said.

"I'm so sorry," I said. "I went by the morgue this morning to identify her."

"How did she look?"

"She looked fine. Peaceful," I said.

"That's good," Adam said.

"How did you get away?" I asked.

"I was hiding in the vent," he said. "Mom told me to hide there. She thought it was Carter coming up to see us. But it wasn't. A huge mean-looking man came into my room. He was looking for me. I saw him through the vent. Then he smashed everything in my room looking for something. I saw him."

"Why didn't you go to the police?" I asked.

"I was very scared. The guy killed Mom because of me."

"Say what?" I asked.

"Mom gave me this laptop computer. He smashed up my room looking for it, but I had it with me. If Mom hadn't bought me the laptop, she would be alive today. I found some old stuff on it and told Mom. She called a number at the FBI or National Security Agency. Then they sent somebody to see us. I think the guy who they sent killed Mom. It's all because of this fucking laptop."

"Adam, what is on the laptop?"

"Stuff about 9/11. Stuff written a year before the attacks. I retrieved it in the hard drive information and showed it to Mom. I explained the information to her. It was instruction on how to do the attacks of 9/11. You see, she bought the computer used at a sale from the Portland airport, stuff people had forgotten at the airport years ago," Adam said.

I pulled the car into an inside garage and parked it in a far away parking spot where no one could see and detect us.

"Come up front here," I said to Adam.

Adam came up into the front seat and I hugged him. He hugged me back and wouldn't let go.

"I was so scared, Uncle Dave," Adam said. "So scared. I couldn't move. I was, like, paralyzed."

"That's okay, that's okay. There was nothing you could do," I said.

"He was huge. I could have stopped him," said Adam. "But Mom told me to hide. She told me not to come out from the vent."

"She saved your life. That's what your Mom did. She did that for you."

Adam started crying on my shoulder now and I tried to comfort him as best I could. The tears came down heavy and I felt my shirt getting wet.

"Here, take a tissue," I said.

Adam blew his nose and wiped away his tears.

"Show me what's on the laptop," I said.

Adam pulled out a black garbage bag. Inside he has some clothes and the laptop. He pulled it out and turned it on. Images of a game came on.

"That's my *King of Persia* game. Wait till I turn it off," he said.

He turned off the game and opened a file that was on the right hand corner of the screen. The screen quickly filled up with English and Arabic writing. There were coordinates and directions for flights and target information for the World Trade Center in New York. I couldn't read the Arabic, but you didn't have to be a genius to understand that the laptop contained instructions for the terrorists to follow. It was an instruction manual for the attacks.

"You called the NSA hotline about this?" I asked Adam.

"Mom did," he said.

"And then this all came down on you."

He nodded a yes.

The National Security Agency was now the most powerful intelligence agency in America. After 9/11, they had acquired unlimited powers to snoop, arrest, and deport possible suspects. If there was a case going on that concerned them, we would have very little time before they would be following me, too. All the airports would definitely be monitored. I needed to find some time to figure out what was happening.

"What are we going to do now, Uncle Dave? Go to a hotel? I'm so hungry and tired."

"That's not a good idea," I said to Adam. "Whoever did this is going to come after us, too. Kid, how would you feel about a cross country road trip back to New York?"

"Now?" asked Adam. "I'm so tired, but as long as I am with you I don't care," said Adam.

"We'll stop by a Wendy's and get you some food first."

I pulled out of the parking lot and headed to a fast food place to get Adam some food. He looked exhausted. Then we would head to the highway. From Portland to New York it would take me about four days driving slowly and stopping overnight to rest. Just to be on the safe side, I would have to make sure to pay cash everywhere and not leave any traces or credit cards. It would be easy for some NSA guy to find me with even one phone call or traceable credit card. I wasn't sure who this large agent was who had been in front of Adam's house and was at his school. I didn't really want to know for the moment. Whatever he wanted, it didn't sound promising. I needed to make a few phone calls that couldn't be traced.

We stopped at the first Wendy's I saw to get some hamburgers and French fries for Adam. I called Kelly in New York from a pay phone, and told her what was going on. I told her to tell Susan in person that Adam was okay and not use the phones in the office. Kelly thought I had finally lost all my marbles.

"Do you want me to use a code name as well?" she asked.

"That would help," I said.

At least Susan would know that Adam was okay. I knew that that would be a great relief to her. I also told Kelly to get in touch with my Moroccan friend named Mehmet Hadji. He was an ex-national soccer team player that I had represented once a while ago. Hadji had later gone to work for the FBI as an Arabic translator on an anti-terrorist unit. Kelly told me she would call me back with his number and a psychiatrist for my paranoid state. I thanked her for her support as always.

After we ate, Adam and I got back in the car. I made a pallet for Adam in the backseat so he could sleep. He was in pitiful condition and fell asleep in a few seconds.

I had accomplished my first goal of finding him, or he had found me. Now, all I had to do was get him back to New York in one piece.

CHAPTER 27

❦

The first motel we stopped in was called the Sunny Roadhouse, and it was in a small town in Idaho. It was one of those motels used by fishermen on weekends and the college kid at the desk was glad to take my $50 cash, no questions asked. Adam was still asleep as I carried him into the room. The room was small with two single beds and a small color TV from the 1950s. I woke Adam up and told him to take a bath. He hadn't had one in three days and smelled like it.

"I just want to sleep," said Adam.

"Take a quick bath and then go to bed. That's what your Aunt Susan would tell you to do." Adam nodded as he went off to the bathroom and shut the door. I took my shoes off and connected his laptop to the wall unit, turning it on. I wanted to look at the information with calm to determine what use it had served.

Instructions in Arabic and English came up on the screen, complete with coordinates, plane reservations, and everything the terrorists would have needed to accomplish their mission. The date of the download was visible as well, and the Internet name that had sent the download also appeared: Pharbor@aol.com.

Clever, I thought to myself. Whoever had created the name had used the moniker Pearl Harbor to recall the Japanese attack on September 7, 1941, that launched the American intervention into World War II. President Franklin Delano Roosevelt had called it "a day that will live in infamy." I read through the material and understood the implications that this computer could possibly have been given to Mohammed Atta, the leader of the terrorists leaving Portland. Somehow, or for some reason, he had left it behind at the airport.

He didn't think he would need it anymore, I thought to myself, *and he wanted to show us that he did these attacks.*

It was bizarre enough that the laptop was now in my hands. But people I knew were being killed because of it. Kelly had given me Mehmet Hadji's home number, and I proceeded to dial it.

"Mehmet Hadji, please?" I said as a Middle Eastern voice answered the phone.

"My friend, Dave Stillati," answered Mehmet enthusiastically. "Don't tell me your calling to offer me a contract with Arsenal."

"Chelsea, they need a left winger. Mehmet, are you ready?"

"I was born ready, Dave. You know that."

Mehmet had been a very skillful left winger in college at St. John's. Fast and skillful, and with blinding pace on the left side, he had played on the Moroccan national team for a few years and had finished a glorious career in Casablanca. Once he retired from football, he came back to New York and started working as a translator for the FBI in the counter-terrorist unit.

"So my friend," I asked, "are you still playing any soccer?"

"I play for the UN team now, and we are undefeated, but we play against overweight diplomats in Central Park. It's like shooting fish in a barrel. How's the sports agency business?"

"Not bad. I get some good players every now and then. Some good young kids, too."

"I have some good players in Morocco I want to show you."

"That will be great," I said. "Send me their curriculums and DVDs so I can see them."

"But that's not what you are calling me about, my friend, is it?"

"No, Mehmet. Unfortunately not. I'm dealing with a personal problem at the moment. My ex-wife, Susan, you remember her.?"

"Beautiful woman. I never understood why you got a divorce," said Mehmet.

"Neither did I, really. Anyway, her sister lived in Portland and she was murdered recently."

"I'm terribly sorry, Dave," Mehmet said.

"So am I. Apparently the attack had something to do with some information she found on a laptop computer. Now, I flew out here to retrieve the computer and her personal items. Some of the information on the computer is in Arabic. Can I e-mail you some of the information for you to translate for me?"

"For you, Dave, of course," said Mehmet. "I'll give you my e-mail address. Send it to me and I will see what it's all about."

"Mehmet," I said, "from what I can tell, it's sensitive stuff about 9/11. If you don't want to see it and get involved, I would understand."

"I'm not with the FBI anymore, Dave. I work for the Moroccan delegation at the UN. I'm a big boy and can make my own decisions. Send me the e-mail so I can have a look at it."

I hung up and took the telephone line and installed it into the laptop. It took me less than a minute to find local access numbers for the Internet and then e-mail Mehmet the information. I blessed the Information Age in which we live. Then I waited for a few minutes watching TV. He soon called me back at the hotel.

"Where did you say you got this stuff, Dave?" Mehmet asked.

"It was on a used laptop that Susan's sister Sandra bought. She was killed in Portland this week. I don't know if her death is related to this information. What do you think, Mehmet?"

"I think you should throw the laptop away. Forget about it and don't get involved. I am telling you this for your own good."

"I'm already involved in it. Don't you understand?" I said to him. "My wife's sister was murdered for this."

"Ex-wife," I heard Mehmet say.

"Same thing," I said.

"It's pretty significant information," said Mehmet. "The person who prepared this document translated directly from English to Arabic first. There are some mistakes in the translation that makes that obvious. The original writer was American. The translator came from Saudi Arabia."

"And was the reader?" I asked.

"This might seem crazy, but the reader had to be one of the 9/11 terrorists, possibly a cell leader. He received these instructions before boarding the plane."

"Have you seen anything like this before? When you were at the FBI?"

"Yes, but I am not allowed to reveal where. The FBI made me sign a mandatory gag order when I left there."

"Was it part of the anti-terrorist investigation prior to 9/11?"

"Yes," Mehmet said. "I wish I could tell you more."

I understood his position and did not want to press him on this. He worked for the Moroccan delegation at the UN. I was putting his life in danger. Also, a phone call from the FBI to his chief delegate at the UN and he would be on his way back to Morocco with his family. I did not want that or anything bad to happen to Mehmet.

"Can you think of anybody who knows more about this sort of thing, Mehmet? I'm out of my water here."

"There is an agent who ran the anti-terrorist department in Minnesota. I worked for her at the FBI. Her name is Kara Murphy. I think she would know how to help you, but I doubt she would," said Mehmet.

Kara Murphy, I thought. *Why does that name sound familiar?*

"She was the head of the anti-terrorist department at the FBI prior to 9/11. She arrested Zacarias Moussaoui, the twentieth terrorist before the attacks but was stopped from opening his laptop or interrogating him. After 9/11, she was incensed at what had happened. She claimed the FBI was involved in a cover-up about her investigation. I worked directly for her," said Mehmet.

"That's right, the whistleblower. Wasn't she on the cover of *Time* magazine one week?" I asked.

"She was. She went to the press when the FBI refused to pursue her allegations about the blocked investigation and subsequent cover-up."

"What happened to her?"

"After she went to the press, she was in a car accident and then was attacked in her home. She barely survived. The FBI worked out a severance deal for her, giving her a pension, but put on a gag order that stopped her from talking to the press. They made a public statement saying it was for her own protection. She now lives in Ely, Minnesota. We still exchange holiday greetings. I can give you her number, but I doubt she will talk to you."

"Thanks, Mehmet. I really appreciate this," I said.

"Watch out for yourself, Dave. There are dangerous connections involved in the information you are carrying around."

"I believe you. One more question, Mehmet. Is this stuff really important? Would somebody kill to stop this information from getting out?" I asked him.

"I think you know the answer already, my friend," Mehmet said. "I wish I could help you more, but I can't. I wish you could just lose the laptop and worry only about soccer."

"I wish it was that simple," I said.

"Then may Allah protect you, my brother. I have a feeling you are going to need it."

"Thanks," I said to him, feeling quite certain he was right.

As I hung up the phone, Adam came out of the bathroom, covering himself with a small towel. He looked almost human again.

"Did your friend tell you anything?" he asked me getting into his bed.

"He said there was something to this information we should look into. He gave me a name of his former boss in Minnesota who might be able to help us."

Adam didn't say anything for a while, then he said, "You know, I saw him."

"Who?" I asked.

"The giant, the one who killed Mom."

"Yes, you told me, through the vent," I said turning on the TV.

"No, I saw him again, the next day in front of the house. He was talking to the cops."

"The killer?" I asked astonished.

"The one who came into our house. The one who killed Mom. He was talking to the cops and waiting outside the apartment complex. I think he was waiting for me to come back."

"I think he was, too," I said. "He must be pretty confident coming back to the house and talking to the cops in broad daylight."

"Maybe he is a cop, too," said Adam.

"Maybe," I said. "Or worse. Don't worry about him. We are far from Portland now."

"Is he going to come after us? After me?" Adam asked me.

"No. Nobody knows we are here. Once I get you back to New York, you will be okay. I'll put you in a safe place once I work out what's going on here."

"Dave?" said Adam getting into bed.

"Yes, Adam?"

"I missed you real bad when we moved to Portland. I missed you coaching me and I missed Aunt Susan and grandpa and grandma."

"We missed you, too," I said. "Now, kid, get some sleep. We have a lot of driving to do tomorrow."

It didn't take real long for him to doze off. He was a good kid in a bad situation. I watched some reality TV show, as if I didn't have enough reality to deal with, and then gradually went to sleep myself.

CHAPTER 28

Szabo Tanovich was sick and tired of being in Portland and dealing with the local police. Above all, he was frustrated by the lame excuses they invented for not locating the Baines woman's kid. It couldn't be that hard for a whole police department to find one boy.

Where the fuck is he? This thing should have been wrapped up by now. Fucking, useless cops, pichca, he thought to himself swearing in Serbian. He dialed Michael Cherry's number to talk to him.

"Hey, Mikael. The police still can't find this boy," said Szabo.

"What you are saying is you can't find him. You should have killed him when you did the woman," said Michael from his office.

Szabo didn't like to receive criticism, even from his boss.

"I went to his school," said Szabo, "and they told me they haven't seen him in days. They don't know this other boy, Dave Stillati, either. He never went to the school."

"Who's Dave Stillati?" asked Michael.

"That's the name the woman gave me before she died. She said her son was spending the night at the house of a boy named Dave Stillati."

"Must be some relative of the kid," said Michael Cherry. "We will put the name into the computer recognition program and see what comes out."

"What should I do now?" asked Szabo.

"Book yourself onto a flight back to Washington today. The police will call us once they find the kid. If we find out who this Stillati character is, you go after him. You took care of the woman. That's good for now. The rest will fall into place. So you fucked up a bit. Happens to everybody."

"Not to me," said Szabo, visibly annoyed that his boss was giving him shtick.

"We can find anybody in America, trust me. There is no place the kid can hide. Nor his friend," said Michael. "Once we know where they are, then we'll take them out. Now get on a plane and come back to headquarters. Leave the rest to us."

"Okay," said Szabo. "I'll be back tonight then."

Michael hung up the phone. No need to extend pleasantries with the Serb. *The man was a psychopath and had killed more people in Serbia than the plague,* thought Michael. *Still, he's my psychopath and has done very well for me. Let me see if I can find this kid Stillati.* Michael turned to his computer and fed the name Dave Stillati and Sandra Baines Carter into the National Security Agency databank. It contained the biggest databank of information in the United States. More than one hundred million names, addresses, phone numbers that he could cross reference with the databanks of the IRS, credit companies, banks, schools, associations, Google and yahoo. *Welcome to the Information Age,* said Michael to himself. It wasn't long before all the Dave Stillatis located throughout America came up on the screen.

Michael Cherry cross-referenced the name to Sandra and Adam Baines. This limited the names to one entry, which read:

> Dave Stillati, travel soccer coach of the New Jersey Terminators. A team of players, which includes ten-year-old Adam Baines have won the New Jersey State Championship.

Further data study revealed that Adam Baines was son of Sandra Baines, sister of Susan Baines and Susan Baines had once been married to Dave Stillati.

So he's the boy's adopted uncle, thought Michael. *How cute.*

Now that he had the exact area, Michael Cherry focused his computer search on all data regarding Dave Stillati. Within a few seconds he had Dave Stillati's entire file on his computer screen:

> Dave Stillati, Professional soccer player, New York City policeman, multiple commendations, medals, partner killed, resigns his position. Opens sports agency representing players. Represents soccer players mostly, but also tennis players, Olympic athletes, skaters. Stillati was involved in prominent skater Naomi Wyatt's involvement in the murder of Charles Ickes III in Jamaica. For his assistance in clearing the case, he was awarded highest

Jamaican decoration by Prime Minister. In 2005, he arranged fundraising game for the tsunami victims in Jakarta, Indonesia.

The man has an interesting file, thought Michael. *$615 in his bank account, an office at a 42nd Street address, a one bedroom apartment on East 56th, divorced, no kids of his own.* He proceeded to put Dave Stillati's name on the high priority terrorism alert list for airlines. The results flashed on his screen and he dialed Szabo's cell phone number.

"Yes, Michael," said Szabo in his thick Serbian accent.

"Forget about coming back to Washington," ordered Michael. "Fly direct to New York City. Dave Stillati is the boy's adopted uncle. He flew into Portland only two days ago."

"Is he still here?" asked the big Serb.

"I wouldn't think so. The guy's an ex-cop. They are probably on their way back to New York. The computer doesn't show him using his return ticket. He's probably driving. Tomorrow I will send out some agents to his office to see if we can get more information on him. I might notify the press as well. That will get his attention. Make sure you get to New York tonight. I'll give Agent Durhling the information on Stillati."

"Okay, when they arrive in New York, I will be there waiting for them."

"You better be, Szabo. We don't want any more fuck ups, understand?" said Michael.

"Okay, okay," said Szabo who felt like killing his boss there and then but knew that Michael had enough information on him lead him straight to the gallows for war crimes. Szabo put down the phone and started packing his belongings. *Besides,* thought Szabo, *only Michael Cherry could have gotten me out of Serbia and gotten me over here to the U.S. to work with the FBI and NSA.* Szabo pulled his suit from the clothes rack and threw it into the Samsonite.

About fucking time that I get the fuck out of here, he thought to himself heading for the hotel lobby to check out.

CHAPTER 29

❁

Ely, Minnesota
Pop. 3800.

It had taken me almost twenty-five hours of tedious winter driving, through sleet and snow to reach the outskirts of Ely, Minnesota. We had had to stop at a Holiday Inn along the way to get me one full night's sleep. At the hotel, I had called Mehmet Hadji again, and he had given me his former boss Kara Murphy's address and phone number. Although he said she probably wouldn't talk to me at all, I still had to take the chance.

"Ely is a small village in the northeast of Minnesota located on the shores of Shagowa Lake," said Adam, reading from a book on Minnesota we had bought at the Mobil gas station. "Fishermen come here to catch the walleye fish."

"Great," I replied. "We should have brought our fishing rods."

"There is even an Independent Fishing Party that won the last mayoral election," said Adam.

"Smart voters. It must be ice fishing," I said to him. "It's only ten degrees Fahrenheit outside."

"Temperatures range from zero to ten degrees in the wintertime," said Adam. "The average temperature is minus three."

"Ideal for sun bathing," I said to him driving through the blinding snow drifts. "Balmy weather. Reminds me of Miami," I said.

"They even have a winter carnival," read Adam, "with snow sculptures of an eight-foot moose and a crystalline rose that is on the banks of Lake Superior."

"Well," I said, "now we know everything about Ely, Minnesota."

"It's said Ely, like steely," said Adam. "Not Ely like the name."

"Okay, Okay, enough. Just help me find a decent hotel we can stay in."

Adam gave me the name of the Grand Ely Lodge and I called in for a reservation. They told me it wouldn't be needed as they weren't busy at this time of the season. The man sounded friendly enough. I took the exit off the highway as directed and stopped in the snow-covered parking lot of the hotel.

The Grand Ely Lodge wasn't as grand as the named suggested, but it looked comfortable. We pulled our luggage out of the car and checked in. I paid in cash again, just to be on the safe side. Adam was wearing a white sweatshirt with Minnesota written on it that we had bought on the road. For the most part, he had recovered from the exhaustion of being on the run in Portland. I knew, however, that he had mental scars and damage that would take him years to recover from.

Who wouldn't after what he's been through? I thought to myself. *But let's face one problem at a time.*

As soon as we got into our room, I called the number Mehmet had given me for Kara Murphy. A gruff female voice answered the phone.

"Is Kara Murphy there?" I asked.

"Who are you?" asked the voice.

"I'm Dave Stillati. Mehmet Hadji recommended I should call Kara Murphy on an issue of some importance."

"I'm her assistant. Leave a number where she can call you back."

I left the number of the hotel and five minutes later the phone rang."

"Ms. Kara Murphy?" I asked.

"Mr. Stillati," she said, "Mehmet told me you were his friend. The only reason I am calling you back is out of respect for Mehmet. What do you want?"

"I need for you to see something that was found at the airport in Portland. A laptop with some information on it. Information regarding September 11, 2001."

"Mr. Stillati, every conspiracy crackpot seems to have made a mission of finding me in Ely. You must be number 1637. I no longer work for the FBI, nor am I interested in anything you might want to say or show me," said Kara Murphy.

"I just wanted to meet with you," I said. "All I want are five minutes of your time. Then you can walk away."

"I'm walking away now. You wasted your time coming to Ely, Mr. Stillati."

"Call me, Dave," I said.

"You wasted your time, Dave."

"Two minutes. Mehmet said you were his boss. He says this is important. He says you will know what it's all about."

For a few seconds the line was silent.

"One minute because it's Mehmet. Meet me at the Chainsaw Sisters Saloon in ten minutes. Come alone."

"Is it in town?" I asked.

"We only have one street and two stop lights in Ely, Dave. I think you can't miss it." She hung up the phone.

I have a small chance to speak to this woman, I thought to myself. *Might as well make the best of it.*

I told Adam where I was going to meet Ms. Murphy. He was already in bed watching one of his favorite TV shows. I told him I would bring him back a burger for dinner. Then, I took his laptop with me and headed out in the freezing sub-zero Minnesota air.

How did the boss of the FBI anti-terrorist unit, Kara Murphy, end up living in Ely, Minnesota? I asked myself. I was keeping all my fingers and toes crossed that she would help me out and headed toward the Chainsaw Sisters Saloon, looking for some answers.

CHAPTER 30

Riyadh, Saudi Arabia, January 15, 2006.

Prince Abdullah was admitted into the Royal Palace waiting for the presence of his older cousin, Aziz bin Sultan, heir to the throne of Saudi Arabia. He had been waiting in the anteroom for some time. The 105-degree heat of the Saudi capital had made him sweat under his white Saudi headdress. His cousin's assistant led him to the gold inlaid table where Prince Aziz bin Sultan was studying some papers.

"*Ukhwa*," his cousin said rising to kiss him, using the term for brother.

"*Malik Aziz*," he replied calling his brother a king.

"It is a sad day for us, as our dear king has gone to meet Allah," said Aziz bin Sultan.

"Yes, a sad and tragic day. Although he had been so sick for so long, it still comes as a shock. I have been mourning him all week," said Prince Abdullah.

"Every mosque from Mecca to Jerusalem is singing hymns in his honor."

"He led our kingdom well for many years, as I can only hope to try to do the same," said Prince Aziz.

"I am at your complete disposal to help you guide our nation in any capacity," said Prince Abdullah as he bowed to him.

"You have been our defense minister for almost six years," said Aziz. "You have built good alliances with the Americans, and in particular this Cherry man who was chairman of Holliwell. He has helped us defeat our common enemy in Iraq. We are a small country and our alliances have saved us from our enemies. We are grateful to you for this."

"I was only doing my duty as a Saudi," said Prince Abdullah.

"As you know, I was the oil minister for many years. It is the most crucial position in our kingdom—our lifeline of prosperity and power. The industrial nations of the world fight for our oil reserves, which will one day be depleted. They would just as soon take us over. The Americans and Chinese compete with each other over our oil. It hasn't been easy to balance such major powers against each other."

"I have admired the work you did as oil minister for many years," said Prince Abdullah.

"With my ascension to the throne next month, that position is now vacant. I would like you to be our new oil minister, if you would care to."

Abdullah felt his heart beat quicker. The oil minister had the greatest power of any of the ministries. His power would be second only to the king's and unrivaled in the world.

"There is nothing that would please me more," said the prince.

"Good, then it is settled. You will occupy the ministry next month after my public coronation as king."

Prince Abdullah bowed deeply and took his cousin's hand and kissed it.

"Thank you from my heart, my king," he said.

"There is only one more thing," said the future king, Aziz bin Sultan.

"Ask me anything," said Prince Abdullah.

"Your cousin, the terrorist Bin Laden. His time is up. We are going to give him to the Americans. You must help me in this task."

"Excuse me, your highness?" asked Abdullah. "I don't understand."

"We are not all fools here, Prince Abdullah. Telephone calls from Kabul and Tora Bora were intercepted from him to you. Your calls to your American partner Michael Cherry were also recorded. We know of your part in helping Osama plan the attacks against the Americans and how you and the American let him escape death many times."

Prince Abdullah felt the sweat drop from his armpits.

"But…" he said, "I swear…I never."

"Don't say anything you will regret, cousin. We have all profited handsomely from America's involvement in Kuwait, Iraq, and Afghanistan. Our oil prices are at a record high. America is wasting billions rebuilding Iraq and buying our goods. Our beloved kingdom has never been stronger or better protected. However, lately Bin Laden has been directing his suicide forces against us here in Riyadh. He is disgracing Islam and putting the kingdom at risk. He is agitating our very own people against us. That cannot be tolerated. Because of Osama, we have already forced our American allies to leave Saudi soil. It's all right for suicide bombers to kill Israelis and Americans, but what he wants is a return to the Middle Ages. Now that I will be king, I will not tolerate his behavior any longer."

"I will speak to him," said Prince Bin Abdullah

"I have a plan I want you to assist me with. Tell your cousin of my ascension to the throne. Tell him I have decided to change the political and religious course of Saudi Arabia in line with a return to the strict letter of the Koran. My ambassador in Pakistan will meet him face to face in person to sign an agreement between us both. We will help him once again with money and protection. Tell him he will be able to return here with his family. All will be forgiven and we will help Al-Queda spread their message to the Arab world."

"He would be very happy to hear that. But why would he believe it?" asked Prince Abdullah.

"He will believe it if you tell him it's true. I will send my ambassador to Pakistan to sign the agreement with him and give him $50 million in cash as guarantee," said Aziz bin Sultan.

"That is very generous of you," said Prince Abdullah.

"I am sacrificing the money and my ambassador in exchange for your cousin, Osama bin Laden. Once the meeting is set up, I will notify the American intelligence. They will plan for his destruction."

Prince Abdullah grew very alarmed at the plan.

"This is much to ask of me," said Prince Abdullah. "After all, he is my first cousin. You are asking me to set him up for a kill."

"Your king is asking you to do your duty to your kingdom. Would you let your family ties interfere with your duty as the oil minister of our Saudi Arabia?" Aziz bin Sultan eyed Prince Abdullah carefully. He had thought out this plan long and hard and decided it was the only way for him to appease the Americans.

Prince Abdullah weighed the one choice against the other. The oil ministry was the prize he was waiting for his whole life. If he refused, Aziz bin Sultan would brand him as a traitor. It could cost him his life. *I have to make a decision*, thought Prince Abdullah. *It is either me or Osama.* He bowed his head to his new king.

"My duty is to my king and my kingdom above all else," said Prince Abdullah. "Your will be done."

"Good. *Allah akbar*," said Prince Aziz bin Sultan, lifting his cousin up and kissing him two times on each cheek.

"*Allah akbar*," replied Prince Abdullah as he prepared to leave the great hall of the palace.

Prince Abdullah left the room with some apprehension. *Protecting Bin Laden has kept me safe from radical Islamics*, he thought to himself. *However, the oil ministry is now mine—billions of dollars in revenue coming to the kingdom through me. Billions in bribes from the Americans and the Chinese oil companies. In a few months, I could be the richest man in the world.* It was sad that he had to sacrifice his terrorist cousin to the Americans. Prince Abdullah had done everything in his power to protect Osama time and time again. Without his assistance and use of the intelligence the American had fed him, Osama and the Al Queda leadership would have died long ago in Afghanistan.

So be it, thought Prince Abdullah to himself. *Osama got the influence and fame he craved. The American has enriched himself many times over. Now, I have achieved the prize I have wanted for so long. It is high time for me to think about myself now.*

He walked out of the Royal Palace and into the cool air-conditioning of the black Maybach Mercedes that was waiting for him in front of the palace.

CHAPTER 31

The Chainsaw Sisters Saloon in Ely, Minnesota, was the kind of dive that my father would have loved. A good soccer player in Italy, my father had come to New York in 1974 to play in the old NASL for the Rochester Rhinos in upstate New York. He had quit playing soccer at the age of thirty-eight and opened an Italian art gallery in Brooklyn with my mother, who was an art student at NYU. They represented starving young artists who seemed to live and eat at our house on a permanent basis. I grew up watching Italian soccer on Rai TV every Sunday and carrying paintings up and down stairs for the rest of the week. My father died when he was sixty-five years old, of a heart attack, while eating a New York strip steak at Peter Luger's restaurant. It was the way he would have wanted to go. He was a man who loved to play soccer, eat, travel, and he lived a rich and entertaining life. It wasn't easy and he wasn't rich, but he was generous with his friends and family, and never boasted about anything in his life. I missed him sometimes when I experienced things we would have enjoyed together.

The Chainsaw Saloon was one of those saloons where people feel more at home than in their own living rooms. About thirty feet deep, the weathered saloon had simple red vinyl booths on one side and a long wooden bar on the other. On the wall, a blackboard showed the daily specials and different types of beers on tap: "Split Pea Soup and Generator Burger—$3.99, Light Spaten On Tap." The restaurant was crowded with local patrons and a friendly waitress took me to the only open booth in the back.

"You here visiting friends?" the silver-haired waitress asked me.

"Yes, they're going to join me soon," I replied.

"I'm Betsy," said the waitress. "We mostly get locals here. Ely is not the biggest town, you know? Take your time." She left me a vinyl one page menu to look at.

Just then the saloon door opened and two women walked inside. One was a tall, strong looking lady with cropped black hair, wearing a police uniform, who looked like she knew how to handle herself. The other woman was very attractive, five feet, five inches tall, with dirty blonde hair, very fair skin, freckles, and piercing green eyes.

"Hi, Susan. Hi, Jenny," said Betsy the waitress, who seemed to know everything. "I think there's some guy waiting for you in the back booth."

I got up expecting the policewoman to come speak to me, but she went to the bar as the petite blonde woman came to sit down in front of me.

"Hi," I said, "I'm Dave Stillati."

"Hi. I'm Kara Murphy," she said shaking my hand.

Her hands were small but her handshake was firm and warm.

"You are not what I expected," I said.

"What were you expecting?" said Kara looking at me.

"Someone more like your friend," I said.

"Jenna is my best friend. She's the local cop here. There are only two cops in Ely. She's here looking out for me."

"Do you need a bodyguard here in Ely?" I asked her.

"People come down sometimes—crackpots looking for a conspiracy theory on 9/11, journalists who want a story, extremists who hate whistleblowers. I'm the local celebrity around here. Your minute is ticking. What are you looking for, Mr. Stillati?" Kara asked me.

"Mehmet told me I should talk to you. I was his soccer agent a long time ago," I said.

"Mehmet Hadji is the reason I am here sitting in front of you. He was my Arabic translator at the FBI, a very good man. He told me just to listen to your story. You have fifty-two seconds left. I'm listening."

I pulled out the laptop and laid it out on the table turning it on. The images of Arabic and English instructions came to life on the screen. Kara looked at it. She showed no reaction.

"Have you ever seen this before?" I asked her.

She said nothing.

"This laptop was purchased by a woman at a flea market for her son. It was found at the Portland airport on or close to September 11," I said. "Mehmet said the information on it might be relevant to things you had seen in the FBI. He thinks this might have belonged to Mohammed Atta."

I put the computer in front of Kara and she casually flipped through the information as I ordered two beers from our waitress.

"Mr. Stillati," Kara said. "If you are a nut looking for some sensational story or conspiracy theory, then I think you should leave now. You're wasting your time and mine. Good night." She got up to leave.

I took her hand.

"Please," I said. "Hear me out."

I took out a picture of Susan Baines' body.

"This is the woman who bought the laptop. She was my sister-in-law. She is dead now. Someone carved her eye out of her head after he raped her. Someone is trying to kill her son who is with me at the Grand Ely Lodge. There is a giant NSA agent after me and the boy. We are on the run. There is no agenda here, Ms. Murphy," I said. "Just survival."

Kara Murphy looked at me with more respect and her eyes softened.

"Mr. Stillati…"

"Call me Dave."

"Very well, then. Dave. Yes, I have seen this information before. On August 15, 2001, and it belonged to a laptop Zacarias Moussaoui had when I arrested him in Minneapolis. You recall that he was the only terrorist who was caught almost a month before the attacks."

"And it contained the same instructions that this did?"

"Same instructions, different target. Now that's all I am allowed to say," said Kara. "I am under twenty different gag orders from both the FBI and the NSA to not reveal anything that occurred at the FBI during my term as leader of the anti-terrorist unit. This includes any mention of my arrest of Zacarias Moussaoui. A judge has placed this gag order on me, upon penalty of arrest and jail time, not to mention the loss of my pension."

"Is that that important to you?" I asked her.

I saw fire come into her eyes.

"You have a big set of balls, questioning me, Dave Stillati," said Kara Murphy. "I was the person who captured Moussaoui. I was also the only person who took on the entire FBI and accused them of impeding the investigation that could have prevented 9/11 and then covering it up. I was accused of being a traitor and attacked twice, raped, and left for dead. Now I work security at the local Wal-Mart. What have you done for your country lately?"

I saw Jenna getting up from the bar ready to come to her defense.

"I'm sorry, I was way out of line," I said.

"Yes, you were," she continued. "Now go home and don't come back for your own good."

"Okay," I said. "But answer just one more question, and then I'll go."

She looked at me waiting for my question, her eyes glaring indignantly.

"I was a cop once in New York. Why would a beautiful and talented young woman like you want to join the FBI?"

"To serve and protect my country, of course," said Kara Murphy without hesitation. "My father served in World War II in the Pacific with forty percent of the other Ely men. I graduated with honors from St. Lawrence and could have gotten any job I wanted. I chose to join the FBI to help my country, to do some good. I thought that was my purpose."

"But something or somebody stopped you, didn't they?" I asked.

She didn't say anything.

"Somebody you know is still out there. The same people who are after us now. Help me find them, Kara. You are the only one who can."

"I'm sorry," she said, getting up. "I must go now."

"I'm staying at the Grand Ely Lodge tonight," I said defeated. "If you change your mind, here is my cell number as well."

"Take care of yourself," she said softly as she walked away. Jenna joined her and they walked out of the saloon.

I sat down in a depressed state. Without help and information from Kara Murphy, my situation went from tragic to hopeless. Betsy the waitress came over to my table and said, "Short meeting? Don't give up. Poor girl's been through a lot. Give her time and she might come around. Want your burger now?"

"You're a good soul," I said. "I'll take mine now with one chainsaw burger to go," I said thinking about Adam.

CHAPTER 32

After chowing down on a burger the size of a basketball, I walked out of the Chainsaw Saloon into the frigid Minnesota winter. *Way to go, Dave,* I thought to myself. *Now I'm completely on my own in Ely, Minnesota, freezing my ass off.* I couldn't blame Kara Murphy for not wanting to get involved in our story. It was pretty far-fetched. Besides, she had arrested one of the terrorists a month before the 9/11 attacks, captured all his information, and was about to break the case wide open, but had been shut down by her own people at the FBI. Basically her bosses had stopped her from foiling the worst terrorist attack against the United States.

How do you live with that? I thought to myself, reaching for the cold hotel key in the pocket of my jeans. After 9/11, she had been discredited, physically violated, and left for dead. No one seemed to make a connection between her attack and what she was saying to the press about a cover-up and possible interference on her investigation. To add insult to injury, after surviving a life-threatening attack, she was then ordered to remain quiet by the very agency she had committed her life to serve.

They paid her off with a pension and a get-lost sign, I thought to myself in disgust. I thought about her blonde hair and delicate skin, the freckles on her nose. Kara Murphy was the best looking FBI agent I had ever seen. There was no way I could ever blame her for anything, even not wanting to help a lost soul like me.

She got a lot of guts, that little woman. More than most guys I know, I thought to myself, already smitten with her memory. I made my way back to the Grand Ely Lodge and walked into my room. Adam practically jumped on top of me and grabbed the bag with the food from my hands.

"Where have you been?" he said. "I'm starving."

"One chainsaw burger with fries and a Coke," I said. "As ordered."

He took out the food and put it on the coffee table in front of the TV. Then he proceeded to squeeze an inordinate amount of ketchup on his fries and burger.

"Do you want some food with that ketchup?" I asked him.

"This is the way I always eat burgers," he said, stuffing his mouth full of food. "Did you talk to the FBI lady? Is she going to help us find who killed Mom?" Adam asked.

I didn't want to disappoint him too much.

"She's going to think about it. The FBI don't want her talking to people about these kind of sensitive issues."

"Oh," said Adam. "So she told you piss off."

So much for tact.

"Well, she doesn't want to risk everything in her life just to help us. I can't blame her," I said to Adam. "I would do the same thing."

"No, you wouldn't," he said. "You came to Portland to get me. You could have stayed home in New York. We're not even real family. I mean, you married my aunt. You got divorced. You could have walked away."

"Walk away from what? You're part of my family," I said. "It's different for this lady."

"What do we do now?" asked Adam as he sipped his Coke.

"Now you eat, we sleep, and leave for New York tomorrow morning."

"Okay by me," said Adam digging back into his burger.

I decided to call Kelly at her home to see what had been happening in my absence. It was about 10:00 PM in New Jersey.

"Hey, Kelly. It's me," I said.

"Mario," said Kelly, "how's your team doing?"

I knew right then that there was big trouble on the horizon. A long time ago Kelly and I had established a code that if anyone of us got into trouble, we would pretend to be talking to some other person in case the calls were tapped. Kelly was telling me that this was one of those times.

"I scored two goals here last Sunday," I said. "But I need a new team. Is Dave around? I want to be traded."

"No, Dave's not here. Besides, he is in a lot of trouble," said Kelly.

"How's that?" I asked her.

"Some NSA agents came into our office today and told me Dave was a suspect in an Al Queda terrorist investigation. Can you believe it? What has that idiot gotten himself into now? They went through everything and took away books, phone records, the whole lot. Seems Dave was in Indonesia in March at a tsunami fundraising match and they say he met some terrorists there. They say he came back here to plan some attack in New York. At least that's what the NSA people are saying."

"Dave?" I said surprised and worried. "Doesn't seem likely."

"Yup, it was even on the cover of the *Post*. A big picture of Dave Stillati with the words NYC TRAITOR? written in red. Great advertising for our agency, isn't it?"

"I don't really think so," I said. "Guess I will have to find myself a new agent," I said.

"That's what all the other players are saying," Kelly said. "An old girlfriend of his was on TV saying she always knew he was a terrorist because he took her to a Turkish restaurant called Omar's Oasis on 65th and 1st. More stupid girlfriends are coming out of the woodwork now. Naomi Wyatt's publicist was interviewed and Naomi only knew him by accident."

"Isn't there anybody supporting him?" I asked in desperation.

"His mother called in to Howard Stern saying the government does't have a clue what they are talking about."

Thank God for Mom, I thought to myself.

"Also the Mayor says he knew Dave Stillati when he was on the force and he thinks the government is chasing windmills. Other cops are defending Dave as well. It's not all bad."

"I'm thinking of coming to New York soon," I said.

"Not a good idea," said Kelly. "But if you do, use the 3rd Avenue Bridge. Much less crowded."

"Good tip," I said to Kelly.

What Kelly was telling me was to avoid coming to the office but to go through Harlem and stop at the uptown apartment of my bodyguard and friend, Marvelous Eddie Carpenter, ex-middleweight contender. The NSA would not be looking for me there.

"I'll remember that," I said to Kelly.

"Oh, and Mario?" she said

"Yes, Kelly?"

"The teams aren't fooling around. Take good care of yourself. I'll have Dave call you if he ever comes back."

"You do that. Bye," I said.

She hung up and I thanked Jehovah for having someone as smart and as loyal as Kelly working for me.

Now I was in an even bigger jam. The National Security Agency had announced to the world that I was a suspected Arab terrorist. Where the hell had they gotten that idea? My picture would be in all the papers and worse than that, every cop, FBI agent, and regular nutcase would be out on the streets looking for me. By all logic, I should turn myself in, to avoid getting shot, but where would that leave Adam? He would be at the mercy of his mother's killer.

Terrific, I thought to myself. *I didn't do anything, and the whole world is already after me. I have an innocent kid whose mom was murdered and who now has put his life and all his hopes in me and it will be a miracle if I get us to New York alive. Plus, there is a giant psycho NSA agent after us. Things have definitely gotten much more interesting now.*

"Everything okay, Dave?" asked Adam.

"No sweat, kid," I replied. "We'll be on our way tomorrow morning, get some sleep now."

Adam got into his bed and pulled the covers up to his neck.

I sat there watching some brainless show about people eating disgusting bugs and worms on television, wondering how the human race ever got so desperate just to be on TV. *There must be a silver lining somewhere in this nightmare*, I said to myself, but I certainly couldn't see it yet. *What chance do I have to unravel this whole thing and keep myself and Adam alive and free from prison?* I thought to myself. *Maybe one in a thousand?*

I turned off the light and tried to go to sleep but to no avail. I tossed and turned and moved around making sure that my nine-millimeter Beretta was underneath my pillow. I had a feeling I would be needing it soon. There are a lot of people that I didn't mind taking on, but the National Security Agency was not among them. They were supposed to defend the citizens of our country, which included Adam, his mom, and me. The NSA also had endless resources and powers and I had close to none. It was a lose-lose situation all the way around. It wasn't even a fair fight.

Then I heard a knock on the door.

I pulled out my Beretta and walked quietly in the darkness.

"Who there?" I cried out keeping the revolver pointed at the door.

"It's me," said a female voice.

"Who's me?" I said.

"Kara Murphy. Open up, Dave."

I opened the door carefully keeping my gun by my side. She was standing outside of my door in her blue parka, shivering.

"Hi," I said. "Lost?"

"Don't be stupid. Let me in," she said.

"I don't usually let good looking ex-FBI agents into my room at night," I said to her. "I have my standards."

"Let me in. I just saw your picture on the nine o'clock news. Everyone thinks you're a terrorist now."

"Oh boy," I said. "Guess my cover is blown."

I opened the door and let her in. Her ice blonde hair was flowing over her blue quilted parka and she stepped out of the snowy walkway into the hotel room. She looked ravishing. I turned my night table light on.

Adam woke up and looked at her. "Who are you?" he said.

"I guess you are Adam," said Kara. "Dave's told me about you. I'm Kara."

"You're the FBI agent," Adam said.

"Retired," she said.

Adam waved a sleepy hand at her and went back to sleep.

"Can we go somewhere and talk?" she said.

"Sure," I said. "We can talk in the car."

We walked outside and got in her beat up Volvo that was sitting in the Grand Ely Lodge parking lot.

"Let's go for a drive," she said. We drove to a Winter Carnival scene in the middle of town where people were ice skating. There were statues of ice flowers and an eight-foot snow sculpture of a moose. She stopped the car and we looked at the skaters flowing by.

"I used to come here with my dad to skate," she said. "My mom passed away when I was little and my dad raised me to be a nice but tough little girl. He taught me how to skate, how to shoot, and how not to be scared of anybody."

"Those are good things to learn," I said.

"But there are people that do terrible things out there, people that did terrible things to me, too. I'm a different person than I was then. I'm scared now," Kara said.

"We all have fears," I said. "But basically you remain the same person you always were. You can come back stronger."

"Jenna didn't want me to come to see you. She says I've suffered enough," Kara said.

"I guess she cares for you," I said.

"It's not what you think. We are just best friends, nothing more. She took me in after I was attacked and nursed me back to life. She has been great to me."

"Kara, you don't need to explain this to me. Your life is your life. I'm in no position to judge you," I said.

"I was a good FBI agent," said Kara. "We had a small anti-terrorist unit: me, Mehmet Hadji, Walter Grey, and Todd Jurgensen. We handled all the information that came in from overseas agents. We would analyze the information and give our recommendations to the upper ups."

"Who were these upper ups?" I asked.

"Director Mueller and Deputy Director Michael Cherry. He was only there a year," Kara said.

"Go on," I said.

"One day we received a report from the Israelis that some Arab men were taking lessons at flights schools throughout the United States. We asked permission to investigate. I followed some of the leads that we had received from the flight schools. That's when I arrested one of them right here in Minneapolis, Zacarias Moussaoui. He had a laptop with him just like the one you showed me. We booted it up and looked into the information he was carrying. A terrible attack was planned. It looked genuine. I reported it to director Mueller, showed him the computer. We expected more arrests to follow. They didn't. Then things became very complicated."

"In what way?" I asked her.

"I can show you," said Kara. "I brought some of the documents here in the car with me. You must understand if I didn't want to help you. My life had regained some sort of normalcy. I was safe. But when I saw you on TV, and saw they were setting you up like they did me, I knew it would never stop. I knew that that I had to help you. That's why I came back to the hotel to see you." Her sparkling green eyes looked into mine, and I felt like diving into them like a dolphin in the Caribbean Sea.

"I understand what you have been through," I said. "You were a good FBI agent. You still are. Just like I'm still a NYC cop, no matter what. We are who we are."

Kara turned on the ignition and said, "You don't know what you are up against. I hope I can help you. Let's go back to my place. If you are going to fight these people, there are a lot of things you should know." She turned the car into the snowy road toward her house.

Kara didn't know it, but it was the best invitation I'd had in a very long while.

CHAPTER 33

Michael Cherry was pacing up and down his office in Washington, speaking to his NSA office in New York on his speakerphone.

"Heard anything yet from this Stillati guy?" Michael Cherry asked the National Security agents who were monitoring phone conversations of suspected terrorists.

"Not so far," said Agent Ron Durhling. "We have tapped his home, office, and his secretary's home so far and are recording all their calls. He rented a car at the Portland airport, but from then there has been no sign of him."

Michael considered the information and said, "Stillati is on the run. He must think somebody is after him to be so careful." The Patriot Act had given him and his associates unlimited powers to listen in and tap phone conversations throughout the United States. There were literally millions of hours of conversations being taped and catalogued every day by the NSA. Any calls that were suspicious were then handed over to the FBI for a more in-depth investigation.

"Can you send over the phone logs on his office phones?" Michael asked.

Ron Durhling send him an e-mail of all calls to and from any of the phones used by Dave Stillati, his secretary, Kelly, or their friends.

"Most of them are from players that are looking for jobs," said Agent Durhling. "We haven't found anything suspicious yet. His secretary is answering all the calls. His mom called. Why are we after this guy anyway? I read he was a New York cop once?"

"His name came up in an investigation on a terrorist cell in Indonesia," said Michael.

"The guy was an ex-New York City cop, decorated as well. Do you really think he could be a traitor?" said agent Durhling.

"We can never be too sure. He may be getting paid off. Looks like he's broke now," said Michael Cherry. He looked at the e-mail that Agent Durhling had sent him, and saw a call from Ely, Minnesota. The name of the town sounded very familiar to him for some reason.

"Who made this call from Minnesota?" said Cherry.

"It's from some soccer player called Mario," said Durhling.

"Let me hear it live," Michael Cherry said.

Ron Durhling went to the computer monitoring the various calls made and replayed the phone call made to Kelly Claire from Ely, Minnesota. A man's voice was heard talking to Kelly.

"I think there's a chance that's him," said Michael Cherry. "He's talking with his secretary in some kind of code. It's worth looking into." They replayed the conversation.

"Real smart this guy. Do you want me to fly up there and arrest him?" said Agent Durhling.

"No, I'll speak about it to Tanovich," said Michael. "You stay here and monitor if there are any more calls coming in." Michael sat back down at his desk. *Ely, Minnesota*, he thought to himself. *That's where the FBI agent lived? What was her name? Carrie? No...Kara. Kara Murphy. The one who arrested Moussaoui.*

Michael Cherry had gotten the scare of his life when Kara Murphy had arrested Zacarias Moussaoui in Minneapolis and confiscated his laptop computer. On his laptop there was the same downloaded e-mail from Pharbor, just like on all the other laptops. Murphy had seen the information on the computer, but she wasn't allowed to use it. If she had, she could have linked the information all the way back to Michael, and eventually uncovered the other terrorists as well.

Cherry had been able to get the FBI lawyers involved to forbid the disclosure of any of the laptop information as it violated Moussaoui's civil rights. Despite Agent Murphy's vehement objections, the laptop was sealed and the information suppressed until after 9/11.

Later, Cherry was able to confiscate the laptop from the Washington evidence room and change the information into showing that Moussaoui planned to spray Anthrax in the air, a highly unlikely and unmanageable scenario for one terrorist. The real target was very different. Michael knew this because he had sent the target to the idiot Moussaoui in an e-mail. Moussaoui was to remain in the U.S. after the attacks and strike again. The attack was to take place in January, 2001, in Washington, D.C., at the inauguration of the newly elected president of the United States. Moussaoui had instructions on how to blow himself up underneath the ceremony stand killing everybody with him. Moussaoui's arrest stopped his plans but not those of the other terrorists. After 9/11, Kara Murphy has gone public and accused the FBI of a cover-up, but by then nobody cared. The FBI had fucked up and everyone in the agency was tarnished. Now the nation was at war. The FBI itself minimized Kara Murphy's importance. They portrayed her as a frustrated agent who was betraying her service by speaking out publicly. She was shunned by the agency and officially gagged from speaking to the press. Szabo had gone to visit her arranging first for a car accident to kill her, and then attacking her in her apartment.

That finally shut her up, thought Cherry.

Michael sat down in his office and called Szabo Tanovich.

"Szabo, I know where the boy and his uncle are," said Michael.

"Where?" asked Szabo in his hotel room in New York.

"They're in Ely, Minnesota. Town sound familiar to you?"

"Ely, that's where the FBI woman lived. Maybe it's a coincidence."

"There are no coincidences," said Michael Cherry. "Get somebody out there and have them find the boy and his uncle. Get rid of them. Have them get rid of the woman, too, if you need to. Understood?"

"Understood," said Szabo. "Why can't I go there myself?"

"You've been there before. She might recognize you. Stay in New York in case they get back there," said Michael. "Send one of your Serbian friends and show them the pictures of the boy and this Stillati guy so they know who they're gunning for."

"Okay, I will send Mirko," said Szabo. Mirko had been his sub lieutenant in Serbia. He was a ruthless killer as well.

"Just make sure he finishes the job," said Michael. "No more excuses."

"There won't be any," said Szabo. "Mirko knows what to do."

Michael hung up the phone. That was taken care of then. He had a Republican fundraising dinner at the Smithsonian Institute tonight and he was already late. The White House chief of staff had personally asked him to be there, as President Branch was expected to make an appearance.

Something's up, if they asked to see me, thought Michael Cherry, He had a very confident feeling that there was more good news coming his way.

CHAPTER 34

We drove back in the snow to Kara's plain, two-story white clapboard house on the far end of Ely. In the driveway, a black Harley Davidson motorcycle with police insignia stood outside the garage. Kara walked up the stairs and into the small but orderly living room. I followed her up the stairs.

"Jenna, I'm home," said Kara as she walked into the house.

Jenna came out of the kitchen with a skinned cucumber in her hand. She was wearing a light blue shirt with Ely police on her lapel.

"Hi, I'm Dave," I said putting out my hand.

"I know. I'm Jenna. I was making some salad," she said pointing the cucumber at me. "You mind if I search you?"

"Jenna's paranoid," Kara said.

"Just because you're paranoid it doesn't mean you don't have enemies," Jenna said.

"Just aim that thing somewhere else," I said referring to the cucumber lifting up my arms. "Skinned cucumbers make me nervous."

Jenna put her hand in my jacket and lifted out my nine-millimeter Beretta and placed it on the dinner table.

"I guess you came prepared," Jenna said.

"I have a permit for that thing in my wallet."

"I don't doubt it," Jenna said. "Kara's told me who you are and why you are here. I think you spell trouble with a capital T."

"Jenna's my personal bodyguard," said Kara. "She thinks I'm still under eighteen, even though I shoot better than her."

"She's right to be nervous, too," I said. "I didn't choose this situation; it chose me," I said.

- 122 -

"You could have kept on driving past Ely," said Jenna.

"I didn't want to," I said. "I need your help."

"Don't say I didn't warn you," said Jenna. "I'll go back to making dinner. I guess you two have work to do."

Kara took me back to her bedroom. The walls were covered with references to 9/11 and her role at the FBI. There some positive and some very negative articles about her. Then there was an article with a headline that read: "FBI Whistleblower Out of Hospital." I saw a picture of her leaving a hospital with her face covered up in gauze.

"I guess you've been through a lot," I said.

"To hell and back," she said taking off her coat. She turned on her Apple computer. "I was fired from the FBI in 2002," said Kara. "They removed all my access cards to central computers. However, on my own, I kept following the investigations." There were books, magazine, articles, and printouts all over her bedroom.

"Seems like it became an obsession," I said.

"I was the leader of the anti-terrorist unit of the FBI. We were supposed to anticipate attacks like the ones that happened. How would you feel if it had happened on your watch?"

"I couldn't forgive myself," I said.

"So, you understand. It's more than an obsession for me. I have to know that I didn't fuck up and let more than 3,000 people be killed."

"Who was in the anti-terrorist unit with you?" I asked.

"Mehmet the translator, Todd Grey, and Walter Jurgensen."

"Are they still at the FBI?" I asked.

"Walter Jurgensen was killed in Afghanistan in 2002 following up on a report about two Western men who had visited Bin Laden's camp. Todd Grey was killed on assignment in Florida last year. Mehmet, as you know, retired right after 9/11 and works in the UN now."

"So, you are the only one left from the unit?" I asked.

"With Mehmet, yes," Kara said.

"To whom did you report at the FBI?"

"We reported directly to Director Mueller but he was heavily involved in Congressional investigations against the agency. He delegated almost all of the real work to Michael Cherry, the deputy director."

"Was he an FBI agent?" I asked.

"No, he was new to the agency. He came to the FBI in December 2000 from the private sector and was previously the chairman of Holliwell Corporation.

He made big bucks there. Cherry was a major fundraiser for the Branch campaign. As a result, Branch gave him the position at the FBI as a reward. Many of us were surprised that he would be interested in it at all."

Kara pulled up his picture on the computer screen. It showed a heavy-set bald man with black glasses and a strong face.

"Where is he now?" I asked.

"He was sent to the NSA as a promotion after 9/11. He is the deputy director there now. They say he is a cinch for vice president in 2008 for the Republicans."

"Did you notice any change in the FBI when he came aboard?" I asked.

"Our unit was created in 1998. We investigated most of the terrorist activity aimed against the U.S. The only change in 2000 was that we were ordered to focus our efforts on American militias within the U.S. This happened because of the Oklahoma City bombing and Tim McVeigh. As we had limited resources, we could hardly do both," Kara said.

"I was the only one concentrating on possible Arab attacks," she continued.

"What did the reports that were coming in say?"

"All of the intelligence prior to 9/11 gave us clear indication that a group of Arab men had infiltrated the United States and was taking flying lessons in different states. This information came from the French, German, and Israeli intelligence."

"What did you do about it?"

"I reported it to Michael Cherry and the director. They sent a team of agents to look into it."

"Did anything happen?"

"No. We even got various calls from the flight school instructors warning us about this. Cherry told us he sent agents there and there was nothing in the reports that suggested the men could be preparing attacks of any kind."

"Anything else?"

"Then I got a tip from the Moussad that a well known Arab terrorist was in our area taking flight lessons," Kara said. "He had ties to radical Islamic groups and fighters in Chechnya."

"What did you do about it?" I asked.

"I decided to take matters in our own hands. Agent Jurgensen and I went to the flight school in Norman, Oklahoma, and interviewed the flight instructor there. He confirmed that Moussaoui trained there but couldn't learn how to fly. He gave us a picture of him and told us he had moved to Minneapolis. We continued our research and found him living in a cheap hotel on the outskirts of town. I arrested him in his apartment complex and confiscated his laptop computer."

"What was on his laptop?" I asked.

"We weren't supposed to look at it, but I did. There were names of other terrorists, flight schools, and instructions on an attack that was supposed to take place in September and another in January," Kara said. "It was the mother load."

"The attack in September was 9/11, I suppose. What was the one in January about?"

Kara looked at me and said, "Zacarias Moussaoui had precise instructions from someone in the United States, close to our government, to kill the president of the United States, the vice president, the chief justice, and their families at the presidential inauguration in Washington with a suicide bombing attack."

"You saw this on the laptop?" I said shocked.

"With all the details worked out. It was supposed to supplement the first attack of the other bombers."

"And what did you do with this information?"

"I submitted it with the laptop and the prisoner to the FBI headquarters in Washington," said Kara. "I urged them to take the information on the laptop and use it."

"And what happened?"

"Director Mueller and Deputy Director Cherry kept it for a week. Then they told us the FBI lawyers had prohibited the search of the laptop as there were no indications that Zacarias Moussaoui could be planning a terrorist attack," Kara said.

"What did you do?"

"I went ballistic. I screamed and shouted and wrote e-mails and memos but nothing was ever done," said Kara.

"Did they say why?"

"No. I was reprimanded officially for being too emotional and unprofessional and put on leave of absence. Moussaoui was put in a holding cell for the time being. No one interviewed him until after 9/11. The laptop sat in the FBI warehouse in Washington."

"I saw a later report that it contained the plans for an Anthrax attack on a farm," I said to her.

"I saw that report, too. But that's not what was on the computer laptop I took from him in his hotel room," Kara said.

"Were there any other episodes like this?" I asked.

"There were reports of misinformation coming from the Pentagon. During the fall of Kabul, the captain of an Apache helicopter had some VIP Taliban and Al Queda in his sights. Intelligence on the ground said it might be Bin Laden and other Al Queda members in a SUV escaping Kabul. The captain of the helicopter asked permission to fire," Kara said.

"And what happened?" I asked.

"Permission was denied by Intel-op ed headquarters in the Pentagon," Kara said. "Also in Tora Bora, Bin Laden and Al-Zawahiri were surrounded by American Ranger forces. There was no way out. Then the intelligence center at the Pentagon gave the order to restrain the Rangers and let the Afghan allied forces go in for him. That decision gave Bin Laden and his forces time to escape to Pakistan."

"How do you know this for sure?" I asked.

"I have friends in the Pentagon who believe the same thing I believe."

"What is that?" I said.

"That there was a powerful mole in the United States helping or even planning the attacks and protecting the terrorists. Agent Todd Jurgensen went to Afghanistan to interview a driver who claimed to have brought two Westerners to Bin Laden's camp in 1998. Jurgensen was killed interviewing that driver and his family. Their house was bombed by a U.S. Air Force jet while they were in it."

"And agent Grey?"

"He was killed in Florida, apparently on a different case. But I don't believe that. He was trying to find out information on Atta for me."

"What happened to the helicopter pilot, the one in the Apache?"

"His helicopter was downed by friendly fire a week later. He was killed on the spot."

"So how can you confirm that it ever really happened?"

"His gunner, Charles Ryan, survived. He was severely burned in the crash and lives in a V.A. hospital in Virginia. I went to see him there. He confirmed the story that my friends at the Pentagon had told me," Kara continued, showing me mounting evidence that she had acquired in the years since she had retired from the FBI.

"This information could explain why somebody would kill Adam's mom in order to get his hands on the laptop," I said.

"Or keep it from getting into somebody else's hands. It's the smoking gun needed to prove there was a traitor behind the attacks," said Kara.

"You must come back with me to New York," I said, "and help me find them."

"Not on your life," Kara said. "I went to war once already and lost. The first time somebody crashed into my car while I was on the highway. I barely survived that. The second time somebody came into my house at night. He was huge and incredibly powerful. He bound and gagged me. Then he raped and beat me. Me, an FBI agent! Have you ever been raped, Dave? It's the most humiliating and painful thing that can happen to somebody. It makes you feel soiled and dirty and sinful. After that, I took the deal the FBI made me and retired. Now I work as a security guard at Wal-Mart. Happy?"

I didn't know what to say. What I was asking her was beyond the pale. She had already suffered way too much for trying to help her country.

"I'm really sorry, Kara."

"So am I, Dave," Kara said. "Understand me well. I have nothing left to give."

"I understand, Kara. I'm on my own."

We looked at each other in mutual disappointment for a while pretending to look at different papers. Then she said, "I told you all I know. I better take you back to the hotel now."

"Okay, Kara," I said. "Take me back."

CHAPTER 35

While driving back to the hotel, Kara was mostly silent. I didn't know what to say, either. We drove through the snowy streets of Ely made more brilliant by a resplendent full moon. The more I looked at her, the more I found myself very attracted to her, smitten by her looks and personality. She drove into the parking lot of the Grand Ely Lodge and parked the car.

"Well, we're here," Kara said.

"I want to thank you for talking to me," I said. "You didn't have to do that."

"I wish I could help you more," she said. "My situation here is still difficult."

"I know you did what you could," I said.

"Bye, David," Kara said and she leaned over and kissed me on the cheek close to my lips.

"Bye, Kara," I said and I leaned over and kissed her full on the mouth. I know it was rude, but I just had to do it.

She was surprised at first, but then kissed me back hard. We were soon making out passionately like teenagers. Then suddenly, she pulled away.

"Whoa, cowboy," she said. "Where did that come from?"

"I don't know, but it felt good," I said. I reached over and kissed her one more time holding the back of her head in my left hand. Her lips were soft and warm and her tongue darted into my mouth like a wet whisper.

"I haven't kissed anybody in five years," Kara said.

"I haven't wanted to kiss anybody in a while," I said.

"Liar," she said. "You're too good at it."

We kissed again and again. It felt too good to stop.

"I should be getting back home," Kara said. "Jenna will get worried."

"Can I call you when I get to New York?" I asked her.

"You better call me," Kara said, "if you're not in jail by then, or in Guantanamo Bay."

"They have to catch me first," I said.

"Don't underestimate who you're up against, Dave. Look what they did to me."

"I'm an old center back defender and an ex-New York City cop," I said. "I can take care of myself."

"Somehow, I don't doubt that," said Kara.

We said goodbye at least three more times as passionately and as long as we could, and I walked back to my hotel room, turning around to look at her departing Volvo only twice.

Kara Murphy, ex-FBI agent, I thought to myself. *Who would have thought I'd have a crush on a Fed?*

I arrived at the door and put the key into the lock. As I opened the door quietly, I hoped Adam would still be asleep. I needn't have bothered. Adam was lying on the bed on his side. He was tied up with his mouth and wrists covered in grey electric tape. In the corner, a very ugly looking man with long, greasy black hair and a scar on his forehead was holding a Mauser revolver aimed right at me.

"Mr. Dave Stillati, I presume?" he said in a heavy Eastern European accent.

"None other," I said. "But you're not Dr. Livingstone."

"My name is Mirko," he said. "Sit down on the bed and keep your hands over your head."

I sat on the bed putting my hands up in the air.

Mirko walked over to me, reached into my jacket, and removed my Beretta.

"Nice piece," he said.

"Everyone seems to like it tonight," I said. "What do you want?"

"I was sent to retrieve a laptop computer," he said. "Do you have it?"

"It's in my car," I said. "I can go get it if you want."

"You're a funny guy," he said. "Pick up the boy."

I walked over to pick up Adam. His eyes were wide with fright. I winked at him to calm him down, but I didn't know where this was going either.

"Now, let's go to the car," he said standing behind me with the Mauser pointed at the small of my back. We walked out of the room and out of the hotel, toward the parking lot.

"Put the boy in the backseat," Mirko said, opening the door. I slid Adam into the backseat.

"Careful," said Mirko putting the gun behind my ear. I considered whether to punch him right there but decided that it would take nothing for him blow my brains all over the snow. I figured he was going to take us out somewhere desolate and do the job there.

"Now, get in the car and drive," he said as he got into the passenger seat.

"Where are we going?" I asked.

"You'll see," he replied.

I put the car into drive and went out onto the main road of Ely. A million plans came to mind—none of them good ones. For anything I could do, he could do better—shooting me or Adam on a whim at any time.

"Go towards the highway," Mirko said.

"Are you a Serb or a Croatian?" I asked.

"None of your fucking business," he said. "Where you are going, you don't need to know anything."

"It's funny because you look a lot like a Serbian whore I once fucked in Zagreb. Might be your mother."

He hit me hard with the gun across the mouth. I elbowed him in the eye and tried to grab his hand but he held it firm against my temple.

"You do that again and you are a dead man," he said and he spit in my right ear.

Things were really going great, I thought. I didn't have to worry about disease because I had a feeling I would be underground in about fifteen minutes. I wasn't scared, just upset that I couldn't get the better of this idiot in the current situation we were in. We continued driving on the highway further and further away from Ely and civilization. Things looked very bleak for me and Adam. Suddenly a motorcycle came up behind us with the sirens flashing. I looked in the rear view mirror and said, "It's the police, what do you want me to do?"

"Pull over," he said. "I'll take care of him."

I pulled the car over to the side of the road.

The motorcycle stopped behind us and the officer started to come over to the passenger side window. I noticed Mirko holding the revolver in his lap. There was no doubt in my mind that he was planning on killing the officer. I reached into my left pocket and grabbed the small four-inch fishing knife I always carried for possible emergencies. I opened it with my left hand while Mirko was waiting for the officer to come around to his side of the car.

"Good evening, guys. Are you in a hurry? You were going eighty miles an hour back there, license and registration, please," said the officer.

Mirko swung his right hand with the gun ready to shoot the cop. In a flash, I pulled out the knife and slashed his wrist to the bone. Mirko yelled out and the gun fell to the floor. A splash of bright red blood splattered across the windshield. The officer pulled out a revolver and put it in Mirko's face.

"Out of the car, now, scumbag!"

I pocketed my knife and Mirko grabbed his bloody wrist getting out of my car cursing in Serbian. The officer removed her helmet and I saw long brown hair falling out. It was Jenna, Kara's roommate.

"Jenna, I've never been so happy to see a cop in my whole life," I said. Jenna put cuffs on Mirko who was moaning about his wrist. She made sure it hurt.

"Kara told me to keep an eye out on you until you left. I was at the hotel and saw you carrying the boy out to the car. I knew something was wrong. Who is this guy?" Jenna asked.

"I don't know," I said. "Some Serbian hit man sent out to kill us. I don't think we will get anything out of him."

"Well, we can keep him in the Ely jail on an attempted carjacking charge. We can hold him for a couple of weeks till he lawyers up."

"I'll be glad to file charges," I said.

"We can do that ourselves. Go back to your hotel and pick up your stuff. You need a good head start if you're going all the way to New York."

"Okay, Jenna," I said. "How can I ever thank you?"

"Be nice to Kara," Jenna said. "She came back all starry-eyed from the hotel. I haven't seen her smile like that in five years. If you ever hurt that girl, I will hunt you down, kill you, and skin you like a deer."

"I promise, I'll be nice to her," I said.

"Now get up," Jenna said to Mirko. "We're going for a cool ride on my chopper." She pulled off his shirt and pants so he would enjoy the ride on the back of her Harley in his underwear in sub-zero weather. I almost felt sorry for him.

I reached into the backseat and freed Adam. He pulled his wrist out of the tape and hugged me crying.

"He wanted to kill us, didn't he, Dave?" he said. "Like my Mom?"

"Yeah, but he didn't," I said. "You and me are a lot harder to kill than what that guy had to offer."

CHAPTER 36

After we went back to the hotel and packed up all our stuff, Adam and I started out on the long journey from Minnesota to New Jersey. The close call with Mirko had put a scare into us and we wanted to get on the road as soon as possible. Adam was my co-pilot and traced our driving route all the way through Wisconsin, Indiana, Ohio, and Pennsylvania. We planned to stop in a motel in Ohio for the night. Like most American cars, the Lincoln Town Car I had rented at the Portland airport was great on comfort, but bad on gas. Luckily, I had just enough cash to pay for gas and the last night at a hotel before heading for New York, without using my credit cards. Now more than ever I was sure my credit cards were being traced. Adam played on his laptop for most of the trip. Having never had a son, I had to admit I enjoyed spending time with him. He was a smart, quick kid who had every reason to be down and out, but instead tried to cheer me up as much as he could.

In Wisconsin, we stopped at a 7-11 to get some Cokes and chips, and I called Mehmet Hadji collect. He accepted the call when I said I was Diego Armando Maradona, the world-renowned Argentinean soccer player.

"Diego, how is Argentina?" Mehmet said in jest.

"Cold for this time of year," I said.

"Where are you, my Arab brother? You have become a big story in the news," Mehmet said. "I had no idea you were a true believer."

"You never really know who your friends are," I said.

"Half the city is calling you an Islamic terrorist and half is defending you."

"Who's doing what?" I said.

"The entire New York City Police Department is rejecting the story as crap, and calling you one of their ex-finest."

"And the others?"

"Mostly politicians and talk show hosts implying you were paid off by the terrorists somehow. But they all have an agenda anyway."

"Mehmet, I need you to do me a favor," I said.

"For an Islamic brother, anything. But I have no guns or money for you."

"Very funny, I don't need them for now. I need for you to help me find an Afghan taxi driver named Ali Mahalati."

"In New York? Impossible. There must be hundreds of them. However, the name sounds familiar," Mehmet said.

"Kara Murphy gave me his name. She said he drove two Westerners to the Al Queda terrorists camps in 1998. Do you think you can find him?"

"Yes, now I remember. He was a driver there and reported to the Afghan resistance that he picked up some Westerners and took them to a camp. An FBI agent went there to find him but I thought they were all killed. What was the driver's name again?"

"Ali Mahalati. See if there is a chance he might still be alive somewhere. He would be a key to this story."

"So you are still pursuing this, despite the warnings I gave you. You really have a hard head, Dave. I will ask my friend who is with the Afghan delegation here at the United Nations. They should be able to help me."

"Thanks, Mehmet. I will call you when I get to New York."

"The Feds are looking for you here," Mehmet said. "Are you sure it's a good idea to come back?"

"I'm a New Yorker, Mehmet. I have an automatic permit to come back to New York whenever I feel like it. It's the New York law of return."

"I just don't want to see you shot while resisting arrest."

"I appreciate the concern. I will call you once I get into the city."

"Okay. Bye, Dave. Call me on my cell. If I help you with this, I will ask you for a favor myself."

"Anything, Mehmet."

"When you come back, you have to lead us in prayers on Friday at the mosque on 96th Street. After all, you are an Islamic celebrity here now."

"You do this for me, and I'll be there, Mehmet. I promise."

"I'll keep you to your word," said Mehmet. We both hung up.

Mehmet was an A-1 stand up guy and I knew he would do his best to find out if this guy Ali Mahalati was still alive.

I saw Adam was talking to the guy at the counter of the 7–11.

"Let's go, Adam," I said to him.

Adam grabbed the bag with the chips and two Cokes and we headed back to the car.

"Can I drive?" Adam asked.

"How old are you? You don't have a license."

"I'm fourteen," said Adam. "How am I going to learn if you don't let me drive?"

"Okay, that makes sense," I said. "Here are the keys. Get in the car."

"Really?" said Adam, totally surprised that I was letting him drive. He got into the driver's seat and put the key into the ignition. I sat besides him hoping I wasn't going to regret the decision. Adam pulled out of the lot and into traffic. There were some stops and starts, but after some initial hesitation he appeared to handle the car pretty well.

"My mom taught me to drive a bit in Portland," said Adam.

"She taught you really well," I said.

"I miss her," said Adam. "I'm never going to see her again, or her me. Who will I live with now?"

"Probably your grandparents or your Aunt Susan."

"Will you be there, Dave?" Adam asked.

"Yes, Adam," I said. "Now concentrate on the road before we get flattened by a twelve-wheel truck. If we survive this adventure, yes, I will definitely be there for you."

"Good," he said. "How do you turn on the windshield wipers?"

The skies had opened up on our road in Wisconsin. I had Adam pull over to the right and changed seats with him.

"Time to change drivers," I said. "No need to take unnecessary risks."

"Ah, shit," said Adam. "I was doing great. Didn't I do well, Dave? Didn't I?" Adam said excitedly.

"Yes, Adam," I said. "You did real well. Now, move over."

CHAPTER 37

❈

There are few sights in the world as majestic as crossing the George Washington Bridge. When you cross it in the early morning, headed toward New York City, you see the glorious Hudson River on your left and the island of Manhattan on your right. The sight is especially glorious if New York is your final destination after a thirteen-hour drive from Ohio. Adam could hardly stay in his seat from his excitement. We had consumed lattes and espresso along the way, which made me wired enough to light up the Empire State Building. I was kind of excited myself about our return, never forgetting the fact that there was a warrant out for my arrest waiting for me in the city.

I'll face that when I get there, I decided.

First I had to drop off Adam at Marvelous Eddie Carpenter's gym in Harlem. We had passed Adam's home in Clinton, New Jersey, on the way to the G.W. Bridge and I had been sorely tempted to drop Adam off with his grandparents. However, I also knew that whoever had killed his mom would be waiting or having somebody waiting there to greet us. I had explained this to Adam and he understood. I followed I-95 through the tunnel that led to Harlem River Drive and drove uptown to the exit on 125th Street. Eddie's townhouse was not far away. He had bought it with the money I got him for the last fight. On the ground floor was a boxing gym where Eddie taught local kids how to box. Eddie's living quarters were on the second and third floors. It was a sweet set-up. I called him from a pay phone on the corner of the street to make sure he was there. He came down to greet us with a smile on his face. I had told Adam a little bit about Eddie's career and he was mesmerized that he would be staying at his place for a few days.

"Let me sort this thing out and I'll be back to get you," I told him. In the meantime, I would hold on to his laptop. We parked on the corner of the street and got out of the car to meet Eddie.

"So this is the little champ," said Eddie talking to Adam. "I hear you're pretty good with your head and your fists."

"Really?" said Adam looking at the big black man with amazement. "I heard you're the champ."

"You see? We're friends already," said Eddie. "A week with me and you'll be a contender for the lightweight title."

"He is a handful," I said to Eddie. "Take good care of him."

"Don't worry, Dave. We'll be sparring every day."

"You promise?" said Adam.

"Absolutely," said Eddie. "Dave says I got to get you into shape."

"Eddie, thanks a lot for taking him in," I said to Eddie as I took him aside. "The kid has been through a lot."

"And what about you?" asked Eddie. "You are all over the news. How you going to work that out? They're looking for you."

"I don't know," I said. "But that's what I'm here to find out. Just be a little careful who comes into the gym. The guy who killed his mom is still out there and might be after him still."

"Dave?" Marvelous Eddie said. "You are talking to the former contender for the middleweight title of the world, a man with a 44-and-3 record. Don't you remember how I took out that Jamaican punk?"

"Yeah," I said. "But I have a feeling this guy who is after us is in a completely different weight class altogether."

"Doesn't scare me a bit," said Eddie. "I'm fast and I'm lethal." He showed off some of his footwork to Adam's delight.

"Okay, kid," I said. "Eddie will look after you."

Adam and I hugged and I told him that I would call him every day. He had tears in his eyes when we said good-bye. As I drove off, I could see Eddie taking him into the gym. Watching them go off together made me feel a lot better.

I took the FDR drive downtown toward the 42nd Street exit. I stopped first at my Wachovia Bank and dropped off Adam's laptop in the safe deposit box so I could keep it there for safekeeping. Then I dropped off the rental car at the Hertz office on 9th Avenue and started walking toward my office on 11th Avenue. There was no doubt in my mind that the NSA might have posted a stakeout there. I knew that I could sneak up the back of the fire escape and climb into my back office window, which was never locked without being noticed. By all means, I should have been dog-tired after the long trip, but I wasn't. Being back on my home turf gave me unsuspected energies and resources that could last me a while. I headed around the building to the fire escape, climbed up the first step, and swung down toward my back window. I opened it and jumped into my office. There in front of me was my faithful secretary, Kelly Claire, hardly surprised at all.

"Well, if it isn't the master terrorist, himself," said Kelly.

"Shhh," I said to her.

"Don't worry," she said. "The Feds were already here this morning. I then had the electronic guys come over and look for bugs. They found two. The place is clean now. But will you tell me what is going on?" she said.

"You're a gem," I said to Kelly. "I've been set up to take a fall of some kind. We need to do some research to see who would want to do this to Susan Baines, her kid, and me."

"It seems a little extreme," said Kelly.

"It is. Someone obviously has a lot to lose. Get Friedland on the phone."

"Who, the professor at NYU?"

"Yes, the one who teaches economics at the NYU business school. Let's try and reach him ASAP."

Kelly went back to her office, got the phone number, and made the call. She found him in his office and passed the line to me.

"David Stillati!" he said. "Soccer agent *and* Arab terrorist. How do you find the time?"

"I try to keep busy," I said.

"Is it serious?" Walter asked concerned.

"It could be if I don't disprove the bad rap."

"Let me know if I can help you," said Walter.

Walter Friedland was one of the smartest men I had every met. His son, Michael, was an aspiring soccer player and I had been his coach in high school. Walter was a graduate professor at the NYU business school and an advisor to just about everybody on Wall Street.

"I need an asset analysis on some people pre- and post-9/11."

"Who would these people be?" said Walter Friedland.

"Director Mueller of the FBI and NSA Deputy Director Michael Cherry, and a general forrester now at Holliwell, among others."

"Big names," said Walter. "Shouldn't be difficult. Most of the information is available on the Internet or on Dunn & Bradstreet. I will have some information to you by this afternoon. Are they related to the investigation on you?"

"They might be, Walter. Thanks for doing this. I owe you one."

"You don't owe me anything. My son Michael wouldn't be at Harvard today if you hadn't pitched him to the soccer coach there. Even with all my degrees and influence, and all of Michael's grades, and 1600 SAT scores, he was still on the waiting list. You made it happen."

"John Kerr, the Harvard coach, needed a striker," I said.

"You got him in, Dave. You know that. I'll try to get some information and send it over by e-mail to Kelly this afternoon," Walter said.

"Top notch Walter, give my best to Michael."

"I will," he said. "He scored a hat-trick on Sunday."

I congratulated him on his son's success and hung up the phone. *To give and not expect anything in return is what real friendship is all about*, I thought, paraphrasing Oscar Wilde. It also can pay hefty dividends when you need them the most.

"There a lady named Kara Murphy on the phone," said Kelly.

I immediately took the call as my heart starting beating faster.

"Kara, it's wonderful to hear your voice," I said.

"I just wanted to make sure you made it back okay," said Kara.

"I did, thanks to Jenna and you."

"Just being careful, I guess," Kara said. "That perp she arrested is still enjoying the hospitality of the two-cell Ely prison system. He hasn't said anything so far."

"He won't," I said. "I think he has done this thing before."

"Makes me nervous," Kara said.

"About what?" I asked.

"Well, it's been so long since I've cared for anybody," Kara said. "I wouldn't want to lose you now."

"You won't, Kara. I'm not that easy to get rid of."

"I've made some calls to get some more information on some of the stuff I told you about. I even called some of my old sources at the Pentagon to see who was running the intelligence operations there pre- and post-9/11. They will get back to me soon," said Kara, changing the topic.

"How does it feel?" I said.

"How does what feel?"

"To be doing investigative police work again?"

"Like I was born to do it."

"You were," I said.

"So look for some faxes to be coming into your office soon."

"I will. Any chance of you coming to New York any time soon?" I asked.

"I might think about it, if you ask nicely," said Kara.

"Will begging help?"

She laughed. I liked making her laugh.

"Go back to work, Dave."

"Okay, Kara. Big kiss," I said.

We both hung up the phone at the same time.

"Who was that?" said Kelly coming into my office.

"An ex-FBI agent I met in Minnesota," I said. "I think I'm crazy about her."

"That's just great," said Kelly. "My boss is an Islamic terrorist who is in love with an ex-FBI agent. I can't wait to see myself on Oprah."

CHAPTER 38

❃

Where the hell is Mirko, and why hasn't he called? thought Szabo to himself as he waited in the New York office of the National Security Agency. There were two possibilities for Mirko's silence. Either Mirko had killed Stillati and the boy, and was taking his time getting back to Washington, or something unexpected had happened to him. *How could Mirko fail to kill a young boy and a civilian? Didn't make any sense at all,* thought Szabo. *Mirko was one of the best killers in our regiment in Serbia, killing two people was nothing for him.* Szabo was sitting in the office with Agent Ron Durhling who was listening in to the phone conversations coming from Dave Stillati's office.

"He's there!" said Ron Durhling, excitedly. "Stillati's in his office in New York making calls right now."

"That's not possible," said Szabo grabbing a set of headphones.

"Listen in yourself," Durhling said to Szabo.

Sure enough, a man's deep voice similar to Stillati's was talking on his office line.

Shit. Mirko fucked up, thought Szabo. *But at least I know where this asshole is now. I can finish the job Mirko couldn't do.*

"Let's go get him," said Agent Durhling.

"I think it's better if I go alone," said the giant Serb.

"No way," said Durhling. "I've been sitting in this shitty office for a week now. I want in on this collar. We're both going."

There was nothing Szabo could do to dissuade Durhling without Michael Cherry present, and Cherry was at a party in Washington, D.C. Officially, Durhling held a higher rank at the National Security Agency, although Cherry clearly favored using Szabo. Both agents got up and headed downstairs toward their cars. It would only take five minutes to get to Stillati's office. *Once he is in custody, I'll find a way to kill him*, thought Szabo to himself. Durhling took the wheel and Szabo got in the passenger seat.

"Call the NSA jet at LaGuardia and make sure they are ready," said Durhling. "If we get him, we can put him straight on a flight to the base in Guantanamo. Then they can take their time interrogating him there."

Szabo just grunted a reply but made the call anyway. Events were unfolding too rapidly for his liking. He couldn't control them this way. He didn't like that, but he would have to make the best of it. Durhling drove the car in the chaotic New York midday traffic and they were soon in front of Dave Stillati's office on 11th Avenue and 42nd street.

"I'm going in the front," said Durhling. "You cover the back of the building."

Szabo headed toward the fire escape ladder in the back. Durhling walked up the stairs and knocked on the door.

"Open up. Federal agents," he said. "We have a warrant for the arrest of Dave Stillati."

Kelly and I were in her office when we heard the knocking. Kelly immediately turned to me.

"Dave, get out of here," she said, as she headed to open the door. I went into the back of my office and opened my window, getting one leg out over the window ledge. From outside, an enormous hand grabbed my throat and another hand pointed a gun against my temple.

"Freeze, asshole," said a deep voice with an Eastern European accent.

"Easy now, big fella," I said lifting my hands. "I'm not resisting arrest."

Szabo pulled me out onto the fire escape. He was a good head taller than me, and had cold, dead, shark-like eyes and a blonde crew cut.

"Say goodbye to your life," Szabo said to me. "First, I'm going to blow your brains out and then I'm going to add your eye to the collection in my fridge."

My hair stood on end knowing I was facing what had to be Susan's killer.

"Are you going to rape me, too?" I asked him.

I could feel his trigger finger start to move when another agent ran into my room and faced the window.

"I got him, Szabo," said Agent Ron Durhling pointing his .45 at me. "Don't shoot. We need him alive."

The big Serbian hesitated for a second. Then with great regret, he lifted his gun from my temple and pushed me back into my office like a rag doll. Falling back in through the window I got a better look at him. He was easily six feet, five inches, blonde, with that kind of sloping forehead that can indicate a mental defect. His eyes were a dead grey like a fish, and there was no doubt in my mind that he was the man responsible for Susan Baines' murder, among many others. He looked like the incarnation of pure evil.

"Looks like you don't get your eye after all," I said.

The big Serb just glared at me.

"Dave Stillati, you are under arrest for suspected terrorist activity. I am NSA agent Ron Durhling and this is NSA agent Szabo Tanovich," said Agent Durhling putting cuffs on me.

"This psychopath is an NSA Agent?" I asked Durhling. "Have you asked him how many people he has murdered and raped lately?"

Agent Szabo Tanovich came in through the window and punched me in the face. I fell backward against the wall, blood spurting from my nose.

"Easy, Szabo. Easy," Durhling said.

"Call Frankenstein off," I said to Durhling.

"Shut up, Stillati. I should let him kill you."

Holding my bloody nose with my hand I said, "Do you even have a real warrant?"

"I showed it to your secretary," said Durhling giving me a tissue.

"She's my executive assistant," I said. "Don't I get to call my lawyer?"

"No, you don't," said Ron Durhling. "This is a Federal terrorist case."

"You can call your lawyer from Cuba," said Szabo Tanovich laughing.

They then dragged me out of my room toward the exit.

"Call McShirley," I screamed to Kelly. "Call my lawyer, McShirley, and tell him what is happening."

"McShirley?" asked Kelly.

"McShirley. Magnus McShirley," I said. "The number is in your Triboro book." Kelly seemed to finally understand what I was trying to tell her. At least I hoped she did.

The two NSA agents dragged me down the stairs and threw me in the back of their unmarked tan Chevrolet.

"I am going to call Michael Cherry. He needs to know about this," said agent Durhling getting into the car. Szabo didn't say anything.

"Guys," I said, "I used to be a cop in this city. Aren't you breaking all sorts of laws here? Ask your mongo friend what he did to my sister-in-law in Portland."

"Shut up," said Szabo.

"No, let him talk," said Durhling. "Where he is going, they're going to find ways to make him talk a lot. It's what he deserves, the fucking traitor."

"I feel like I'm in a b-grade horror movie here," I said, "being driven away to oblivion by Boris Karloff and Peter Lorre."

CHAPTER 39

❁

The Republican fundraiser, held every January in Washington, was always one of the most talked about events of the season. Michael Cherry surveyed the Smithsonian Museum and saw many faces that he knew well, elegantly clad in black tie. Here in the Great Hall of the Smithsonian, the technology of the United States of America was on permanent exhibit with examples of the Wright Brothers' plane, *Kitty Hawk,* Lindbergh's *Spirit of St. Louis,* the Lem Modular that landed on the moon, and even the *Enola Gay,* the plane that had dropped the atomic bomb on Hiroshima. Power and wealth were also on exhibit as the most powerful senators, congressmen, lobbyists, and businessmen gathered to celebrate the success of their party both in politics and in business.

*This is what it must have been to have been a Roman at the epicenter of the ancient worl*d, thought Michael Cherry. He felt he was part of the ruling elite and was proud to have earned his position in the continuous power struggle that was life in Washington, D.C.

"Great crowd, eh, Michael?" said Colonel Forrester.

"Bob, I didn't see you," said Michael Cherry.

"Came here early with the Missus. Everybody who is anybody is here. Did you see Holliwell's latest figures?"

"An increase in profits of forty-five percent, stock at an all time high. Pretty good work, I would say," said Michael.

"The world's a dangerous place and we are here to arm those who protect us," said Bob Forrester.

"Hear, hear," said Michael.

Just then Michael's cell phone rang. It was Szabo.

"Sorry, Bob. Gotta get this," said Cherry.

Michael listened for a second and said, "Well, good. It's not what we wanted, but it takes care of our problem anyway. So go with it. One less person to worry about. Stillati's history now. Let Durhling put him on a plane to Cuba immediately. I'll tell them there what needs to be done. He will never come back from Cuba alive."

"Problems?" asked Forrester.

"A small pebble in my shoe, but it's been taken care of."

"You know, Michael, I hope some of the stuff we did, you know, doesn't ever come out."

"Why would it?" asked Michael. "We made history, didn't we?"

"Not everybody would see it that way," said Colonel Forrester.

"Doesn't concern us," said Michael. "You were very well compensated for what you did, and so was I. Plus it was all for the good of the nation."

"I really believe so," said Bob Forrester. "In the end, it turned out the way we wanted."

"Look, there's the president," said Michael Cherry as he left Bob Forrester to move toward the president of the United States.

President Branch made his appearance into the Great Hall of the Smithsonian Museum and all the guests turned to him like bees to honey. With his youthful boyish looks, President Branch was a captivating presence, shaking hands and joking with senators and congressman as if he didn't have a care in the world. They all knew that behind that joyous façade was a fiercely competitive political animal that had defeated all those that had underestimated him. He was forever loyal to his friends and devastatingly destructive to his enemies. His strength was in power and political infighting and he left policy to his aides. The president made his way through the room posing a few seconds with big contributors for photo opportunities. For the first time in a century, the Republican Party controlled both Houses of Congress and the Executive branch. Thanks to President Branch, they had never been so powerful. President Branch had three more years left in his term of office and was looking for a successor who would continue his legacy of power.

"Michael C!" President Branch said when he came upon Michael Cherry.

"Mr. President," said Michael, humbly.

"You're doing a heck of a job at the NSA," said President Branch. "A heckuva job. Give those terrorists some of their own medicine."

"Thank you, Mr. President."

"And we appreciated our Saudi friends' generous contribution. Thank Prince Abdullah for us."

"My honor, Mr. President."

The president went on to shake hands with the other prominent guests in the Smithsonian. Charles Trove, head of the White House staff stopped by Michael Cherry to talk to him.

"It's amazing how he handles a crowd," said Michael.

"Nobody like him," said Charles Trove. "It will be hard to find a replacement for the next election."

"I thought you had a favorite already," said Michael.

"Oh, definitely," said Trove. "But we need to find a vice-presidential running mate that has served this country honorably during these difficult five years. Someone who can be seen to have been tough on terrorism. The president seems to think you might make an ideal candidate. Interested?"

"Is that a formal request?" asked Cherry, feeling the anticipation grow in his gut.

"As formal as it can be at this point," said Trove.

"Then I would be honored to serve my country in any capacity, especially as a candidate for vice president."

"The president was sure you would say that. He will be delighted." The two men shook hands and Trove went on to rejoin the Presidential party.

Vice president, said Michael to himself. *That's something to celebrate*. He downed his drink in one gulp. *That calls for a toast to myself. It's been nothing but good news all around tonight*. He couldn't wait to tell his wife the news. *Vice president*, he thought to himself in excitement. *Just a heartbeat away from being the most powerful man on earth*.

CHAPTER 40

❀

The tan Chevrolet headed up FDR drive toward the Triboro Bridge. Sitting in the back of a Federal vehicle with my hands in handcuffs, I got that feeling of hopelessness and helplessness that suspects must get all the time. This time, I was the one on the receiving end. I figured they were taking me to either LaGuardia or Kennedy airport. From there I could be on a flight directly to Cuba. It would all be over in a half hour at the most. This was habeas without corpus or corpus without habeas; in any case, it felt more like something that would happen in Russia with the KGB than to me in New York City. I figured I had, at most, twenty-five minutes before we arrived at LaGuardia. My only hope was that Kelly had figured out what I was trying to tell her. If not, I was on a one-way ticket to Guantanamo Bay.

"Agent Durhling," I said. "Are you aware that your partner killed a woman in Portland, raped her, and cut her eye out?"

"Shut the fuck up," said Szabo turning around to look at me.

"Plus, he sent a friend of his to Ely, Minnesota, to kill me and a fourteen-year-old boy. Do you know about that?" I said trying to gauge his reaction.

"Ely, Minnesota?" said agent Durhling. "Weren't you supposed to go there, Szabo?"

"Cherry sent another agent," said Szabo.

"He was a Serb lowlife who is in jail now, and he is spilling his guts out to the local police there as we speak," I said.

"What could he say?" said Durhling. "That he went to arrest a possible Islamic terrorist and you escaped somehow? The agency will get him released in a heartbeat. You're the one who is under arrest."

"Agent Durhling," I said, "I was a New York City cop for four years, and a sports agent for another five. I was born a Catholic and baptized at St. Patrick's. Do I look like a fanatical Muslim to you?"

"Traitors can come in different guises," said Durhling. "Maybe you needed money. Maybe it was drugs or women. Whatever you did, the agency has put you high on their list of suspects."

"Who's your boss at the NSA?" I asked.

"Enough talking!" yelled Szabo at me.

"No, it's okay," said Durhling. "My boss is Michael Cherry, deputy commissioner of the NSA and former deputy director of the FBI."

"Don't you think it's strange that he would use a troglodyte like this crazy Serb here to work in the NSA?"

At that Szabo went crazy and turned around punching me several times on the side of my head. I tried to duck but he got in some good ones around my eyebrows. Agent Durhling was trying to stop him while driving the car.

"Easy there, Szabo, easy. Don't let him bait you into hitting him."

"I bet you he goes on all field assignments, doesn't he? Gets all the collars, doesn't that upset you?" I said trying to duck and avoid as much damage as possible. Durhling looked surprised that I would know this.

"He's in the field. I'm in the offices. That's the way they want it."

"Bet there are a lot of accidental deaths on his beat," I said.

Szabo pulled out his gun. "You are dead now," he said.

"No! Don't kill him," said Agent Durhling. "Cherry wants him alive."

The Serb's face was so red he could have lit up the Cross-Bronx Expressway. He put the gun away.

"Stillati, do yourself a favor and shut up before I let Szabo kill you once and for all. If you have anything to say, you can say it to the interrogators at Guantanamo Bay."

We approached the toll booth at the Triboro Bridge and Durhling waited in a car line to pay the toll. My eyes looked around in desperation but I couldn't see anything there that looked unusual. The toll attendant took Durhling's money and handed him some change. We waited for the little yellow bar to go up allowing us to pass but it didn't.

"Must be broken or something," said the tollbooth officer. The cars behind us started to honk.

"Buddy, we are kind of in a rush here," said Durhling. "Can you lift it up already?"

"I'm going to have to call my supervisor," said the attendant, and he put up the electronic closed sign on the overhead board. The attendant made the call.

"Fucking great," said Szabo.

Three officers walked over to the car.

"What's the problem?" said the sergeant.

"The gate is stuck," said the attendant.

"Sergeant," said Durhling, showing his badge, "we are transporting a prisoner here to LaGuardia airport and are in a rush. Get the gate up."

"It's Sergeant Magnus McShirley," said the officer. "And I need to see your warrant as I wasn't notified of any prisoner movement going on at all by our people or the Feds. Get out of the car."

"Sergeant, you are impeding an investigation," said Durhling raising his voice.

"Get out of the fucking car now," said Sergeant McShirley. The other two officers drew their weapons and pointed them toward Szabo and Durhling. Both of them got out of the car.

"Hands on the hood," said McShirley. "You, too. Get out of the car," he said to me.

I showed the sergeant my handcuffs. He opened the door and pulled me out and slammed me against the car.

"If it's something I can't stand, it's the Feds trying to show us how to work here in New York City. Now show me the fucking warrants."

Szabo looked like he was about to kill all three policemen but knew that he couldn't go that far. Durhling gingerly pulled the warrant out of his jacket pocket and showed it to Sergeant McShirley. In the meantime, one of the policemen came behind me and quietly undid my cuffs. I felt my hands go free. As McShirley looked over the warrant I started to step away from the car. I turned toward the Triboro Bridge and took off running on foot as fast as I could. Szabo and Durhling tried to go after me, but the cops kept their weapons trained on them.

"You're letting him go free!" screamed Durhling at McShirley. "I'll have your badge for this."

"I'm still checking your paperwork," said McShirley. "Don't you move. We can always catch him later." The two other cops kept their weapons trained on Durhling and Szabo Tanovich, ready to shoot them if necessary. Szabo and Durhling couldn't believe what was happening but by then I was long gone.

I ran past the cars and the tolls, toward the Randall's Island exit on the left of the bridge. Running down the ramp, I headed to an old stadium that I had played in long ago, which now lay in ruins. It was where the Cosmos had played their first game with Pele in the old NASL league. I had gone there many a time to see my father play and had also played there back in the day. It was directly in front of the hospital for the criminal insane and when we trained there the inmates used to cheer for us. As I ran, I blessed Kelly Claire for being so quick and my police old sergeant Magnus McShirley for showing his loyalty to me. Sergeant McShirley had been the squad leader of my old Brooklyn precinct when I was a cop and he had been there when John, my partner, was killed. He was a cop in the old Irish tradition and would always stand up for his men. The sergeant and I still drank beers at Gallagher's every Wednesday night. I knew he had been transferred to running the Triboro Bridge. I prayed that Kelly would understand my hints and contact him. I also prayed that he would come up with something to help me. He did and with flying colors.

I knew that he had just put his thirty-four-year career and his pension on the line for me. There was no way I could ever repay that. I pulled up at the old stadium, gasping for breath. I knew that McShirley would not be able to hold Durhling and the Serb for long. They would soon be after me again. I had precious little time to get something going. I pulled out my phone and called Eddie. No answer. I left Marvelous Eddie Carpenter a recorded message where to come find me. I knew the call would be monitored but I had no other choice. It was either him or the NSA agents who would find me first. Then I also called Father Dolnic at the Croatian church on 40th Street. He was also the president of the Croatian football team in the Metropolitan league of New York.

"Father Dolnic," I gasped for breath.

"Dave," he said. "You sound like you did when you played for me, slow and out of shape."

"Father, sorry to rush you, but I'm in a jam," I said.

"I read the papers, it's a ridiculous accusation," he said.

"Do you know a Serb military guy called Szabo Tanovich?"

"I know a Szabo Danovic who was the right hand man of the Serb militia—criminal, Arkan, very tall, brutal man. You don't want to know him," said Father Dolnic.

"Well, a guy with a slightly different name, but the same description is after me now."

"He is a brutal killer that has killed hundreds of Croatian men and did worse things to the women," said Father Dolnic. "They said he was killed in Serbia, but nobody here believed it."

"Well, he is here in New York, and I believe is working for the U.S. government now in some capacity. I need for you to pull out as much information as you can on him."

"That won't be hard. Where can I reach you?"

"Nowhere, I'm on the run," I said. "I will call you."

"God protect you, Dave," said Father Dolnic.

I hung up my cell phone and hid behind the old battered concession stand of the stadium. I had to hope somehow that Eddie Carpenter would find me before the NSA agents did. Coming from uptown in Harlem, he wasn't far away. But they were already right on the Triboro Bridge. One way or the other, it would be a very close call.

CHAPTER 41

❀

Kara Murphy was packing her Samsonite bag in the small house she shared with Jenna Davison in Ely, Minnesota.

"Are you sure you want to do this?" said Jenna facing her roommate of five years. "You're risking everything for this guy you just met."

"It's not just him," Kara said putting some shirts and skirts into the bag. "It's about me. I need to do this."

"What are you going to do?" asked Jenna.

"I'm going to Washington to speak to my friend at the Pentagon. He says he has some information for me about things Colonel Forrester did at the Info-ops center—things that might explain what happened to me and what is going on with Dave."

"How is this going to help you?" said Jenna.

"Ever since 9/11, and my attack, I've been living in shock," said Kara. "I was a good FBI agent who discovered the worst terrorist attack was going to happen on U.S. soil, and I wasn't allowed to stop it. Then someone hurt me bad, and scared me into living half of an existence. I was shut up, retired, and almost killed. None of it made any sense to me until Dave showed up with the kid and his laptop."

"But here you are safe," said Jenna. "I don't want to see you hurt. You are setting yourself up for them to get you. They will come after you again—the FBI, CIA, all the ones who tried to hurt you five years ago. They are still out there, Kara."

"I know that, Jenna. You know the saying, 'A ship in port is safe,'" said Kara. "But that's not what it was made for. I didn't become an FBI agent to be safe. I wanted to serve my country. Now I work security at Wal-Mart. That's not what

I wanted to do with my life. I still want to serve my country, and I believe this is the only way for me to do it—even if it may costs me everything I have. You know what I mean. You're a cop. You do it everyday."

"I know," Jenna said. "I always thought this day would come, the day you became yourself again."

"In a way, Dave helped me do that. I owe it to him to help him now," said Kara. "He's the one on the run now."

"You sure he's on the level?" said Jenna.

"He's the first guy I've wanted to be with in five years."

"What should we do with this guy in jail here?" asked Jenna. "We got his license. He's some kind of private investigator for the NSA."

"Has he said anything?" asked Kara.

"Not so far. Not even asking for a lawyer. I figure his arrest has embarrassed him with his superiors and he is wondering how to get out of this. I have him in a cell with 'Stinky' McGee, the town drunk. I figure after a couple of weeks in there with him, he will be begging us to get him out."

"Well, hold him for at least a week, till I get back from Washington, D.C.," said Kara. "I shouldn't be long."

"I have a feeling once you get back in the game, you're not going to want to come back to live in Ely," said Jenna in sadness.

"Ely will always be my hometown, the place where I was born, where my father lived and my best friend still lives today," said Kara. "Don't worry. I'll be back." The two girls hugged in a moment of tenderness.

"Nothing could ever repay what you did for me," Kara said to Jenna. "You took me in and saved my life."

"Don't get all soft on me," said Jenna. "I'll drive you to the airport."

The two women went out to the squad car that was outside of the small house. It was a typical winter morning in Ely, Minnesota, and the temperature read a balmy one degree. Kara felt sad to be leaving her best friend, but she knew she was doing the right thing in trying to help Dave and help uncover the truth. For the first time in five years, she felt that her life had a purpose once again—serving her country. The fact that she was also doing something to help a tall, lanky ex-cop, sports agent with curly black hair, to whom she was also desperately attracted, didn't hurt either.

CHAPTER 42

❈

Riyadh, Saudi Arabia.

Prince Abdullah sat in the back of the Maybach Mercedes limousine talking on his cell phone. The Al Queda operative to whom he was talking was in a small house on the outskirts of Karachi, Pakistan.

"The new king wants a meeting set up in Karachi and will send his personal envoy to Pakistan," said Prince Abdullah. "He wants a conference set up with all the major leaders present. It's an unprecedented event."

"What is the purpose of this meeting?" said the operative.

"The new king, Aziz bin Saud, wants a truce with Al Queda. No more bombings in Saudi Arabia in exchange for financing, weapons, and extensive support in Afghanistan, Sudan, and Iraq. It's truly a breakthrough."

"Your cousin will be very pleased," said the operative.

"Osama will be able to come home finally," said Prince Abdullah. "Covertly of course, but with the support of his king. His family cannot wait to see him. His mother has missed him all of these years."

"When is this meeting to take place?" asked the operative.

"You must tell me the time. When Osama and Al-Zawahiri feel safe enough to travel to Islamabad from the mountains, you must inform me of the time and place. The king's ambassador will be there."

"Will you be coming out as well?"

"The new king thinks my ties to Osama would make my trip suspect and alert the Americans."

"The new king is wise. At last, our Arab brothers are starting to support our cause against the infidels."

"All foreigners will be out of Saudi Arabia by year's end. The king personally told me that. Then other countries will be pressured into doing the same thing, Arab troops will pour into Iraq and defeat the Americans there. They will never recover from the humiliation," said Prince Abdullah. "It will be worst than Vietnam."

"A unified Arab front, a return to the lands we owned before the Crusades," said the operative. "Death and expulsion to the infidels."

"Allah Akbar," said Prince Abdullah.

"I will call you with the information you need very soon," said the operative. "We will succeed."

"*Inshallah*," replied Prince Abdullah. "If it's God's will." He hung up the diamond-crusted phone in its leather case. The phone itself had been a gift from the Mobil Oil Company and cost $25,000. All calls were untraceable and garbled automatically.

Prince Abdullah was relishing in his new position as the oil minister for Saudi Arabia and OPEC, oil was at seventy-seven dollars-per-barrel. He had just sealed a new ten-year contact with the Chinese that dwarfed the sales to the United States. The value of the contract was $250 billion and his commission was $2 billion, which had already been placed in his numbered account in Geneva.

There is a new order in the world, indeed, thought Prince Abdullah to himself. *But it isn't a return to the Middle Ages as Al Queda wanted. It is the expansion of the Orient with China as a world power. They would be ordering oil and gas for years to come in exponential increases.* It didn't bother Abdullah much that he was purposefully setting up his cousin and the other Al-Queda leaders to be killed. As soon as the Al Queda operative called him with the information, he would pass it on to Saudi intelligence, who would then relay to the Pentagon. The Pentagon would send up a Stealth bomber to launch the missile attack that would kill all of the participants, including the king's envoy. That was already decided. The Saudi envoy had to arrive in Islamabad to make the meeting more plausible. King Aziz bin Saud had already selected the sacrificial lamb for the slaughter. It was to be the Saudi ambassador to Pakistan. Prince Abdullah recognized that this was the best way to uphold the deal that he had made with the new king, Aziz bin Saud. He really had no choice. The new king had been clear and forceful about satisfying the Americans.

Osama bin Laden had served both his and Michael Cherry's purposes admirably making them rich beyond anybody's imagination. Now it was time for his cousin and his allies to disappear into the sands of time, to be honored as martyrs like the thousands of young Arab men that were sent to their fiery deaths as suicide bombers. In the meantime, all connections to him and Michael Cherry would vanish as well.

The game is coming to the end now, laughed Prince Abdullah to himself. *And I am the biggest winner by far.*

CHAPTER 43

❦

Michael Cherry received the call about Dave Stillati's escape sitting in his office in Washington. He became so angry that his face turned a beet red and he lost his usually impassive demeanor. He took off his glasses and started screaming into the phone.

"What you are saying, Agent Durhling, is that the New York City police purposefully let Stillati get away!"

"That's what I am saying, Deputy Commissioner. They had their guns trained on us while he ran through the tollbooth. As soon as we were able to leave, we followed him to Randall's Island but there was no trace of him."

"What was the name of the commanding officer who stopped you?" Cherry asked.

"Sergeant Magnus McShirley, sir."

"I'll have his badge and his pension revoked," said Michael Cherry as he wrote down the name of the sergeant.

"Now, Agent Durhling, you were in a car, armed, and the suspect got away on foot. Do your realize what a lame excuse you are handing me? Do you realize what a pathetic excuse for a Federal agent you make?"

"Yes, I realize it, but…"

"No buts! You just let a dangerous terrorist escape, a man who may well be plotting to blow up New York at this very moment. You are relieved of any future field duty. This will weigh heavily on your career, Agent Durhling. Now pass me to Szabo, now!"

Shit, thought Agent Durhling. *There goes my career.* "Here," he said as he passed the phone to the giant Serb.

"Szabo here."

"You had him. What happened?" Cherry asked.

"The police here stopped us," said Szabo. "He ran away at the toll booths on the Triboro Bridge. I was with Durhling and couldn't do anything."

"You understand that he must be taken care of. This is the second time you let him get away. There cannot be a third."

"There won't be," said Szabo.

"Or you're back on the plane to Zagreb," said Michael Cherry. "Kill this bastard once and for all. Where is the kid?"

"We haven't found him yet," said Szabo.

"Do you know anything? Why do I have to do all the thinking all the time? Trace Stillati's phone calls. He must be checking up on the kid somehow. Find the kid. Once you have him you can smoke out this ex cop. This has to be done and done fast. If not, you'll be back in your former country within a week."

"Yes, sir," said Szabo who didn't relish the idea of appearing in front of a United Nations tribunal for war crimes.

"In the meantime, I'm going to call the chief of police in New York and give him a shitstorm of trouble. They are going to help us find this motherfucker. Now, get to work!"

Szabo hung up the phone.

"He's really pissed," said Agent Ron Durhling.

"Get me all the phone records of the last calls Stillati made," said Szabo. "This time, I go get him alone."

Michael Cherry hung up with Durhling and asked his secretary to dial Frank Curtis's number in New York. Frank Curtis was the chief of police for the City of New York, a respected veteran appointed by Mayor Bloomfield in 2004.

"Mr. Curtis, this is Michael Cherry, Deputy Commissioner of the NSA here. It appears we had a major problem in your city."

"Oh, really, Deputy Commissioner?" said Frank Curtis who had an aversion to Federal representatives.

"Seems some of your dumb cops messed up an arrest we made yesterday of a suspected terrorist in your city."

"Where did this happen?" said Curtis recoiling at the insult of his men.

"At the tollbooth of the Triboro Bridge. My agents had apprehended Dave Stillati, a suspected Islamic terrorist and he was allowed to escape by the actions of a Sergeant Magnus McShirley. I want that officer suspended pending investigation, if not arrested."

Curtis smiled to himself. He knew McShirley for thirty years and Stillati for the past six years. They were both good men who had served their departments with honor.

"I'm afraid I can't do that, commissioner. McShirley has been on the force for thirty years. If I suspended him, the police union would go on strike," said Frank Curtis.

"He allowed a terrorist to escape—one we had apprehended without your help."

"First of all," said the chief of police, "I know Dave Stillati personally and I doubt very strongly that he has become an Islamic terrorist. He was an excellent cop and left the force with full honors." Frank Curtis didn't add that Dave Stillati still coached the police soccer team every year. "Second of all, you should have forewarned me that you were planning any arrests in my city. That way we could have made sure your agents didn't lose their man on their way to the airport."

"Chief, with all due respect, I don't think you understand the terrorist threat we are facing every day," said Michael Cherry. "The president has asked me personally to undertake every effort to protect our citizens and cities. I can speak directly to the Mayor Bloomfield, if you would prefer."

"I don't need any threats or a lecture on terrorism from you," said Chief Curtis, who was getting pissed off. "While I was digging out the bodies of my men in the World Trade Center debris, you were sitting in Washington wondering how you got your finger stuck up your ass at the FBI. You can call whoever you like. I am the police chief here. Next time you want to make an arrest in my city, you call me first."

"I'm just trying to get us all on the same side," said Cherry, backing off.

"It shouldn't be that hard to figure out," said Frank Curtis hanging up.

Cherry let it slide. He knew he could get the president to call the mayor of New York, but didn't want this issue to escalate any further. With any luck, Szabo would find the boy and kill him and Stillati and that would put an end to any connection to his involvement.

"Get me McShirley!" yelled Chief Curtis to his assistant.

"Yes, chief," said Magnus McShirley.

"What the hell happened yesterday on the bridge, Magnus?"

"Well, there was a wee bit of confusion. Apparently, some federal agents came through and while we were asking them some questions a suspect escaped."

"That wouldn't be an ex-officer and current soccer coach, Dave Stillati, escaping, would it, Magnus?"

"I'm not quite sure about the name, but it could be something like that," said Sergeant Magnus McShirley.

"Magnus, I know these charges are pretty far-fetched, but there's a federal warrant out for Dave's arrest. We should be helping the Feds find him, not stopping them," Chief Curtis said.

"Oh, here on the Triboro Bridge I will make every effort to look for him. We got quite a view here. I have men with binoculars searching the skyline as we speak."

Curtis couldn't help himself from laughing. "Don't be a smart-ass, Magnus. If you hear from Dave, tell him to turn himself in. That will make it much easier on him and us, okay?"

"We'll do that, Chief," McShirley said and hung up.

Frank Curtis knew full well that McShirley must have assisted Dave Stillati's escape. However, he was not going to punish the thirty-year veteran for this. Loyalty was the biggest trait Curtis admired because it was so rare. Sergeant McShirley was Stillati's precinct leader in Brooklyn and he would put his life on the line for one of his men. *Fuck Cherry*, anyway, thought Curtis to himself. *Politician asshole.*

If he wants to call the mayor, let him. Won't get him very far, as I got almost all the force to vote for the mayor in the last elections. This isn't Washington, D.C. He'll learn that New Yorkers don't spook so easy.

CHAPTER 44

❦

I was still in my hiding place underneath the concession stand of the dilapidated Randall's Island stadium. Twice, the tan brown Chevrolet swung around slowly looking for me and I held my breath hoping they would leave, which they did. There was still no sign of Marvelous Eddie, and it was getting dark. A rat as big as Volkswagen came up to me wondering if I was a relative of his or just a big chunk of cheese to bite into. Luckily, the tan Chevy had pulled out by then and I was able to move out into the open before he and his rat friends had me for dinner. Just then a Good Humor ice-cream truck pulled in front of the stadium. A big black man jumped out and said, "Ice-cream, get your tootsy-fruitsy ice cream."

"Very funny," I said, coming out from behind the concession stand. "What took you so long, Eddie?"

"I got your message on my machine and had to find a suitable car for cover."

"Do you think you could have found something less conspicuous?" I said getting into the truck.

"No," he said. "This belongs to my cousin, Albert. It's perfect for hiding a felon such as yourself. I could be arrested helping you."

"I'm still a suspect, Eddie. I'm not a felon, yet."

"That's what all prisoners say," said Eddie as he started up the truck. "Good thing you finally came by or the Feds would have had me by now. How's Adam?"

"He's fine. He's at the gym now working out. I tell you, that boy has the makings of a fine bantamweight. We've been working out every day. Nice boy."

"That he is. Does this thing have a phone? An untraceable one?" I asked.

"Sure. Look at the plastic ice cream cone."

I picked up the cone-phone and dialed my secretary Kelly's cell phone number.

"Guess who?" I said.

"*My Favorite Martian?*" said Kelly.

"Close, more like the *Fugitive*," I said. "Thanks for the McShirley call."

"Don't mention it. I wouldn't get paid if they send you to Gitmo."

"Anybody call?" I asked.

"You are all the rage," Kelly said. "I've gotten phone calls from the mayor, the police chief, the commissioner, and numerous lawyers who want to represent you. They all want you to turn yourself in."

"In due time," I said. "Did you get any calls or faxes from Mehmet Hadji or the NYU professor?"

"I got two faxes."

"Read them to me."

"Mehmet says he traced down the taxi driver, Ali Mahalati, thanks to help from the Afghan ambassador at the U.N. Former driver, Ali Mahalati, lives in Staten Island and now drives a cab in Manhattan. Mehmet gave us his phone number to call and an address."

"A lucky break for us," I said writing down the number and address. "Anything else?"

"The professor sent a bunch of economic value charts on various names you gave him, with net worth, pre- and post-9/11."

"And the conclusion is?" I asked.

"Director Mueller's net worth actually went down in value after 9/11. He retired from the FBI and teaches at Florida State University. Same with many of other CIA and FBI chiefs."

"Any exceptions?"

"I'm getting to that. Don't be so pushy," Kelly said.

"We escaped suspects are always in a rush," I said.

"The big wingo winners in post-9/11 were Deputy Director Michael Cherry and Colonel Forrester of Oped Info at the Pentagon."

"How's that?" I asked as Eddie sped onto FDR Drive.

"Holliwell Corporation has won huge bids in Afghanistan and Iraq. Cherry was the chairman before 9/11 and Forrester became the chairman after Cherry went to the FBI. Their stock values skyrocketed after 9/11."

"What are they worth now?" I asked.

"Cherry is worth upwards of $300 million; Forrester about $50 million and climbing," said Kelly.

"How did Forrester become chairman of Holliwell after working Intelligence at the Pentagon?"

"Cherry convinced the Holliwell board that he would be the best man for the job. With the stock value at what it is, he wasn't too wrong."

"Curious connection…" I said on the phone.

"It gets weirder. Cherry supposedly left a million-dollar-a-year job at Holliwell to become deputy director first at the FBI and then at the NSA, where he still is now."

"Why would he do that?" I said.

"He said he wanted to serve his country. It's reputed he will be the next vice presidential candidate for the Republican Party."

"Great," I said. "I can pick my enemies, can't I?"

"Oh, and your friend Kara called, too. She says she flew to Washington to get some information for you."

I couldn't believe Kara would do that for me—leave her safe home in Ely to put it all on the line to help me. She was as good as gold, that one.

"Dave, you still there?"

"Yes," I said. "She's a great gal."

"She sounds too good for you. I am sure she will bake cookies to send you in Cuba every week."

"Funny. Anything else, Kelly?"

"Yup, a couple of players you have as clients called up to say they don't want an Islamic terrorist as an agent."

"What a surprise," I said. "Any of the good ones?"

"No. They don't read the papers, thank God. Angelo called and said he will forgive you if you find the two brothers you saw in Queens a pro team in England to play with."

"Nice guy," I said. "It's hard for me to make calls to teams when I'm on the lam."

"Dave," Kelly said, "your ex-wife has been calling. Susan's worried about you and Adam, and so I am. Maybe it is better if you turn yourself in now."

"To who, Kelly?" I asked. "The NSA? They want me dead or buried in Cuba and finally I'm beginning to see why."

"Well, do it with the New York Police Department. You were one of them, after all. They'll look after you.

"That's a better idea. I'll call you later and let you know. First, I have to do some things." I hung up the phone-cone.

"Where to, big mon?" asked Marvelous Eddie Carpenter, driving his Good Humor truck down FDR Drive.

"Staten Island," I said as I reached for a Popsicle. "We have a date with a cabbie."

CHAPTER 45

Adam was in the worn boxing ring, in the center of Marvelous Eddie's gym, sparring lightly with a tall, black boy called Lebron. They were circling each other in the ring throwing light blows that would bounce off their head gear harmlessly. Adam couldn't believe he was actually boxing in a ring. Eddie had spent the first few days showing him how to throw punches, and then went on to explain how combinations work. He then paired Adam with Lebron, who was the same age, and the two worked the heavy and speed bags together. They were about the same weight, 105 pounds, but Lebron was a much faster and more experienced boxer. Eddie had told them they could spar if they wanted to but told Lebron to take it easy on Adam. Lebron was throwing left jabs and right crosses that just missed Adam by a hair. The other boxers were going about their own business.

"You're not really trying," said Adam through his mouthpiece.

"Yes, I am," said Lebron, skipping out of the way of a wild right by Adam. He threw a left jab that caught Adam in the face and immediately excused himself.

"Sorry, man," Lebron said.

"I walked right into that one," Adam said. They continued to circle each other and throw punches.

"Knock him out," said a deep voice from one of the corners. Adam turned to the right and saw a huge man getting into the ring. Adam recognized him immediately. It was the huge Serb that had killed his mother, and he was walking over to him.

"Who da fuck are you?" Lebron asked though his mouthpiece.

"Nobody you need to know," said Szabo picking up Adam and lifting him over his shoulder like a sack of rice. Adam tried to punch and kick his way out of the Serb's iron hold but it was impossible.

"Hey, leave him alone," Lebron said charging the Serb.

Szabo turned around and with his free right hand punched the young boy in the face knocking him out instantly. He climbed out of the ring as Lebron lay bleeding on the canvas. The other boxers came toward him menacingly.

"I would like to kick all of your black asses," said Szabo to the boxers. "But I don't have the time now." He pulled out his Magnum 357-millimeter revolver and waved them away. "Get the fuck away from me," he said, backing up toward the exit. The boxers didn't know what to do but stepped backward.

"Tell Stillati he can call me at this number if he wants the kid back," said Szabo, leaving his card on the floor.

Adam was still wiggling to get out of the Serb's grip when he was thrown into the backseat of the tan Chevy. Szabo got in the car and drove off. Adam spit out his mouthpiece and tried to take his glove off. "Let me out of here, you asshole," said Adam.

Szabo turned around and slapped him with the back of his hand. The blow would have knocked Adam out but he was still wearing his boxing headgear. Instead, his head hit the back of the seat dazing him.

"Another word out of you and I'll kill you like I killed your mother. Understand?"

Adam's eyes got teary and he felt like crying but kept it in.

"Fuck you," he said. "Why did you kill her?"

"You got spirit," Szabo said. "She found something she shouldn't have. A laptop. People wanted her dead. I work for those people. It wasn't personal."

"It was to me," said Adam. "She was my mom."

"My mom died in a war, many years ago too. You'll get used to it. We're all sons of whores in the end," said Szabo

"My Uncle Dave will come after you," said Adam.

"That's what I hope," said Szabo. "Then I can kill him."

"He's an ex-cop, not a kid like me," said Adam. "It won't be that easy."

"It always is, brat," said Szabo, heading toward the West Side. "Take my word on that. As soon as your uncle shows up, he's dead and so are you, and this story is over."

Adam didn't say anything but just started to pray that Dave Stillati would not come after him and get killed by this psychopath. He started to use his teeth to get rid of the ropes that held the gloves and was trying to formulate a plan to escape from the car. He figured his chances were close to nil but he was going to try his best anyway to survive and warn Dave. *If only I can get my gloves off and call Dave*, Adam thought. He slowly but surely continued chewing on the ropes that kept his hands together.

CHAPTER 46

❦

The Pentagon's electronic information center was a huge database run by Colonel Dwight Summers. It contained the history of every decision made during combat and registered or recorded by the Pentagon for further review. Colonel Summers was a veteran who commanded the center like a personal fiefdom. He was a disabled veteran who had been wounded at the battle of Khe Sanh in Vietnam and still walked with a limp. Kara Murphy had flown down to Washington to meet him.

"How is my favorite and beautiful FBI agent?" asked Colonel Summers.

"Ex-FBI," said Kara leaning over to kiss him on his cheek. "Retired mostly."

"I always thought you got the raw end of the deal," said Colonel Summers. "All your instincts were right about 9/11, after all, and you were the one put out to pasture."

"While others moved on to greater things," said Kara.

"That's the way of the world," said Colonel Summers. "But you didn't fly all the way here from Ely, Minnesota, to talk about life's fickle arrows, did you?"

"If I had some questions to ask you about personnel that was part of the Pentagon," asked Kara, "could you help me?"

"As long as I didn't betray classified information to you, I could," said Summers. "What do you want to know?"

"Colonel Bob Forrester."

"Retired two years ago," said Dwight Summers. "A full colonel and went into the business world. Believe he is the chairman of Holliwell International right now. Doing very well, they tell me."

"What was his last position at the Pentagon?" asked Kara.

"Let's look it up," said Colonel Dwight Summers, punching in the name on his main computer database. "You realize you will not be able to use anything I tell you."

"Of course. It's all classified, isn't it?" said Kara.

"Most of it," replied Summers. "Ah, here it is. Colonel Bob Forrester, awarded Medal of Honor in 2004 for service to his country, upon retirement."

"Any flaws on his record?" Kara asked.

Summers looked into the computer screen.

"There were no black marks or dishonorable mentions," said Summers. "But he committed several judgment mistakes when he was the co-op intelligence director at the Pentagon."

"What kind of mistakes?"

"In January, 2001, a drone picked up the possibility that a group of Al Queda leaders were fleeing Kabul. A helicopter picked up a black SUV heading toward Tora Bora. Permission was asked to destroy the SUV by the captain of an Apache Helicopter. Permission was denied by Colonel Bob Forrester."

"Any reason given?" asked Kara.

"He said that the drone couldn't confirm who the passengers were. It was later determined that Bin Laden, Al-Zawahiri, and other Taliban leaders were traveling on board the SUV," said Colonel Summers.

"What happened to the helicopter pilot?"

"He was shot down by friendly fire a week later. The gunner survived and is living at the Virginia Veteran hospital. His report clearly stated who he saw in the SUV."

"Were there any other episodes?"

"Yes, when Tora Bora was surrounded by the U.S. Ranger division," said Summers.

"What happened then?" asked Kara.

"A decision had to be made whether the Rangers would be sent it to fight Bin Laden cave by cave, or to use the Air Force to launch bunker buster bombs to destroy the caves and then send in our Afghan allies to clean up after the bombing."

"Who made that decision?"

"One again it was Colonel Bob Forrester's decision and he picked the latter course. His opinion was that he was saving American lives by sending in the bombers and the Afghan troops. In a way it was true."

"But Bin Laden escaped because of it."

"Apparently," said Dwight Summers.

"What was his punishment for these decisions?" asked Kara.

"Punishment? There was no punishment. He was deemed to be too cautious and promoted to procurement and Army weapon deployment. Two years later he retired on full pay and with honors."

"And now he runs Holliwell, the largest arms contractor to the Pentagon."

"Welcome to the land of opportunity," said Colonel Summers.

"And who put him there?" asked Kara.

"You should know that it was your former boss and now deputy director of the NSA, Michael Cherry," said Summers. "Why all the questions?"

"This is off the record," said Kara.

"As was all of my information," said Summers.

"Do you think it is possible that someone in the Pentagon and FBI could have been involved in the 9/11 attacks and was protecting Bin Laden, someone on our side? Someone who had strong interest to see the attacks take place?"

"Anything is possible," said Colonel Summers. "But you suspect Colonel Forrester? That seems very far-fetched. What would his motive be?"

"Huge financial success, if he had an ally who would benefit greatly from pushing America into war," said Kara.

"And that would be?"

"My former boss, Michael Cherry," said Kara. "Who did everything he could at the FBI to stop us from arresting the terrorists before the attacks. Together, with Forrester, they could have planned this whole thing with the terrorists. Holliwell made them both immensely rich after the attacks. They might have wanted this war to take place."

"Kara, anything is possible," said Summers. "But even if it was, and it's really a pretty wild notion, you could never prove it. You would be seen as a jealous ex-FBI agent ranting and raving once again, and this time yelling at the Pentagon. I would advise against it for your own sake and health."

"And your information? The one you just gave me?"

"You could never use it in court. As I told you, it is classified," said Summers.

"But between us, do you think it could have happened?" asked Kara looking straight into his eyes.

"Between us, not officially?" asked Dwight Summers.

"Yes, just a conversation between friends," said Kara.

"I think it's probable that it did, but I will forever deny saying it," said Summers. "There were too many coincidences, too many things that worked in favor of the terrorists, without thinking of a mole or agent that was helping them from the inside. We conducted several investigations but nothing serious ever came out of it. If you find something you will tell me, yes?"

"Unofficially?" asked Kara.

"No, officially," said Summers. "If you get even a shred of real evidence, bring it to me, and I will frag Forrester's ass personally. A lot of my close friends were killed in the Pentagon attacks, and, now that I think about it, I don't recall Colonel Forrester being in the building on that day."

"Just another coincidence?" asked Kara.

"I don't believe in coincidences," said Colonel Dwight Summers.

"Could you get me to meet Forrester?" Kara asked.

"Under what excuse?" said Summers.

"Tell him I'm a reporter for the *Atlantic Review* here doing a story on the Pentagon."

"It shouldn't be hard. I'll set it up. It's almost as if you were back on the job with the FBI again. Will you use a real name or a fake?"

"Real name will be fine," said Kara Murphy. "But let's try and do it as soon as possible. I have a friend who is in a lot of trouble and need all the information I can get."

CHAPTER 47

❁

Marvelous Eddie drove us downtown in his Good Humor ice cream truck to Lower Manhattan to catch the Staten Island Ferry. Mehmet Ḥadji had given me the taxi driver's address at 444 Manor Road in Staten Island. According to Mehmet, Ali Mahalati had been living there and driving a cab in New York City for the past two years. We parked the truck waiting for the ferry to arrive. Eddie started to sell some ice-cream to a few customers while we were waiting.

"What are you doing?" I asked.

"Selling ice cream, what does it look like? Might was well make some money while we are here," he said, very practically handing out two snow cones. I couldn't argue his logic and helped him hand out a few ice creams as well. Needless to say, we were the only truck selling ice cream in January in New York City. Finally, the ferry arrived and we drove the truck on board.

The Staten Island Ferry is the cheapest way to see the Statue of Liberty and I always marvel at that magnificent gift that France gave us to celebrate our help to them. The ferry was also a very safe and sane way to travel to and from Manhattan, until the captain of one of the ferry's fell asleep at the wheel and tore into the wood pilings, killing a number of people. We spent the half-hour trip looking back on the island of Manhattan and the seagulls flying past the Statue of Liberty. "What a sight," I said to Eddie.

"People forget what it stands for," said Eddie.

"The inscription says give us your poor, your sick, and your hungry," I said. "It didn't talk about building walls on our borders to keep them out."

"Different times, big mon," said Eddie.

"Same times. Different leaders," I said.

We finally made it over and drove the truck to 444 Manor Road in about ten minutes. A Yellow Cab was parked in front of a flower shop at that address. We rang the bell and a lady from the store opened the door.

"Yes," she said. "Can I help you gentlemen?"

"I am looking for Ali Mahalati. They gave us this address for him."

"He lives in the apartment upstairs," said the lady. "Ring the doorbell."

I rang the doorbell and waited for an answer. After about five minutes, a sleepy voice answered the buzzer.

"Yes, what you want?" the voice said.

"Ali Mahalati?" I said.

"Yes, that's me."

"I was given your name by a member of the Afghan UN council," I said. "He told me you may have some information that might interest me."

"Just a second," the voice said. The buzzer rang letting us into the door. The stairs were dark and worn, and Eddie and I walked up the two flights of stairs that led to the small apartment.

Ali Mahalati was waiting for us in a white Afghan robe. He had a short black beard and was wearing an Arab head wrap.

"I am sorry. I was asleep," said Ali. "I drive the night shift."

"No problem," I said. "We should have called first."

His home was a sparsely-furnished, one-bedroom apartment with an Oriental prayer rug in the middle. On one side, a Koran lay open with candlesticks next to it. On the walls, there were some pictures of a pretty woman in a traditional sari dress and two children, a boy and a girl.

"Would you like some tea?" Ali asked us.

"Sure," I said. "Eddie?"

"Tea would be fine," he said.

"I rarely get visitors here," said Ali. "Excuse me for the mess. Who sent you here?"

"Mehmet Hadji, of the Moroccan delegation. He spoke to the Afghan delegation and they tracked you here and gave us the address."

Ali came out with the hot tea for the both of us.

"And to what do I owe the pleasure of your company?" asked Ali.

"We are investigating some leads in the 9/11 attack. Your name came up in an FBI investigation that an Inspector Todd Jurgensen was conducting. Something regarding two Westerners you reportedly drove to see Osama bin Laden in 1998."

Ali looked at us with tremendous sadness in his eyes.

"Are you here to kill me?" asked Ali Mahalati looking at me.

"No," I said. "Of course not."

"Somehow, I doubt that," he said. "I have been praying for two years that this moment would come, and that I would join my family in heaven." He pointed to the pictures on the wall. "Now you are here. Get it over with." He lowered his head as if offering it for sacrifice. Eddie and I looked at each other in wonderment.

"I assure you, I am not here to kill anybody," I said. "I am just looking for some answers. My sister-in-law was murdered. I believe you might know who did it."

Ali looked up at us with fire in his eyes.

"Answers? I have been looking for answers for five years. What answers are you looking for then? I told everything to that FBI agent Jurgensen in Afghanistan."

"Did you drive two Westerners to meet Bin Laden in Khost, Afghanistan, in 1998, as was reported, and who were you working for then?" I asked.

"I was working for myself and for my family as always on that accursed day that ruined my life forever," Ali said. "I was hired by one of the Taliban to pick up two Western men at the Kabul airport and drive them to Khost. I was to wait for them there and bring them back to the airport, which I did."

"Why did you report this to Massoud's men?" I asked him.

"Because I had lived in the U.S. and hated the Taliban. I figured it would be information that Massoud could use. Had I known what would happen, I would have kept my mouth shut forever."

"What happened?"

"After the attacks that killed Massoud in Afghanistan and the plane attacks here in the U.S., Agent Jurgensen came to Afghanistan to ask me what I had seen. He asked me to describe the two men I had driven."

"And did you?"

"Yes, I told them one of the men was very tall, blonde, a killer, with an Eastern European accent. The second man was the leader. He was bald and fat, with dark-rimmed glasses."

"Do you have a computer?" I asked.

"Yes," said Ali taking me to his bedroom. An old Mac computer was on a nightstand. I turned it on, googled the name Michael Cherry, and found a recent picture of him with the president.

"Do you recognize the person in this picture?"

Ali looked at the photo and said, "Yes, that was him—the fat one, the one next to President Branch. He was the one I drove to Khost with the other one."

"Are you sure?" I asked.

"As sure as my family is dead," he said with a grave tone.

"When did they die?" I asked him, shocked by his revelation.

"The same day agent Jurgensen was killed. He was supposed to show me some photos to identify and we had an appointment in my home. As soon as he arrived, we started talking. My family was with me in my home. My wife was cooking and my children were studying. Everything seemed to be fine and then the world just exploded. When I awoke I was in a hospital in Kabul, my body was severely burned and I had lost my memory. A neighbor had pulled me from the rubble thinking I was dead."

"How did it happen?" I asked.

"An American jet dropped a bomb on the wrong house, my house. As they thought everybody was dead the army didn't even make any apologies. Someone from the FBI came and recovered the remains of Jurgensen's body. No one thought to question who were the Afghans who had died. That was my family. It should have been me. I killed them by bringing that FBI man into our house. They said it was an accident. I know different."

Ali started to let tears come down his face. "My daughter was eight and my son was eleven. My wife was twenty-six. She was a doctor. We were so happy the Americans had come to free us. I could never have imagined this could have happened to us."

"When did you come to live here?" I asked as Eddie brought him a tissue.

"I had nothing more to live for," said Ali. "I decided to move to the U.S. again to make money for my cousins who were still alive and lived in Afghanistan. As you can see, I live alone and always will now. I pray that I might be allowed to join them soon. I thought you were finally going to deliver me from this life."

"No," I said. "That is not my intent. I may, however, be able to bring you vengeance on the people who did this to your family."

"The man in the photograph?" asked Ali. "Did he do this to me?"

"I think so," I said. "The other man killed my sister-in-law."

"They must be made to pay for their evil," said Ali.

"Will you help me exact vengeance?" I said to Ali.

"With every bone in my body," said Ali. "By Allah, I swear I will make it my life's work to track these men down and kill them."

"I will not ask you that," I said. "Just to help me if you can when I will need it."

We shook hands on it and hugged. Ali hugged Eddie whose eyes were wet as well. "My friends, you have brought me a reason to live, the possibility of avenging the death of my family. I am grateful to you for that," said Ali as he saw us out.

"Ali, be patient," I said heading out. "Remember the old Mafia saying: vengeance is a plate best served cold."

"As long as it is served at last," said Ali. "I have been waiting for five long years."

CHAPTER 48

Marvelous Eddie Carpenter and I walked down the creaky stairs of Ali's building together and walked toward the Good Humor truck parked on the corner.

"Seems like a decent guy," said Eddie.

"He's a guy who's lost everything," I said. "And yet he is still willing to help us. If I was him, I'd have bought an Uzi long ago and wiped everybody out."

"Maybe the papers are right about you being a terrorist lunatic," said Eddie. "You got a temper, boy. Instead he's put his faith into his God. Maybe you should, too."

"Thanks for the lecture, but church is on Sunday," I said.

Just then Eddie's cell phone rang.

"Talk to me," said Eddie. "Damn," he said. Then he nodded a few times and said, "Okay, give me the number." He took a pen and wrote down a number on a yellow pad. He turned off his phone and turned to me.

"What's the matter?" I asked.

"We got trouble, Dave."

"What happened?" I said, feeling my blood run cold.

"Some huge white guy came into the gym and grabbed Adam," said Eddie.

"Shit," I said. "In a boxing gym packed with fighters? Couldn't anybody stop him?"

"Seems he was huge, and was packing some heat as well. He knocked the boy who was sparring with Adam unconscious with one punch."

"Big hero, beating up on a kid. Do they know who it was?" I said, knowing full well that it was probably the huge Serb.

"His name is Szabo. He threw his card on the floor of the gym," said Eddie. "He wants you to call him, now. Want the number?"

I looked at the number for what seemed like an eternity wondering what to do next. This was the guy who had killed Sandra. He had tried to get me before, but now he had Adam and he wanted me. I would certainly sacrifice myself to get Adam free. That wasn't the problem. The problem would be surviving my encounter with him long enough to beat him and clear my name. Not an easy thing to do.

Finally, I took Eddie's phone and dialed the number he had written down. It rang twice and an Eastern European accent answered the phone.

"Szabo here," the voice said.

"Dave Stillati, here," I said. "You were looking for me?"

"It's about time you called," Szabo said. "Your little boy has been waiting for you to call us. For a while, I thought you were too scared to call. You were shitting in your pants, I bet."

"It must feel real good kidnapping young boys," I said. "You are graduating up from raping and killing single mothers."

"Don't lecture me, asshole. This was my way of getting you to call me," said Szabo. "It worked, no?"

"What do you want?" I said.

"You," said Szabo. "Alone. Meeting with me."

"Where?" I asked.

"At the base of the aircraft carrier Enterprise, at 6:00 PM tonight."

"If I come, will you release Adam?" I asked him.

"I don't need him," said Szabo. "You come with the laptop and I will let the boy go. You don't come and I kill the boy and then I kill you."

"I guess I'll see you at 6:00 PM then," I said. "On the street."

"You have three hours," said Szabo, "or the boy dies."

"Fuck you. I can count," I said. "I'll be there."

I hung up. I had the feeling I had just signed my death warrant. I would have to go to this meeting alone, facing a federal officer who was also a stone cold killer. He was armed and had killed many times before. In fact, according to the Croatian Father Dolnic, he was a psychotic killing machine who had worked for the infamous militia leader, Arkan.

"Terrific," I said out loud.

"We going together, Dave," Eddie asked more like a statement.

"No," I said. "I told him I would do this alone. Just drive me to my bank so I can get the laptop out of the safe deposit box." Eddie headed in that direction.

"This guy is going to kill you," Eddie said. "You need me there with you."

"You're retired, Eddie, and I appreciate your offer. I need you to be there just to take Adam out of there. Then you leave, understand? Or he will kill you, too. It has to be him against me. I owe Susan and Sandra that for Adam, to make him safe."

"What about the truth?" asked Eddie. "If you get killed, it will never come out."

"I'm an old dog," I said. "Old dogs are hard to kill. Center backs and old dogs, moles, cockroaches, and rats are hard to kill."

"Is there anything you want me to do now?" Eddie asked as he parked the van in front of the bank on 42nd Street.

"While I am at the bank getting the laptop, call Father Dolnic at the Croatian church on 39th Street. Tell him exactly what's happening. He'll know what to do," I said.

"You want him to be there to administer the last rites?" asked Eddie worrying about me.

"Yes, that's it," I said. "But not my last rites, Szabo Tanovich's."

"At least you're confident," said Marvelous Eddie, looking at me strangely. "That's good in a fighter—a little insane, but good."

CHAPTER 49

The Enterprise Museum is one of the modern wonders of New York City, housing the famous aircraft carrier, a submarine, different types of interesting military aircraft, and the Concorde on its deck. The aircraft carrier, permanently moored on the West Side of New York, is visited annually by thousands of tourists and normally is one of my favorite places to be in New York. Not this time. I knew my life was going to be put at risk in a very short time. That also made me a little edgy. Not scared or anything like that, just edgy. I had to get myself in a frame of mind that didn't care whether I lived or died. That way, my chances of surviving were increased, but not by much.

My meeting with Szabo Tanovich was to take place in the abandoned underpass of the West Side Highway within a few minutes. I had stopped to pick up the laptop at my bank and Eddie and I were now waiting for Tanovich to show up. I double-checked my nine-millimeter Beretta to see that it was loaded with all fifteen bullets. I took off the safety. Then I checked my ankle knife. I was as ready as I could ever be.

"Do you have a Kevlar vest?" asked Eddie.

"Didn't have the time to get it," I said.

"You could use my help," said Eddie.

"I know, but I need you to get Adam out of here."

Just then the brown tan Chevy drove up and parked directly opposite to us in the underpath. The door opened and the Serb got out of the car holding Adam with his right hand. Adam was still dressed in his boxing gear. I got out of the truck with the laptop in my hand.

"Let the kid go," I said.

"Put the laptop on the ground," Szabo said.

I put the laptop on the ground.

"Now take out your gun," he said, "and put it on the ground as well."

"*Jebem ti sense*," I said in the little Serbian I had learned playing for their team in New York. "You first," I said.

He took out his gun and placed it against Adam's temple.

"Say good-bye to the boy, *supak* (asshole)."

"Okay, Okay," I said, taking out my gun. "I'm putting it down."

"Dave, don't," said Eddie.

"Whose the *shwarza*?" said Szabo, looking at Eddie.

"He's here to get the boy and take him home."

"Put your gun down on the ground," Szabo said. "This is just going to be between me and you. No guns."

Great, I thought to myself. *This animal outweighs me by fifty pounds and is three feet taller than me. Fair fight.* I put my gun on the pavement and kicked it to him. He laughed and pushed Adam toward us, kicking him in the ass. Adam ran to me and hugged me.

"Dave," Adam said, "I'm so sorry. Don't get killed because of me."

"Don't worry, kid. Now go home with Eddie."

Adam got into the van, and Eddie said, "Dave, you sure about this?"

"I'm sure, Eddie. Now go!"

"Get the fuck out of here before I change my mind and kill you, too," Szabo said to Eddie.

"You and me," said Eddie to him. "We have an open account no matter what happens here."

"Go home, old man," said Szabo.

"Go, Eddie," I said. "Get Adam out of here."

Eddie and Adam got into the Good Humor truck and drove away. In a way, after they left, I felt like the loneliest guy in the world. Szabo took out his gun.

"So now you're going to shoot me," I said.

"No need to use guns," he replied. "I'm going to kill you very slowly, with my bare hands. I will break every bone in your body before I kill you."

"*Jebem ti sense* (fuck you)," I said. "Did Michael Cherry tell you to do this?"

He was surprised that I would know about his relationship and showed it.

"He's my boss at NSA," Szabo said.

"He's more than that," I replied. "Didn't you guys go to Afghanistan together to meet the terrorists before 9/11?"

"How did you know that?" Szabo asked, coming toward me.

"A taxi driver told me," I said crouching into a boxer's stance. "He drove you there."

"He's dead," said Szabo.

"Nah, you got his family, but not him," I said.

"All the more reason to kill you now and him later," said Szabo, swinging a kick toward my head that just missed by inches.

"So, you set up the attacks and then what? Kill off anybody who might stop them from happening?" I asked throwing out a left jab.

"You want to talk? *Perderchino* (faggot), why not? Talk now, 'cause you won't have a chance when you are dead," said Szabo catching me in the head with a right hook. I bobbed backward parrying his blows with my arms.

"You helped the attacks happen," I said. "And then you had Grey and Jurgensen, the two FBI agents who were looking into it, killed," I said.

"No," Szabo said. "I killed Grey myself with my hands and took his eye out just like I will yours, *Ubiq te klozeca*. I'll kill you like a rabbit."

The giant Serb had a five-inch reach advantage over me and hit me flush on the chin with a right cross. It felt like a train had smashed into my face. I shook off the daze and circled around him trying to duck his blows.

"You killed Susan Baines and raped her because she found the laptop," I said. "Did Cherry order you to do that, too?" I asked, getting in a good left hook to the body. A normal man would have felt it and backed away. Not this guy. I felt like I was punching a steel door.

"That was the fun part," Szabo said. "I raped your FBI friend Kara Murphy, too, *kurva* (whore). That shut her up for a while. I wanted to kill her, but Cherry said no. She's too famous, *Pizda*."

At that statement, my blood boiled, and I attacked him, catching him high on the right eyebrow and making him bleed. I followed up by kicking him in the left knee, which caused him to buckle for a second. He actually backed away for a minute, and I thought I might actually get the upper hand. My mistake.

"So, it bothers you, eh? I raped hundreds of women in Croatia, but she seemed to really enjoy it." He then recovered and lashed out at me with his right foot and caught me with a kick in the gut that took the air out of my body. The strength, which my anger and adrenalin had put in my punches, went out of me like air from a balloon. He followed up with a left to my nose and an uppercut to my chin. I fell to the ground and felt wet, sticky stuff come out of my nose. It was my red blood that was spilling to the ground.

"You don't understand," said Szabo. "Michael Cherry and I changed history." He kicked me twice in the ribs, and caught me flush in the face with a punch. I rolled back with it, falling into the street, smelling the oil and urine of the pavement seep into my skin.

"You're just his errand boy," I said, spitting out my front tooth. "His psycho bitch. *Yedi Govna* (eat shit)."

He walked over to me and stomped on my hand. I heard something snap and felt a pain in wrist that told me he had broken my wristbone.

"And what are you?" he asked. "A man who is about to die. *Yebem te supak* (I fuck you in the ass)."

He leaned over and punched me repeatedly in the head. Then he took my head and banged it hard against the pavement. I felt myself black out but tried to keep fighting. The blood was flowing now from my face and the back of my head. With the little strength I had left I threw out some punches that caught him in the kidneys but had little power to hurt him. He finally got up off of me and pulled out a serrated knife he was carrying with him.

"Get up," he said to me. "I don't want to get dirty when I cut your eye out." He pointed the knife at me like a matador about to kill his bull. I got up on my feet holding my wrist. Every inch of my body was screaming in pain now, and I could see there was little chance of me winning this fight. He was bigger, stronger and more ruthless than I could ever be. His body seemed made of steel and I couldn't hurt him with a two-by-four. I wished I still had my Beretta on me. As I was getting weaker with every minute, I had few choices left.

"Come on," he said. "Let's finish this."

"Okay," I said, getting to my feet. "Get ready, here I come. *Mama ti ye Kurva*," I said, calling his mother a whore. He looked at me strangely as I prepared to attack him. I started running right toward him, and he got ready to knife me, coming in and quite possibly killing me on the spot. Except that was not my intention. Instead of running right at him, I ran toward him and then ducked at the last second, letting his blade swing over my head. Then I ran by him to the exit of the tunnel. By the time he realized what I had done, I had a twenty-foot advantage and was running out of the tunnel like my life depended on it, which it did. He turned around and started running after me as I sprinted toward 11th Avenue.

"You chicken piece of shit," he said coming after me. "You have no balls. Come back and die like a man."

I admit I wasn't proud of what I was doing, but survival was foremost in my mind. I kept running as fast as I could up the wet pavement. Szabo, using his long strides, was gaining on me as I rounded the corner and headed toward the Croatian Church of Mary the Immaculate on 41st and 11th Avenue. As I ran up the marble stairs, he caught my ankle and I fell in front of the church. I pulled out my ankle knife but he kicked it away and it clattered down the steps.

"Die bastard," he said plunging his knife into my thigh.

I screamed and pulled back, crawling into the dark church as he followed me in.

"I'm going to cut out your eye while you're still alive so you can see it in my hand before you die," he said walking into the church and standing above me. He leaned down and pulled out the knife from my thigh letting my blood gush out onto the marble church floor. The heavy door of the church closed behind him with a loud bang. It was very dark and through the light from one of the stained glass windows I could see him making a three finger sign with his thumb and fingers over me.

"The Serbian sign of the Trinity," I muttered, sure that I was facing my death.

"The last thing you will ever see," said the giant Serb coming toward me with his knife. "*Ubit cute* (I will kill you)."

"*Zao mi je* (I don't think so)," said a voice in Croatian in the darkness of the church. "*Govno Yedno* (you piece of shit)."

"Who's there?" said the Serb turning around to the shadows in the church. "*Yebem ti svestro* (I fuck your saint)," he said.

A group of men came out of the shadows. There must have been ten to fifteen of them. They were armed. "We are the Croatian brothers and fathers of the women you killed and raped. Now you will pay for your sins, *svinge* (wild pig)."

"*Yebem ti sestru*. I fuck your sisters, and I spit on you and your Croatian whore mothers," said Szabo spitting on the floor of the church. "I will take you all on like I did them. *Nemog da me drkas* (don't fuck with me)."

The group of men encircled the giant Serb. Each man had an axe, or a knife or a blade in his hand. There were at least twelve of them. I painfully turned to my side to watch what was happening. Szabo kicked out at one man catching him in the side, but one of the other Croatian men stabbed him in the back with a knife screaming "*Dabogda crko!* (May God make you dead!)" The giant Serb yelled out and turned around punching him, but another man sliced his thigh with a sickle. Szabo dropped to one knee. Soon the other men were slashing at him stabbing him with their blades as blood spurted out on the church floor. Szabo roared helplessly like a gored bull as the men continued stabbing him and he rolled to the ground trying to fend off the blows. Finally, the leader of the pack told the other men to stand back. He lifted up his ax and swung it in the air several times like he had done this many times before. With all of his might he sent his axe crashing into the giant Serb's neck severing it cleanly from his head.

"*Djavli te ponesli* (go to hell)," said the man.

The head rolled away and came to rest a few inches from me. I looked into Szabo's face as his eyes rolled back into his head. It was a horrifying sight that would stay with me for the rest of my life.

"That's how you kill a vicious *supak* (asshole)," said the Croatian man to me wiping the blood from his axes as he walked toward the exit with the other men.

Father Tony Dolnic came from behind the sacristy running to my side and said, "Dave? Dave, are you okay?"

"Father, I've feel like I've been through a meat crusher," I said, coughing up blood. "I thought you might not have been here, that the men had refused to come or something. I thought it was all over."

Father Dolnic replied, "After Eddie called, I called a meeting of all the Croatian men. They were just waiting for this opportunity to avenge what this animal had done to their loved ones. I'm sorry it had to happen in my church."

"It had to happen. It was him or me," I said.

"I know," Father Dolnic said. "Justice was done here."

"Yes, Father," I said. "Justice was done."

"Now let's get you to Mount Sinai Hospital," said Father Dolnic. Then his voice got farther and farther away and everything became black and I went into a dark world from which I never thought I'd return.

CHAPTER 50

❈

Kara Murphy walked into the opulent marble-walled reception area of Holliwell International in the trendy Georgetown area. Kara had read that Holliwell had recently bought the aging, ten-story building and was spending more than $200 million refurbishing it. Bob Forrester, CEO of Holliwell, had told the press that he was doing this to show his commitment and gratitude to the nation's capital. *For a company that was making more than $5 billion in sales to the Pentagon, Holliwell could afford it,* thought Kara.

The receptionist asked her name. "Kara Murray, from the *Atlantic Review*," she said. "I have a 10 o'clock appointment with Mr. Forrester." Dwight Summers, her friend at the Pentagon, had arranged the interview for her, telling Forrester she was writing an article on Pentagon intelligence. Kara used an alias and some fake ID just in case anybody recognized her from her *Time* magazine article but she knew the chances of that were very small. It had been almost five years and memory spans were very short in the capital. The receptionist took down her name and sent her on through to security. Kara passed through a metal detector and the security guard checked her purse. He sent her on her way and she took the elevator to the tenth floor. There the whole process was repeated again.

"Mr. Forrester will be with you shortly," said the receptionist on the tenth floor. A cute blonde secretary came up to her and said, "Are you Ms. Murray?"

"Yes," said Kara.

"Mr. Forrester has been expecting you. I'm his secretary, Sonya Bennaker. Come this way." Kara walked through the crowded hallway where workers were installing all-leather wallpaper.

"It's been nothing but work and noise here since we moved in," said Sonya to Kara.

"I am sure it's not easy to work through this type of construction," said Kara, putting Sonya at ease.

"Well, we all must sacrifice somewhere," said Sonya. "As Mr. Forrester says, 'There's a war going on out there.'"

And Holliwell is making the most of it, thought Kara.

Sonya showed her into a huge corner office that was covered in cherry wood paneling, leather couches and wall-to-wall carpeting. A huge electronic map covered one wall and showed all the subsidiaries of Holliwell International throughout the world. On another wall were pictures of Robert Forrester in uniform, with President Branch, and with various other political leaders. Kara recognized the president of Italy, Silvio Berlusconi, Tony Blair, and many others.

"Impressive, isn't it?" asked Bob Forrester walking into the room.

"Certainly, sir," said Kara turning around to him. Forrester sat down in his black leather chair and invited Kara to sit as well. He was a tall, handsome man with grayish black hair and was wearing an expensive Italian grey Brioni suit with a yellow tie. *He looks like he belongs in an insurance ad*, thought Kara.

"They are the famous ones. I only live off reflected light," said Forrester with false modesty.

"As the head of a billion-dollar multinational, I would say you are famous, too," said Kara.

"I serve their countries, so the leaders are gracious to appear in pictures with me. It's all PR," said Forrester. "Dwight Summers speaks very highly of you, says you write articles favorable towards the Pentagon."

"He is too kind," said Kara. "And I thank him. I am writing an article about intelligence at the Pentagon and you were the director of Intelligence Ops."

"Five years, from 1998 to 2003," said Bob Forrester. "Then I moved here to the private sector."

"What were your specific duties there?" asked Kara pulling out a notepad.

"We gathered satellite information electronically and relayed it to units throughout the globe for immediate military action," said Bob Forrester. "It's a vital service to the Pentagon."

"Images from drones, satellite targets, this kind of stuff," said Kara.

"Exactly, sometime the turnover time was in micro-seconds. We had to be totally organized so that the targets could be destroyed seconds after the information was relayed to our centers."

"Would you say you accomplished your task?" asked Kara, writing down the information.

"We couldn't have conquered Afghanistan and Iraq in such a short time had we not been so organized and efficient. We were the eyes and ears of the Army, Navy, Air Force, and Marines."

"How many people worked for you?" asked Kara.

"In total, about thirty-five operatives in the Pentagon," said Bob Forrester.

"Were there any mishaps, mistakes?" asked Kara.

"There are always some mistakes. That's human nature," replied Mr. Forrester. "But I like to think they were small compared to the successes we had."

"In particular, wasn't there a purported leak on launching of the Tomahawk missiles in 1998 towards Osama bin Laden's camp in Khost in which he received a warning that saved his life? As if there had been a leak in the Pentagon?"

"There were no leaks that I am aware of, Ms. Murray," said Forrester getting red in the face.

"Also, wasn't there a decision made in 2001? A decision made by your team that stopped an Apache helicopter from destroying an SUV fleeing Kabul—an SUV that purportedly was carrying top Al Queda officials?"

"This is classified information, Ms. Murray, isn't it? I cannot discuss this in any way and I don't see what this has to do with an article."

"It's just that there seems to have been a pattern of misinformation coming from your department, and with you in command there, the responsibility would fall on your shoulders."

"There was no pattern of misinformation. Who have you been talking to?" asked Forrester getting agitated.

"At Tora Bora, a decision was made to destroy the caves from the air while the Rangers were waiting to kill Osama bin Laden. You made that decision, Mr. Forrester, didn't you?"

Forrester stood up suddenly. "This interview is over. I am going to tell Dwight Summers what kind of a reporter you are."

"Oh, he knows," said Kara. "You see, I'm not a reporter at all. I am an ex-FBI agent, and my real name is Kara Murphy. I was the whistleblower on the cover of *Time* magazine. Remember me? I know what you did. You conspired with Michael Cherry at the NSA to protect the terrorists and allow the worst attack against your country. You are a traitor, sir."

"Get out," screamed Bob Forrester. "Get out! Security!" he yelled into his desk microphone.

Two members of the security team came into the room brandishing their weapons.

"You were not at the Pentagon on 9/11, were you? Why not? Why not? Because you knew what was going to happen. Michael Cherry told you. You have blood on your hands, sir. Lots of blood. You sold your soul for thirty pieces of silver," said Kara as the men escorted her out. Sonya had run into the room and was looking at Kara in amazement.

"Your boss is a traitor," said Kara on her way out. "Start looking for a new job and a lawyer."

The security guards dragged Kara into the elevator and escorted her through the lobby to the exit. All the employees and the receptionist looked at the scene in disbelief. Kara raised her right fist and yelled, "No justice, no peace!" just to confuse the issue. One of the security guards threw her out of the building. "Don't come back, you fucking liberal," said one of the security guards as he walked away.

Back in his office, Bob Forrester sat down, sweating profusely. He couldn't fathom what had just happened. In one minute, his entire life had come crashing down in front of him. What he dreaded most—discovery, exposure as a traitor—had just happened. This girl, Kara Murphy, had set him up, and she could be working alone. But that meant that Dwight Summers in the Pentagon knew something, too. And there must be others as well.

I'm not going to be the only fall guy in this, thought Forrester. *Michael Cherry has got to help me out of this.*

"Get me Michael Cherry on the phone, now," he ordered Sonya. Sonya went to make the call immediately. She had never seen her boss so agitated. It made her nervous.

"His office says he's playing golf," said Sonya.

"Keep trying. Tell them to get him on the fucking phone immediately!" yelled Forrester.

Sonya's eyes welled up with tears. She couldn't handle pressure very well, That's why she had gotten a job at Holliwell working as a personal assistant. She thought her boss was a calm, controlled, successful guy. Now, she was seeing otherwise.

CHAPTER 51

Michael Cherry was preparing to hit a nine iron from the edge of the lush fairway onto the green. The secretary of defense, Harold Rushman, had already gotten on in two strokes and was waiting for Michael to join him on the green of the seventh hole at the prestigious McLean Golf Club. Michael set up and took a practice swing first. He was a good enough golfer to beat Rushman on any given day, but that was not the purpose of the game. He knew he must lose by one or two strokes at the worst to make the game close and give Rushman the satisfaction of winning. The Pentagon had just received an additional $225 billion for the wars in Iraq and Afghanistan from Congress, and Holliwell International was well poised to get at least twenty-five percent of that in the next three years. *Enough to raise my stock value to $500 million*, thought Cherry to himself. He concentrated his large bulk behind the ball and executed a perfect shot. Too perfect. The ball flew up in the air and dropped onto the green, rolling downhill and stopping only ten inches short from the hole.

"Great shot, Mike," yelled Rushman from the green.

Too good, thought Cherry to himself. *No way I can miss that putt and make it look natural.*

As he walked toward the green, the cell phone in his pocket vibrated. He looked at the number and realized it was Bob Forrester calling. Michael's secretary had left him a voice message that Forrester was urgently looking for him.

"Bob," Cherry said. "What's up? I'm on the green with the secretary of defense. This better be important."

"This woman came to my office pretending to be a reporter," said Forester sounding agitated. "Turns out she's Kara Murphy from the FBI. She said she knows everything about me: what I did at the Pentagon, what you did with the attacks. She knows everything and she says she has proof."

"Calm down, Bob," said Cherry. "Kara Murphy, that's the ex-FBI whistleblower. I thought we had shut her up. She was out of the game, like, four years ago."

"Well, she's back and she is coming after me. She said she will go to the press, to the FBI to get me. She's after you, too. You got to do something about her."

"She's got nothing," said Michael. "I'll get my man on her. Besides, she was already branded a traitor for finking on the FBI. Now no one will believe her anyway. We can spin the story in a thousand ways."

"I'm worried," said Forrester. "I'm the one on the line here. You don't understand. She says she has proof. There are other people who know now, too."

"Who?" asked Cherry.

"Dwight Summers at the Pentagon. He set the interview up."

Michael Cherry made a mental note of the name.

"I tell you, Bob, don't panic. They don't have anything," Michael Cherry said. "It's just a hysterical bitch. I will take care of her."

"Do that," said Bob. "But do it fast."

"Don't give me any fucking orders," said Cherry. "I put you where you are. I made you. Now calm down and let me sort it out." He hung up the phone and continued walking to the green.

What the fuck is going on? he thought to himself. *Some lady finds Atta's laptop, her fifteen year old kid in Portland gets away, his uncle the sports agent Stillati finds him and escapes, a hit man blows the job in Ely, and now this bitch from Minnesota makes a big scene spooking Forrester. Crazy shit. And where the fuck is the Serb?*

Michael pulled out his cell phone and called Szabo Tanovich's phone number but a recording just said, "The number you requested is out of service." *It's not like the Serb to disappear*, thought Michael. *He should have called me about the Stillati matter hours ago. The sports agent should have been dead and buried, the boy eliminated, and the laptop recovered and destroyed.* After that he could send Szabo out to kill Kara Murphy and this Dwight Summers at the Pentagon as well. He needed to clean up the mess once and for all.

"Trouble at the office?" asked Rushman.

"Nothing I can't handle," said Michael Cherry. "Just a potential terrorist case I've been working on. An ex-cop from New York turned Al Queda traitor."

"That's what I like about you, Michael," said Rushman. "You are like me. We don't like to delegate. Hands on approach. On the job 24/7 keeping our nation safe. I like that in you, and the president does, too."

At the mention of President Branch, Michael's mood brightened. "I'm honored that the president has noticed my work," said Michael tapping in his putt.

"Quit the false modesty," said Rushman. "We both know you might be the vice-presidential candidate of our party at the next elections. The president asked me about it and I told him you were ideal for the job. Give Maclain some backbone."

"Thanks, Harold," said Michael Cherry, stepping back to let the secretary complete his hole with two putts.

"This nation has many enemies, Michael. We have many enemies. The Democrats are after us for this fucking war in Iraq. We have to count on every good man we've got," said the secretary of defense.

"I'm there for you," said Cherry smiling, but inside he was worried about the situation he had created for the first time. *So much is at stake for me*, thought Michael.

"Now, if you could hit some lousy shots, that would help me plenty," laughed Harold Rushman.

"I'll see what I can do about that, too," said Michael Cherry, thinking about the possibility that he could actually become the next vice president of the United States. *Then no one could touch me*, thought Michael. *I'd have earned my place in history. I'd have the power in my hands, a heartbeat from the presidency and all the money I could want. All I have to do is clean up these loose ends. Now where the fuck is that Serb?*

CHAPTER 52

❀

Darkness. Oblivion. Nothing. The empty void. I was floating through the darkness, spinning like the dead astronaut in *2001: A Space Odyssey*. There were no shining bright lights, no men in beards and robes greeting me to heaven—only emptiness. It wasn't unpleasant; in fact it felt good that my body didn't hurt anymore. A voice called out to me. It was my old partner, Dougie Gardner, the one who had been killed many years ago when I was a cop.

"Dave," he called to me. "Over here." He was sitting at a desk, looking over some files. "Where are you going?" he said to me in a matter of fact voice.

"I don't know," I said. "Looks like I'm joining you. Is this where you live now?" I asked.

"No, this is my office," he said. "Don't be in such a rush, It's not your time yet."

"How do you know?" I asked him. "It sure looks like my time."

"Trust me, it's not," he said. "I'll let you know when it is."

Just then a bright light started shining into my eyes. I tried to get away from it, but it kept going from one eye to another and I couldn't see Dougie anymore.

"Dougie!" I yelled out. "Dougie, what's going on?" I asked. He just shrugged and walked away. I opened my eyes. A flood of harsh light ran into my brain and a woman dressed in white was standing over me. I was in a room of some kind, a hospital room.

"He's coming to," said the doctor's voice as he turned around.

I tried to shield my eyes from the harsh light but my right arm was attached to an IV tube.

"Be careful," said the doctor holding down my wrist. "I'm Dr. Rachael Ungerer, resident doctor here at Mt. Sinai. You were in a coma."

I noticed my left arm was real heavy as if in some kind of a cast. Then intense pain shot all through my body. My head was killing me and a sharp pain jolted through my thigh. I grimaced in pain.

"God, it hurts," I said.

I saw three other women come up around the bed and join the doctor.

"Don't be such a wimp," said Kelly Claire.

"Yeah, we were wondering when you would wake up," said my ex-wife Susan.

"We all have better things to do than sit here wondering about you," said Kara Murphy.

"It feels like I'm in the *Witches of Eastwick*," I said.

"Much worse than that," said the doctor. "This must be a fan club. They've been here for three days, waiting for you to wake up. Your head was smashed pretty badly. If it wasn't so hard, you would be dead."

"He's always had a hard head," said my ex-wife Susan.

"Where's Adam?" I asked.

"He's at the house with my kids, safe," said Susan. "Eddie Carpenter brought him over with your gun and a laptop."

"How long have I been out?" I asked, trying unsuccessfully to get up.

"Three days," said the doctor. "A Father Dolnic brought you into the emergency room here at Mt. Sinai. You had a broken wrist, a perforated thigh, a concussion, a bruised kidney, brain, and spleen, a broken nose, contusions on your face, and you were out cold. You had lost a lot of blood. It was touch and go for some days here."

"You should see the other guy," I said grimacing.

"The father said you were run over by a car. A hit and run. But it doesn't seem consistent with your injuries. He says there were a lot of witnesses. Do you remember anything?"

"I think I was jaywalking on 11th Avenue. Then a cab ran me down. That's all I remember," I said, thinking how smart Father Dolnic was.

"That's my Dave," said Kara. "Always walking around with his head in the clouds."

"You can't walk anywhere in this city without some cab running you down," said Kelly Claire. "It's a disgrace."

"Well," the doctor said. "I will prescribe some morphine for your pain and let you get some rest."

"Thanks, Doc," I said as she walked out.

Kara walked around the bed and kissed me. She updated me on her meeting with Bob Forrester and the other investigations she had done at the Pentagon.

"I can't believe you put yourself out on a limb for me," I said to Kara.

"It wasn't just you. I did it for me, too. It felt good to scare the shit out of him," said Kara.

"Little good it will do, if we can't tie him directly to Cherry," I said. "He still holds all the cards."

"If what Kara has told me is true, I can't believe what these guys did," said Susan. "They are responsible as much as the terrorists for 9/11. We must make them pay for this."

"We will," I said. "As soon as I get out of this bed."

"Oh, there's some more bad news," Kelly said.

"What's the more bad news?" I asked.

"You're under arrest. There's a cop sitting outside in the hallway. Remember that the NSA issued a warrant for your arrest. You're a wanted suspected terrorist. The police commissioner Frank Curtis is on his way over. He's pissed. Doesn't like the NSA but likes Islamic fanatics even less. I think he wants to arrest you personally on national TV," said Kelly. "It might be a good time to formulate another plan."

"I think escape is out of the question," I said raising my arm to show the IV. "Besides, I know Curtis, he's a good man."

"Then I think a negotiated surrender might be a better idea before he shoots you," said Susan.

"I'll consider that," I said.

"What are you going to do?" said Susan.

"Wait till Chief Curtis arrives," I said as I pulled myself up. "And then, hopefully, I'll tell him a story that might interest him. It's got to or I'm sunk."

"The old Stillati charm," said Kelly.

"When all else fails," I said. "I pull out my charisma and a completely unrealistic plan. They go for it every time."

"Save it for the cameras," said Kara Murphy. "There are still a lot of things we need to discuss now before the chief gets here."

CHAPTER 53

The most wanted criminal in the world prepared his long trip to the secret rendezvous with the Saudi ambassador to Pakistan. Osama bin Laden would be traveling to Islamabad, the Pakistani capital, at night, hidden in a donkey cart carrying dates and honey, to meet Ayman al-Zawahiri in about five days time. Bin Laden prepared his Koran and the few clothes he would need for the trip. He would be carried in a wooden compartment under the cart invisible to American drones and the Pakistani army. It was a crude, simple, and effective method of travel, undetectable among the many farmers bringing product from the mountains to sell in Islamabad. Al-Zawahiri was already at the location, in the safe house, waiting for him, along with the Saudi ambassador.

The meeting with the Saudi ambassador, set up by his cousin Prince Abdullah now the new oil minister, would signal the cessation of all hostilities between the Saudi Kingdom and Al Queda. It was a risky gamble for both Bin Laden and Al-Zawahiri to be present at a meeting at the same time, but the new Saudi king had requested they meet with his ambassador. As a sign of good will, the king had given up his ambassador as a hostage to the Al Queda forces in Pakistan, with a gift of $50 million in cash. It was money they desperately needed to continue their activities in Afghanistan and Iraq. The ambassador from Saudi Arabia was also waiting for Bin Laden with the money in hand to give it to him. Al-Zawahiri had communicated with Bin Laden that it was safe for him to travel.

The ambassador and the money were in safe Al Queda hands in a new luxurious house on the outskirts of Islamabad near the new airport, called the Shaheen development. Bin Laden longed for the day he and his family could return to Saudi Arabia and make a hadj, a pilgrimage to Mecca and Medina.

Now with this agreement, he would be able to do it. Al-Zawahiri had negotiated personally with the ambassador for a one-billion-dollar-per-year subsidiary from the Saudis to stop terrorist activities there and promote attacks outside of the kingdom against American and Western forces only.

As in the ancient days, Al Queda could fight to rid the Middle East of all crusaders and infidels, thought Bin Laden, and he would lead the way with money, fighters, and weapons. The war in Iraq had radicalized the Middle East, which had been the main goal that Bin Laden had envisioned with his initial terrorist attacks. The Americans had fallen into the trap of a long and costly war in the Middle East—a war they could never hope to win and which only fueled more anti-American sentiment throughout the world. *Arabs now had to pick sides,* thought the terrorist leader. *So Al Queda grows in popularity no matter what happens.* From a small radical splinter group, Al Queda now had volunteers from all over the Arab world flocking to Iraq to kill westerners.

The terrorist prepared to climb into the donkey cart helped by one of his sons. They were still inside the large cave that housed him in the Afghan mountains, lit only by candlelight. His eldest son, Mohammed, came to say good-bye to him.

"Now, with Allah's help, and Saudi Arabia's money, we will be able to finally go home," said Mohammed. "We will be safe from the drones and the Americans."

"This is the day we have been waiting for," said Bin Laden. "With the new king in Saudi Arabia as our ally, supplying us with money and weapons, Al Queda will be able to topple the governments in Iraq, Egypt, Lebanon, Morocco, and Algeria, and to lead the liberation of the Middle East and Palestine. We will unify our ancient lands with fire and destroy the infidels and Jews that are on our lands. Like our prophet before us, we will use Saudi Arabia as the base for our religion and political power. Our future is glorious."

"*Allah Akbar*, safe travel, Father," said his son, kissing him three times on his cheeks.

"*Allah Akbar*, be safe," replied the terrorist. "I will be back in ten days and then we will leave these caves for good." His son then helped him slip into the wooden box under the donkey cart that was specially equipped to house him. It would not be comfortable but Bin Laden would read his Koran throughout the whole trip and drink only water, and eat dates and bread that he brought with him. Special Al Queda fighters would carefully guard the cart from afar so that any intervention or potential danger would be spotted. Bin Laden wasn't worried about the trip or the meeting. Everything was working to his favor. He felt he was protected by his faith, and considered himself a direct messenger from Allah.

CHAPTER 54

The offices of the National Security Agency overlooked the red sunset shedding pink rays over the Potomac. It was a view that Michael Cherry always enjoyed, the sense of being in the political capital of the world—the Rome of modern times. *Soon, I will be one of the governors of that world*, thought Cherry to himself with the same ambition that had fueled the various Caesars that governed ancient Rome. Still, Michael Cherry had reason to be nervous. It had been forty-eight hours since he had last heard from Szabo Tanovich. Dave Stillati, the boy, and the laptop must be still at large somewhere in New York City. Kara Murphy had gone to Bob Forrester at Holliwell and threatened to expose him. There were enemies that he still had to destroy. *I must call the Pentagon to have Dwight Summers reassigned to Iceland*, thought Michael Cherry, making a mental note.

Michael picked up the phone and called agent Ron Durhling in the NSA office in New York.

"Have you heard from Szabo?" asked Michael.

"Not a thing since he left two days ago to go after Stillati."

"Anything on Stillati?"

"His cell phone has been quiet. No calls from his office. He has disappeared as well. I have a man in front of his home and one in front of his office. As soon as he shows, I'll get right over."

"It's not like the big Serb not to call in," said Michael.

"I think we have to assume he might be dead," said Ron Durhling.

"What could ever kill him?" asked Michael Cherry in amazement.

"This Stillati guy is tougher than we thought," said Durhling. "He might have found a way to do it."

"And you let him get away," said Cherry. "You had him in your car."

"The New York police helped him escape. He was one of their own," said Durhling defensively.

"I know," said Cherry. "I told Chief Curtis that, but he denied it. I'll get his badge for this."

"What do you want me to do?" said Agent Durhling.

"Stay put until I call you. It seems I have to do everything around here myself." Cherry slammed down the phone and paced up and down in front of his desk. Five minutes later the phone rang.

"New York City Chief Curtis on the line for you, sir," said Cherry's secretary.

"Put him on."

"Chief Curtis, what can I do for you?"

"I think I have good news for you, Cherry. We got the guy you are looking for. Dave Stillati," said Chief Curtis.

Michael Cherry breathed a sigh of relief. "Where is he?"

"Mount Sinai hospital notified us that they were holding a man that was seriously injured in a fight. We rushed over there immediately, but he escaped grabbing some hostages. Now he has taken them to the NBC building in hope of getting a TV interview. He is clearly desperate and deranged. He says he wants to negotiate only with you at the NSA office. We have kept him isolated so far from the press and are talking him into releasing the hostages," said Chief Curtis. "How quick can you get down here?"

"I will be in LaGuardia in two hours," said Cherry. "Keep Stillati there and don't kill him before I get there."

"I wouldn't dream of it. We will wait for you to do that," said Chief Curtis.

"Oh, and, Chief?" said Michael getting up from his chair. "This more than makes up for the snafu on the bridge. The mayor and the president will both hear how you helped this investigation."

"I'm counting on it," said Chief Curtis, hanging up the phone.

Michael Cherry quickly called Agent Durhling again in New York and told him to expect him to arrive at LaGuardia Airport at the private plane section. The NSA Gulfstream airplane would be landing in less than one hour. He also told him to alert the press that they would have a truly big story in couple of hours. Cherry hung up and had his secretary call his driver.

This will be a massive coup for my reputation, thought Cherry. *Capturing a wanted terrorist on live TV. It will guarantee me the vice-presidential nomination.*

Back in his small office in New York City, Agent Durhling also put down his headphones. He didn't like taking orders from his boss, Michael Cherry. He also had disliked Szabo Tanovich intensely and was almost relieved he was now missing. It seemed to Durhling that Cherry and Tanovich were running the NSA like a personal fiefdom, breaking all the rules for their own self-promoting purposes. *The Serb was a criminal if I ever saw one*, thought Durhling. *How Cherry can have had him work here at the NSA I don't know. It was all bad news.*

Ron Durhling looked at the picture of his dead baby brother that sat on his desk. Private Jimmy Durhling had volunteered for the Marines after 9/11. He was killed by a roadside bomb outside of Fallujah while riding in his Hummer. He was only nineteen and was a promising quarterback in college before he volunteered for the Marines.

That's why we fight, said Ron Durhling to himself. *Guys like Cherry and Tanovich will never understand that.*

CHAPTER 55

❀

The new king, Aziz bin Saud, listened patiently to his counselors in the Great Hall of the Royal Palace in Riyadh, Saudi Arabia. The pictures of his ancestors and former kings in their resplendent robes looked down on him from the gilded walls of the palace. He had inherited a heavy package of responsibility as the guardian of the Islamic faith's holiest shrines. Every year, millions of faithful traveled to renew their faith to Mecca and Medina and the king was personally responsible for their safety and well-being. With the extension of the Islamic terrorist movement throughout Islam, the king had his security forces on high alert for suicide bombers. He listened patiently as the details of airport security and travel arrangements to the shrines were exposed to him. The king was somewhat impatient as he waited for his ambassador in Pakistan to call him. There was a lot at stake in the action he was about to undertake. His oil minister, Prince Abdullah, was in the anteroom waiting to be summoned.

Finally, at 3:00 PM Riyadh time, his secretary indicated that the Saudi ambassador to Pakistan was calling him from the capital, Islamabad. The king personally got on the line with his ambassador.

"Your Royal Highness, it is an honor to speak to you," said the ambassador.

"Yes, yes," said the king. "Is the meeting scheduled?"

"As planned," said the ambassador. "Tonight we will be signing all agreements at 1:00 PM."

"Are all members present?" asked the king.

"Both Al Queda leaders are here in the house with me. I have shown them the agreement and they had some corrections to be made, how the monies were to be sent to them, when they could arrive in Saudi Arabia officially with their families. I think they are very relieved to be getting away safely from the Americans and coming under your protection."

"They value their lives very highly," said the king. "But not the lives of their followers that they send to their suicide deaths so happily."

"They are opportunists and fanatics," said the ambassador. "Your highness, are you sure this is the right policy for working with them. Legitimizing their cause, paying and protecting them?"

"Are you questioning your king, ambassador?"

"Never," said the ambassador. "But won't the Americans be angry with us?"

"Let me worry about our American friends," he said. "Just make sure that your agreement is signed tonight by all of you. There is more at stake here than you know."

"I am but a humble, ignorant servant of the kingdom," said the ambassador.

"Do your duty to your country, and you and your family will be amply rewarded."

"I am forever in your debt," said the ambassador.

"May Allah protect you in your journey," said the king.

The king hung up the phone. *The ambassador is a good man and a loyal servant*, thought the king. *It will be sad that he has to die.* But he had to be there, present at the house, signing the agreement. That was the only way Bin Laden and Al-Zawahiri would ever agree to appear in person.

He called his assistant to bring Prince Abdullah over to him. Prince Abdullah walked into the Great Hall where the king held court.

"Your Royal Highness," said Prince Abdullah, bending over in reverence.

"The meeting with your cousin in Pakistan has now been confirmed," said the king. "I thank you for your collaboration in this matter. I know it did not come easily to you."

"It is my duty to obey my king and country. Do you want me to relay the information to the Americans?" said Prince Abdullah.

"No, I will have my intelligence chief inform the Pentagon. You have done enough, Prince Abdullah, to help our faith and our kingdom."

Abdullah did not like the fact that the king would not be using him as a conduit with the Americans. It meant that the king did not fully trust him yet. *That will change in time*, thought Abdullah. *I am the oil minister now, one of the most powerful men in the kingdom. I don't need to work with minor intelligence matters anymore.*

"Have you negotiated the Chinese agreement yet?" asked the king.

"We are in the final draft of the contracts. They are easier to work with than the Americans."

"Give them time," said the king. "They will learn to barter and negotiate."

"My king is very wise," said Abdullah.

"Let me know when the agreements are ready," said the king.

"*Salaam Aleichem*," said Prince Abdullah backing away to the exit.

"*Aleichem Salaam*," said the king to his oil minister.

King Aziz called the head of Saudi intelligence personally and relayed the information with the address his ambassador had given him, and the coordinates of the house. The precise time at which the agreement was to be signed was also conveyed. The king did not want any last-minute mistakes to happen, or any "accidental" leaks that would alert the terrorists. The head of Saudi intelligence would personally relay the same information in code to the Americans at the Pentagon. *The Americans will finally kill Bin Laden and Al-Zawahiri. President Branch and the American people will be forever grateful to us,* thought the king. *We will have destroyed the leadership of Al Queda once and for all, and Saudi Arabia will regain its spiritual political and religious leadership in the Arab world. There will be no interference this time.*

King Aziz waived his counselors away and had the Great Hall cleared. He wanted a moment to be alone to read his Koran and pray that the decisions and actions he had undertaken were the right ones. *Even a king needs assurances once in a while,* thought King Aziz to himself as he opened his holy book.

CHAPTER 56

The restaurant known as the Rainbow Room was on the 65th floor of the NBC building and was one of the most renowned and romantic places in Manhattan. I was well aware of this because when I was wooing my ex-wife, Susan, I brought her there to dance with me on the revolving dance floor. We gazed lovingly over the sparkling lights of the island of Manhattan as the snow fell over the city. Thousands of other couples had done the same thing over the many years, and despite different ownerships and mediocre food, the Rainbow Room continued to rightly be a favorite New York City romantic landmark.

"Is everybody here?" I asked Kara Murphy.

"Some are here already. Some are on their way," said Kara.

"And Chief Curtis?" I asked.

"He is outside with most of his men. I can't believe he's letting you try this."

"He's giving me enough rope to hang myself. Chief Curtis is a true New York cop," I said. "He was in one of the World Trade towers when it went down and got out just in time. He lost a lot of friends and colleagues that day. I think he wants to know what the truth is more than anybody. Besides, he's not risking anything. If we lose, I can't exactly run away."

"How do you feel?" Kara asked as she touched the cast on my wrist.

"There isn't a part of my body that isn't screaming in agony," I said. "I've got a headache the size of the Brooklyn Bridge, but I'll live."

"There's so much at stake here for both of us," said Kara.

"I know, Kara. My freedom among other things, the future of our country," I said.

"Why did you pick this place?" Kara asked.

"I always liked the Rainbow Room. I took Susan here. Under the circumstances, it's probably the only way I could get to dance with you," I said to Kara.

"Maybe, once this is all over, we can come here again," Kara said.

"Kara, I want to thank you for helping me," I said. "I know you put your life on the line for me. You could have just stayed in Ely, minding your own business."

"And miss all this excitement?" said Kara. "I've got more at stake here than you do. Someone ruined my career. Someone allowed or even encouraged 9/11 to happen. Maybe tonight we can nab the bad guys and give our country some justice."

"Maybe," I said. "But it's a long shot, that's for sure."

"You're a long shot, too, Dave," said Kara as she kissed me on the only part of my body that wasn't bruised. "But my money's on you."

"Now let's not get lovey-dovey here," said Kelly, coming toward us. "Dave's still a dangerous terrorist on the lam."

"That's what attracts me to him," said Kara.

"Is Susan here?" I asked Kelly.

"She is on her way with Adam," said Kelly.

"And the others?" I asked Kara again.

"Colonel Summers and Charles Ryan are expected any minute. The taxi driver Ali Mahalati and Hadji are already here. Jenna is personally bringing in that creep, Mirko, from Minnesota."

"Pity the big Serb Szabo himself isn't here," said Kara. "Ready to confess."

At his name parts of my body started to scream in discomfort, places and bones the giant Serb had tried his best to break.

"Trust me, we are much better off without him. Besides, he's more comfortable where he is now," I said.

"And where's that?" asked Kelly.

"You'd have to ask Father Dolnic," I said in a whisper. "But I believe what remains of his body is being fed to some pigs at the Croatian farm in Mountain Lakes, New Jersey. They needed some pig feed up there."

"Much more information than I needed to know," said Kelly.

"It's a Buddhist rebirth," I said. "From human shit to pig shit."

"It's a step up for a monster like him," said Kelly. "I feel sorry for the pigs."

"When is Michael Cherry arriving?" Kara asked.

"Chief Curtis says he is landing at LaGuardia airport in thirty minutes. We have to have everything ready to greet him in style when he arrives."

"Everything will be fine, Dave. Don't worry," said Kara.

"That's easy for you to say," I said. "You're not facing deportation to Guantanamo Bay and torture if this goes bad."

"No, just possible jail time for breaking my FBI gag agreement," said Kara. "Losing my pension and possible physical elimination as well."

"I know that," I said. "Sorry for the smart-ass remark."

"They say the weather in Cuba is great at this time," said Kelly. "Maybe we'll all go down there with you."

"Dave and his harem," I said. "That would be just great. It would definitely improve my status in the Arab world. I would be the celebrity prisoner at Gitmo."

Chief Curtis stormed into the dance hall of the Rainbow Room glaring at me. "I must be crazy giving you a chance like this, Stillati," he said. "My career is on the line here. You only get one chance, Stillati. Only one."

"That's all I'm asking for. That's more than the people in the Twin Towers or the Pentagon or on that flight to Washington got. One chance to nail this bastard is all I want."

"Well, then, you've got it," said Chief Curtis. "Make sure it's your best shot."

CHAPTER 57

❀

Asiago NATO Air Force Base, Italy, 7:00 PM.

In the twilight dusk of the small Italian town of Asiago, in the hangar of the NATP Air Force base, Captain James Meriwether and Gunnery Sergeant Sheldon Gilgore waited patiently for their F-117A Stealth bomber to be armed with the payload of sixteen satellite guided missiles. The pilot had received his orders after lunch and entered the planned route to Pakistan into his EFIS (Electronic Flight Instrumentation System).

"Latitude 24:54:53 North, Longitude 67:01:20," said Captain Meriwether to his gunnery sergeant. The F-117A Nighthawk known as the Stealth Bomber cost $45 million-per-plane and was to be retired from the Air Force in 2007. It could fly undetected into enemy territory and was the perfect tool for the top secret mission Captain Meriwether had just been ordered to conduct into Pakistan by the Pentagon Op-ed center in Washington.

Captain Meriwether was a highly-decorated veteran of two Desert Storm wars and knew Pakistan very well. Technically, Pakistan was an ally of the United States, and Captain James Meriwether knew that the bombing was too close to the capital of Islamabad to be officially sanctioned. However, the mission called for the precision bombing of one particular house, next to the new airport of Islamabad at 1:00 AM and Meriwether did not envision any particular problems in concluding his mission.

The ground crew finally gave their okay for take off. Captain Meriwether warmed the four large GE F-118-GE-100 Turbofan engines that powered the F-117A Nighthawk. The plane resembled a large wing with its 172-foot wingspan, and moved toward the runway. The captain ordered the gunnery sergeant to go through the traditional weapon checks before takeoff. The plane was armed with sixteen missiles that were guided by the JDAM (Joint Direct Attack Munitions) computer. Each satellite could hit a dime in the street of Islamabad. The plane could also carry nuclear weapons.

Not needed for this mission, thought Gunnery Sergeant Gilgore. The Stealth bomber would fly at an altitude of 50,000 feet and could go on a 6,000-mile mission without refueling. However Pakistan was not that far from Italy. Captain Meriwether envisioned a five-hour trip that would get him over the target at 1:00 AM Islamabad time. He would discharge his bombs on the single target and return to Asiago. The gunnery sergeant entered the destination coordinates into the Rockwell Collins TCN-250 tactical air navigation system (better known as TACAN). The plane would essentially guide itself to the target with little intervention from the pilots.

"Ready for takeoff," said Captain Meriwether to the control tower.

"You are good to go, Captain," said the radar controller. "God speed, and have a safe trip."

"Up, up, and away," said the captain as the bomber accelerated onto the runway. The four jet engines of the plane roared their approval as the ominous bomber lifted up into the darkness over the snow-filled Italian Alps. Soon, the Stealth bomber would be crossing over Austria, Germany, Poland, Russia, Afghanistan, and Pakistan at near subsonic speeds unnoticeable by radar or human eye, ready to deliver its package of death and destruction to the inhabitants of a newly-constructed house in Islamabad. Captain Meriwether had been fully briefed as to who the target was in the house he was ordered to bomb in Pakistan.

No one in the world deserves this more, he thought to himself, guiding the plane through the night clouds to deliver his deadly payload. *No one in the world.*

CHAPTER 58

❈

I had turned the dance floor of the Rainbow Room into something out of *Les Miserables* by barricading the entrance using upturned tables and screens. New York City Police Chief Frank Curtis had given me my unloaded Beretta nine-millimeter with which to threaten my so-called "hostages," which consisted of Kara Murphy, Ali Mahalati, Gunner Charles Ryan, Adam, and my ex-wife Susan. The chief himself had placed his uniformed men across the entrance of the dance floor to make it look credible. We waited patiently for our expected guest, Michael Cherry, to arrive. Finally, I heard a loudspeaker come to life.

"Dave Stillati," the voice said. "This is Police Chief Frank Curtis. Let the hostages go."

"No!" I yelled back. "You know my conditions. I won't speak to you. I want to speak to Cherry at the NSA."

"Come on, Stillati," said Curtis. "Give it up. You are placing civilians in danger."

"Once I speak to Cherry of the NSA, I will let them go," I yelled back.

After a few moments of silence, the loudspeaker came on.

"This is Michael Cherry," said the voice. "I have come from Washington, D.C. and am here ready to talk to you. Don't hurt the hostages."

Like if you would care, I thought to myself.

"Show yourself with your hands up," I said.

A rather rotund bald man with dark-rimmed glasses stepped out into the light.

"I am not armed," said the voice.

"Come forward," I said.

Another man came close to him.

"Whose that?" I yelled out, alarmed.

"That's NSA agent, Ron Durhling. He is unarmed as well."

"He can't come," I said. "Only you, come forward."

Michael Cherry walked forward wearing a very expensive Italian grey suit with a white handkerchief in his vest pocket. It took him about two minutes to come through the opening I had made in the barricade. I waved the gun at his head making him turn around and patted him down. He wasn't carrying any weapons. Then I had him sit down on a restaurant stool while looking at him closely.

"So you are the famous Michael Cherry?" I said.

"And you are Dave Stillati, the unlikely hero," he said.

"Just a question, Mr. Cherry. Why did the NSA put out a warrant for my arrest?"

"Your name came up in the investigation of the killing of Sandra Baines in Portland, Oregon, and the disappearance of her son. We believe terrorists were involved in that. We wanted to ask you some questions."

"All you had to do was call," I said. "Is that why you sent that goon, Szabo Tanovich, to Portland?" I asked him.

He dried his head with his handkerchief. "Szabo Tanovich is an agent of the NSA. I sent him out there to investigate. Unfortunately, he has not returned as of yet."

"Somehow, I doubt that he will," I said.

Cherry looked at me strangely.

"Mr. Stillati, if you had a hand in his disappearance, you will have to answer for that, too. He was a federal agent. That would mean the death penalty for you."

"I didn't kill him," I said.

"Then let the hostages go and turn yourself in," Cherry said to me as if he thought he had all the answers.

"Ask them yourself and see if they want to go," I said. "But let me introduce them to you." I brought Cherry over to the chairs where my friends were waiting to see him.

"This is Kara Murphy," I said. "She used to work at the FBI as an agent when you were there. Maybe you remember her? She worked for you back then. She arrested the twentieth terrorist, Zacarias Moussaoui, and grabbed his laptop in Minneapolis in August of 2001. You did everything you could to stop her from using the laptop to stop 9/11. Unfortunately, you were successful."

Kara came up to Cherry and looked at him with disdain. "You are going down, Michael Cherry, for betraying your country."

"What is the meaning of this?" asked Cherry shocked. "What are you talking about? Who are you people?"

"This is Ali Mahalati. Remember him?" I asked. "He remembers you. He was your driver in Afghanistan and drove you from Kabul to Khost to meet Bin Laden in 1998. That was when you made the agreement with the terrorists to protect them and offer them information to use in their attacks. You knew the attack would cause the U.S. to retaliate. That would enrich you and your company, Holliwell, and it did beyond anything you imagined."

"That is complete bullshit," said Cherry. "Holliwell was doing great before the attacks."

"Liar," I said. "Holliwell was bankrupt in 2001. The attacks saved you and your company. This man saw you in the camps with Bin Laden. Do you deny that?"

"Absolutely. I was never there. I never saw this man."

"You thought you had killed him and his family by bombing his house. He alone survived the bombings."

The driver came over to Cherry and looked at him. Then he pulled back and spit in his face. "I remember you well. You were there in my taxi with the Serbian monster. The huge man. You spent the day with the terrorists in Khost. Then when I told the Americans, you killed my family, you animal. You will pay for that in hell for eternity," said Ali Mahalati.

Cherry wiped the spit from his nose. "I didn't kill anybody," he said. "You are mistaken."

"This is Gunnery Sergeant Charles Ryan," I said. A dignified man with a limp stood up to look at Cherry.

"He and Captain Derek Wight had lined their sights on an SUV with Bin Laden, Sheik Omar, and Al-Zawahiri, fleeing Kabul in January of 2002. They were about to blow up the SUV. You ordered Colonel Bob Forrester at the Pentagon to abort the mission."

"I had no such powers," Cherry said.

"I talked to Bob Forrester," said Kara. "You paid him well to take your orders. You put him in as chairman of Holliwell. He aborted the mission and then ordered the Apache taken down by friendly fire."

"Is this true?" Sergeant Charles Ryan asked Kara.

"We believe so," said Kara. "Dwight Summers, Intel director now at the Pentagon, has assembled a plethora of evidence against Forrester."

"It's not true," said Cherry. "They are lying to you."

Sergeant Charles Ryan walked up to Cherry and said, "You killed my captain and I spent two years in a vet hospital because of you, you bastard."

"I don't have to take accusations and orders from you people. Police Chief Curtis, Agent Durhling!" yelled Cherry.

"Shut up," I said as I placed my Beretta on his forehead. "I still have some introductions to make." Adam and Susan came over.

"This is my ex-wife, Susan. The 9/11 attacks killed her husband. The Serb killer, Szabo Tanovich, was the one you sent to Portland that killed and raped her sister. This is her sister's son Adam—the one Sandra bought the laptop for. He recognized Szabo in Portland and hid out. Then Szabo kidnapped him here."

"I know no such story about a laptop," said Cherry.

"Funny," I said. "So you don't know of an e-mail address named Pharbor@aol.com?"

"This is ridiculous," Cherry said.

"It's registered in your daughter's name. PearlHarbor.com. It gave the terrorists instructions on when and how to hijack the planes. Only that Mohammed Atta left his laptop at the airport. He didn't need it anymore. It was placed in the lost and found at the airport. Five years later, Sandra bought it for Adam. When they found out what the laptop contained, they reported it to the NSA hotline. You got the information and relayed it to the Serb. He went there to kill her and Adam."

Susan went up to Cherry and slapped him. "My sister had nothing to do with this," Susan said.

"You killed my mom," Adam said and threw out a right hook that hit Cherry in the left ear. Cherry shook it off.

"It's easy for all of you to accuse an unarmed man. Prove it," spat Michael Cherry, looking at me with hate.

"We have a Mirko in custody who has identified the Serb Szabo Tanovich as the man who hired him to kill Dave and Adam," said Kara. "He has confessed."

"The Serb must have done it on his own, then," said Cherry.

"Like he killed FBI agents Todd Grey and Walter Jurgensen?" asked Kara.

"I never told him to do that," said Cherry, talking to me. "Now let me leave this place immediately. You have no right to question me. You are the one wanted for murder. The police are outside waiting to arrest you."

"Exactly," I said aiming my revolver at the middle of his forehead. "One murder, more or less. What difference does it make? You're next."

"Now, wait a minute," he said. "You don't want to do that."

"Why not?" I asked.

"I can make you all very rich. I'm worth millions, hundreds of millions now. I can give each of you $10 million," said Cherry.

"That's a lot of money," I said. "What do you say, guys? $10 million each to let this piece of shit go? What do you say?"

"No," said Kara Murphy.

"No," said Ali Mahalati.

"No," said my ex-wife, Susan.

"No," said Adam.

"I'm afraid it's unanimous," I said cocking the Beretta.

"Please, don't kill me," cried Michael Cherry. "Not now that I'm so close. I am almost vice president. I can make you all rich and powerful."

"Is that why you did it?" I asked again.

"I only wanted to help my country re-arm. I wanted us to be ready to fight wars and be prepared."

"So you worked out a plan with the terrorists to kill Americans."

"A few had to be sacrificed for the greater good," said Cherry. "It happens in war."

"And you decided this?" I asked. "For your greater good?"

"For the good of the country. Now we are dominant once more in Afghanistan and Iraq, our arms budget has never been higher."

"And more than 2,200 Americans and 40,000 Iraqis are dead," I said. "And you helped Al Queda and unleashed them onto the world."

"Soldiers are born to die anyway. What counts is who wins. We have already won this war. Al Queda are just a gang of fanatics. We were going to have them all killed once this war was over," Cherry said.

"But it's not over, is it? But it is for you," I said.

"You think you have something?" Cherry said. "You have nothing. You are just a lowly sports agent, an ex-cop that couldn't save his dying partner. This whore here is an ex-FBI agent who has broken every law in the book. The rest of you are civilians and illegal aliens. You don't have anything on me that could be proven in court. Nothing. I will spin this away and then I'll come after you. No jury of my peers would ever convict me. Not a man of my power and wealth."

"Not a jury of your peers, but one of your superiors, yes," said Police Chief Frank Curtis, who had been listening to the recorded conversations as planned.

"Chief!" said Michael Cherry. "Thank God you are here. These people forced me to say terrible things. None of it is true."

"Get the fuck away from me," said Police Chief Curtis. "My men died in the World Trade towers because of you."

"It's not true," said Cherry, almost hysterical now.

Agent Ron Durhling was standing on the right of Police Chief Curtis.

"Durhling," ordered Cherry, "take out your gun and shoot this man," He said, pointing at me. I turned around and faced Durhling with my unloaded gun in my hand. Ron Durhling took out his revolver and pointed it at me.

"Shoot," said Michael Cherry. "Shoot him now."

"Put down your gun," said Police Chief Curtis. "That's an order. Nobody is shooting anybody."

"I am your superior, Durhling. Shoot that man!" Cherry yelled. I thought for sure that Durhling would shoot and kill me on the spot. Durhling aimed the gun at me, then he spun around and a shot rang out. Michael Cherry grabbed his thigh and went down. The bullet from Ron Durhling's 45-millimeter had caught him above the knee going clean through the flesh of his thigh. He went down moaning in considerable pain.

"You shot me, goddammit! You're going to pay for this," Cherry said as his blood spilled on the wooden dance floor.

"Fuck you. My baby brother died in Iraq, you miserable pig," Durhling bent down to yell at Cherry who lay on the ground moaning in pain. "He didn't deserve to die for you."

"Shit, what do we do now?" Chief Curtis said.

"I think I have an idea," I said to my audience in general.

"You might be the only one," said Susan.

CHAPTER 59

Islamabad, Pakistan, February 14, 2006, 1:00 AM

In a modern, two-story house, on the outskirts of Islamabad, next to the new airport, Osama bin Laden and Ayman al-Zawahiri, the two most wanted men on the planet, were about to sign the final draft of their agreement with the Saudi government. Prince Zayoob, the Saudi ambassador, had already affixed his signature with the royal seal of the House of Saud. Bin Laden pulled up the sleeve of his black robe and with little fanfare scribbled his signature at the bottom of the document. Al-Zawahiri followed suit. The three men hugged and exchanged traditional kisses on their cheeks drinking warm tea in celebration. The agreement was a landmark for Al-Queda and Bin Laden. The terrorists would be receiving official recognition and protection from the new Saudi king, plus one billion dollars-per-year of financing to continue their terrorist activities. The Saudi king would receive Al-Queda's pledge to stop terrorist attacks within Saudi Arabia, once and for all.

"This is a glorious day for our fatwa," said Al-Zawahiri.

"We will unify all Arabs in the fight against the infidel from our sacred lands in Saudi Arabia. We will destroy Israel. We will place Califates in every Arab land," said Bin Laden.

"*Insha Allah*," said Prince Zayoob, who personally would have preferred to have the fanatics executed. However, he was following a direct order from his king and could do little but participate in the celebrations. "We will soon have a transport plane land in the mountains to pick up your family and loved ones," said Prince Zayoob.

"Our families have suffered so much from the American attacks," said Bin Laden. "We have lost many soldiers in our sacred struggle."

"We will soon fill our ranks again with loyal Arab brothers," said Al-Zawahiri. "With Saudi support and the billions they will pay us, all of Islam will rise as one man behind us. We will kick all foreign infidels out of the Middle East once and for all."

"*Allah Akbar*," they both said looking out of the window to the stars, sure that the God to whom they prayed five times a day was favoring them at last.

Over the small house in Islamabad, at an altitude of 42,000 feet, Captain James Meriwether gave the final bombing instructions to Sergeant Sheldon Gilgore. He shifted the plane into a go-to-war mode that activated the bombing sequences. The sergeant entered the coordinates the Pentagon Ops intelligence operator had forwarded him into the JDAM system. The Lockheed Martin Defense Management System would instruct the sixteen satellite guided bombs to hit the small house on the ground.

"Bombs armed. Portal open. Ready to release bombs," said Gunnery Sergeant Gilgore into his helmet's microphone.

"Fire," said Captain Meriwether.

Sergeant Gilgore pushed the red button that released the bombs. The rotary bomb launcher released the sixteen satellite bombs into the freezing atmosphere.

"Bombs released," said the sergeant.

"Awaiting confirmation of strike to return to base," said Captain Meriwether turning the Stealth bomber into a wide turn. The sixteen satellite guided bombs headed simultaneously toward the small modern house next to the airport. It would take them twenty-five seconds to reach their destination. Four bombs would each strike the north, south, west, and east sides of the house at the same time. There would be no possibility of escape as the TNT equivalent of a small nuclear bomb would devastate the house and all of its inhabitants.

Saudi Prince Zayoob was placing the signed agreement into his briefcase when the bombs first hit the building. He heard a huge blast that tore his clothes off, and he felt himself flying in the air, followed by a burning fireball. In his last moments of life, he saw the dismembered bodies of Osama bin Laden and Al-Zawahiri exploding against the crumbling sides of the building. It was only then, in the very last microsecond of his life, that he finally understood the mission his king had sent him on. *It was the ultimate suicide mission*, thought the prince to himself as his body disintegrated into a bloody mist.

Captain Meriwether surveyed the explosion and took some infrared night scope pictures to relay back to the Pentagon. "Mission accomplished," he said into his microphone.

"We finally got the motherfuckers," said Sergeant Sheldon Gilgore.

"Looks like it," said Captain Meriwether in an even voice, as he banked his plane on the direction home. "I hope they burn in hell."

CHAPTER 60

Kara had applied a tourniquet to Michael Cherry's leg to stop the bleeding. The bullet from Agent Durhling's .45 had gone straight through the meaty part of Cherry's thigh. That didn't stop him from threatening us with dire retribution.

"You're all going to jail for this," said Michael Cherry in between his moans. "You too, Chief Curtis. It's over for all of you. I will never be convicted of anything. The president and the party have picked me as their next vice-presidential candidate. Don't you realize that? You'll be lucky if you see my inauguration from Ryker's Island Prison."

"Pick him up," I said to Durhling and Ali.

They went over to Cherry and lifted him up by his wrist and ankles. Cherry let out a groan as his leg was being touched.

"Don't touch me. Put me down," he complained.

"Where are we going?" asked Kara.

"We're going to the Top of the Rock," I said. "The recently-refurbished observation deck on the seventieth floor. I want Cherry here to have the same view he gave to the poor people who died in the World Trade Center towers. What do you say, Chief?"

All eyes turned to Chief Frank Curtis. His face was completely white and his eyes burned intensely as if he was fighting an inside battle between what he wanted to do and was his job told him to do.

"We should take him into custody," said Chief Curtis.

"He wouldn't be there long," I said. "With his connections, money, and lawyers, he would be out within a few hours. We would be the ones taking his place."

"I have proof I can present to the FBI," said Kara. "Real evidence."

"It looks real now," I said. "But it would disappear like your request to open Moussaoui's laptop. If you give this man time, we will all be dead and he will get away with the worst mass murder in history."

"Kill him now," Ali Mahalati said. "Look what he did to my family."

"And to my sister and husband," said Susan.

"And to my Mom," said Adam.

"He had my captain killed," said Charles Ryan.

"He had two FBI agents murdered," said Kara.

"My brother died because of him," said Durhling.

The chief looked at us all. Then he made a decision and said, "I lost one hundred of my best men in the 9/11 attacks—policeman, firefighters, people that I loved and knew. My own brother was among them. Someone has to pay for that. He has to pay for that," he said to Michael Cherry.

"You are the ones that will pay," Cherry screamed back. "Don't do this, you will all regret it."

"Let's go to the Top of the Rock," said the chief. We left the ballroom with Ali and agent Durhling carrying a screaming Michael Cherry up the three flights of stairs that led to the observation deck. We opened the door to the terrace and a strong, cold wind almost pushed us back in. It was a bright clear winter day in New York, and you could see the city of Manhattan below you in all its splendor, just as it had been on September 11, 2001. The observation deck had recently been renovated and it looked elegant in its Art Deco Style. In the January cold, there was no one out there. On my way up I had grabbed a thick rope, which I proceeded to put under Cherry's armpits. Then with the help of Durhling and Ali we pushed Michael Cherry to the edge of the terrace. He struggled in vain against the three of us, screaming in terror.

"Don't do this. I have $300 million in Holliwell shares," he begged. "I will give them all to you. I will, I promise."

"Blood money," I said. "Too many people died for you to make that money. Your wife will enjoy it now." We lifted Cherry over the terrace ledge and pushed him over, holding the thick rope. He screamed again dangling over the side of the NBC building. His weight tugged at the rope, and it took three of us to hold the rope steady.

"This was the view that the poor people had on the top of the World Trade Center towers," I said. "Enjoy it."

"Pull me up. Pull me up, for God's sake," said Cherry.

"Now you think about God," said Ali back to him.

"I'm going to fall. Pull me up," begged Cherry.

I took the rope and tied it tightly to the banister, like a stretched guitar string.

"Pull me up. Pull me up," he screamed as he dangled back and forth from the side of the building seventy stories above the ground. I pulled out my knife and said to the group, "You have all suffered greatly because of this man. I have not. It is up to you to decide his fate, not me." I held the knife out in my hand. "It's up to you all to cut this rope if you want to. Decide now, life or death for Michael Cherry."

Susan was the first to come up to me without hesitation. "I vote for death for Susan and my husband John," she said. She took the knife and made the first cut into the thick rope.

Ali was next. He took the knife from Susan and said, "This is for my family. Death to the bastard." He sliced more of the rope.

Gunner Charles Ryan took the knife next. "This is for my captain. Death to the traitor," he said, slicing deep into the rope. The rope started to splinter.

"What are you doing, you bastards?" screamed Michael Cherry. "Pull me up. You will all die for this."

Kara took the knife from Ryan. "This is for what was done to me and my fellow agents. I vote for death," she said.

Michael Cherry screamed hysterically from the side of the building, "I'm falling, I'm falling! Please pull me up!"

Agent Ron Durhling was next. "Death. This is for my brother," he said simply and cut into the rope.

Frank Curtis, chief of police, took the knife from him. "This is for every officer, firefighter, friends, and family that died on that miserable day. Death," said Chief Curtis. "May he rot in hell." He cut into the cords, leaving slim tatters of rope that were barely keeping Michael Cherry alive.

Adam came to him and asked for the knife. "You are too young, my boy, to do this," said Curtis.

"He had my mom killed," Adam said. "I have a right."

Chief Curtis looked at me, and I nodded. He gave Adam the serrated knife.

"This is for my mom," said Adam, and he sliced the reminder of the rope in half with a deft stroke. The rope slid through the banister like a scared snake and went over the side of the terrace. I raced over the side to watch Michael Cherry look up at me in terror as he plunged seventy stories to his death. His piercing scream was a sound that will be with me for the rest of my days. I waited to hear the crash of the body, but from that height all I heard was a slight thud.

Chief Curtis's handheld walkie-talkie soon came to life. "Chief, a man just fell off the building and hit the street. What happened?"

The chief looked at us all with a sad look. He pushed the speak button and said, "It was a jumper. I tried to talk him out of it, but he jumped at the last minute. I'll be down in a second."

"There's not much left of him, sir."

"Let me come down and do the identification," said the chief.

"Who was he?" said the voice.

"Michael Cherry, deputy director of the NSA," said the chief.

"Holy shit, there's a ton of reporters down here. He must have known he was going to do this. Why did he jump?" said the voice.

"He cracked under the pressure of his job," said the chief, who was thinking quickly. "Could happen to any of us."

We all looked at each other in relief but also in shame as if we had done something not quite right.

"This is what we had to do," I said quietly.

"I know," said Kara.

"He had it coming," said Susan.

"But it's best if we never talk about it to anybody," said the chief. "To anybody, understood? Otherwise I have to arrest all of us for murder, me included."

"Understood," said everybody.

"Can I keep the knife?" asked Adam. "I never killed anybody before."

"Sure kid," I said. "But this wasn't a killing. It was an execution."

"Amen," said Gunnery Sergeant Charles Ryan.

CHAPTER 61

Colonel Bob Forrester looked at the 10:00 PM evening news on his flat screen TV panel from his home in Bethesda, Maryland. President Branch's press secretary had made a live announcement on the destruction of a home in Islamabad, Pakistan, thought to contain the terrorist leader Osama bin Laden and his second in command, Ayman al-Zawahiri. DNA tests were being conducted on the remains of the bodies. A camera crew was filming the obliterated rubble that used to be a house. The administration was confident that the bombing raid had been completely successful marking a turn around in the war against terror and Al-Queda. The president would be fielding questions on the raid in a press conference the following day.

In a related story, the administration mourned the tragic suicide of NSA Deputy Director Michael Cherry, who had jumped from the Rockefeller observation center in New York. A short obituary showed all of the accomplishments of Michael Cherry during his career with the government and in business with Holliwell. They stressed the pressure that he was under to protect and safeguard America from terrorism. President Branch called him a "great American hero" and awarded him a purple heart medal posthumously. The entire story on Michael Cherry took fifteen seconds.

Bob Forrester turned off the TV. His hands were shaking as he poured himself a glass of Jack Daniels. It was crystal clear in his mind that he had very few options left open to him. Michael Cherry's death was obviously not a suicide. Whoever had killed Michael Cherry would be coming to expose him next. Kara Murphy's visit to his office had been a harbinger of things to come. An investigation would ruin his reputation and possibly put him in jail for the rest of his life as a traitor. His wife and children would be branded for life and probably forced to leave Washington and return all their Holliwell stock. His name would be synonymous with the worst terrorist attack against the United States on U.S. soil. He couldn't let that happen.

Forrester went to his desk and took out his nine-millimeter revolver. "Honey, I'm going out," he yelled upstairs to his wife.

"Have fun," yelled his wife back to him.

Colonel Bob Forrester walked into his garage and opened the door to the bright blue 1962 Corvette that he had lovingly restored with his own hands. He started up the car and heard the hum of the powerful engine come to life. Then he turned on the radio and put on one of his favorite songs, "Time Is on Our Side" by the Rolling Stones. He placed the muzzle of the nine-millimeter into his mouth and waited for the refrain to end. Then he pulled the trigger. For Colonel Robert Forrester, time had finally run out.

Six thousand miles away from Bethesda, Saudi Prince Bin Abdullah was feeling particularly pleased with himself. He had just signed a ten-year multi-billion-dollar oil agreement with the Chinese government. King Aziz would be very pleased with him and reward him with an annual bonus in the millions. This, together with the bribe he was receiving from the Chinese, would make him one of the richest men in the world. He smiled to himself as the chauffeur opened the door to his Maybach Mercedes limousine. True, he thought, the death of his cousin Osama bin Laden was personally sad to him, but great men had to make sacrifices sometimes. Osama served his purpose admirably, beyond all expectations.

Michael Cherry's death had surprised him, however. He knew that the suicide story was make believe, but couldn't fathom who had wanted Cherry killed. *Probably a turf battle between the CIA and the FBI. Squabbles among Americans. Not a concern of mine*, he thought to himself. Prince Bin Abdullah tapped the window for the chauffeur to drive the big limousine away. The driver put the car in drive, and the limousine left the oil ministry to head onto the busy morning traffic of Riyadh.

Two seconds later, the remote control mechanism placed in the five pounds of plastic explosive attached to chassis of the Maybach detonated into a fireball. A shower of debris, metal, and blood sprayed across the street. Prince Abdullah's head was found 300 meters from the explosion. It was all that was left of him.

The chief security guard of King Aziz bin Saud brought the king the news while he was taking his royal breakfast. The king smiled and said, "Well done, Mohammed. The traitor Abdullah is dead. The terrorists are dead. Now we will retrieve the bribe the Chinese deposited in Abdullah's UBS Swiss bank for our national coffers. It's time for us to look for a new oil minister."

"As you wish, Your Highness," said the security guard to his king.

"Yes, it's as I wish," said the king, wolfing down his morning quail eggs with a cup of thick Turkish coffee as he picked up the *London Times* for what he envisioned was going to be a very good day.

Epilogue

❦

We buried Sandra Baines in her family plot at the Clinton Municipal Cemetery on a cold, windy day in late January. Her body had been flown in from Portland and embalmed by the mortuaries of the Frank Hammond Funeral Home. As we filed in front of the open casket in the church, Sandra looked at peace. At the grave, I stood to the right of my ex-wife. Kara Murphy was with me, too, at my left, holding my hand. Kelly Claire was there with her husband. Even Ali Mahalati and Charles Ryan had shown up to lay some flowers on her tomb. The reverend read a few lines from the Bible. Then Adam got up and spoke. He was dressed in a blue suit and looked much older than his fourteen years.

"You all knew my mom," he said. "She took care of me for fourteen years. She never hurt a soul. If anybody deserves to go to heaven, it's her. I know she will always be there looking out for me." He wiped the tears from his eyes. Everybody cried. "Because of her, a traitor was exposed and our country is a better place. Her death was not in vain." He placed a white rose over the casket. Then he went over to Susan and her parents who embraced him. Her kids hugged him as well. I felt sure that Sandra was watching him join his new family.

We walked away from the ceremony in the stillness of the cemetery. Susan came up to me and Kara and said, "Can I borrow him for a minute?"

"Of course, Susan. Just give him back," said Kara. Susan smiled at her and we walked through the trees.

"I never had a chance to thank you, Dave," said Susan. "You risked your life for Adam and me."

"No need to, Susan. They were family to me as well."

"Are you going to be okay now, Dave?" she asked.

"The mayor and Police Chief Curtis issued a statement saying that I was cleared of any terrorist charges. The *New York Post* carried it on page fifteen underneath the announcement of alternate side parking. I figure I lost a couple of clients I didn't want anyway. But yeah, I'm fine."

"How are you feeling?" Susan said.

"Most of my wounds have healed," I said. "And the cast comes off next week, so I will be good as new."

"That's good, Dave. She's pretty special," Susan said.

"Who?" I asked jokingly.

"You know? Kara. Don't blow this one," Susan said.

"Like I did with you?"

"We were way too young to get married," she said.

"I know. I'm lucky to have found Kara. She's moving back to Washington. The FBI have put her back in charge of the counter-terrorism department on the recommendation of Colonel Summers of the Pentagon."

"She deserves all of it," said Susan.

"I know. I guess I'll have to commute on weekends to Washington. I am lucky to have found her," I said.

"And she's lucky to have found you, too," said my ex wife, kissing me on my cheek. "Thanks for everything, Dave. We all love you."

The word love and a kiss from a woman I still loved and respected made my heart skip a beat. But I knew that despite all the love we felt for each other, Susan and I could not share our lives together.

I went up to Kara and grabbed her hand. "Feeling hungry?" I asked.

"After a funeral?"

"Kara, funerals and cemeteries are for the living. Sandra is in heaven now. Let's go get some pancakes, eggs, and bacon at a roadhouse I know just a few exits down on the New Jersey Turnpike."

"Dave Stillati, you are incorrigible," said Kara, walking with me to my car.

"I guess you will expect me to fly to Washington every weekend now," I said to her.

"At the very least," Kara said. "What about moving your office to D.C.? You could work your sports business out of anywhere."

"Me leave New York?" I asked. "Now if you had spent any time at all with me, you would know that that is an impossibility."

"I plan on spending a lot of time getting to know you, Dave," Kara said.

"That's works just fine with me, too," I said, kissing her on her lips.

"So, what are we doing this weekend?" asked Kara.

"Anything you want, darling. But first I have to fulfill a promise I made to the man who introduced us, Mehmet Hadji."

"What promise did you make to Mehmet?" she asked.

"You'll see," I said trying my best to be mysterious. "I always keep my promises."

"That's what I like about you," said Kara.

We got into my ice blue Mustang and drove away from the Clinton Cemetery toward the New Jersey Turnpike. In my rearview mirror, I caught a last glimpse of young Adam as he was getting into the car with Susan and her kids. He looked happy enough. I felt certain now that he was finally in the best of hands. He was a man now. Kara and I drove through the Lincoln Tunnel into New York City.

On the following day, Friday afternoon, at 1:00 PM, I met with Mehmet Hadji at the mosque on 96th Street and 3rd Avenue. It is the biggest and most visited mosque in New York City. Thousands of Muslims worship there every Friday, enjoying the great freedom and diversity that New York City offers above all else. The Iman lead me first to the Wadu where I washed my hands, arms, face, mouth, and ears before leading the congregation in the Juma'a Khutbah, or Friday prayer, to accept the words of the prophet. I'm sure I was the first non-Muslim to lead the congregation in an English prayer, but Mehmet Hadji got great satisfaction organizing this for me with his Imam. I knew I owed it to him for the help he had given me in finding both Kara Murphy and Ali Mahalati. Besides we had made a deal about my participating in his Friday night prayer service. Both the Iman and Mehmet Hadji beamed at me as I was reading my lines, leading the congregation in prayer. I felt strangely nervous like I was a young boy doing his Christening or a thirteen-year-old completing his Bar Mitzvah. After the ceremony, members of the congregation congratulated me in Arabic thinking I understood.

"How do you feel?" said Hadji after the service was over and we were walking out into the street.

"The same, but cleaner," I said.

"Holier, you mean. Better," said Mehmet.

"No. Mostly cleaner," I said trying to give him a dig.

"Mehmet!" said Kara, who was waiting out on the sidewalk. "What are you trying to do to Dave? First you get us together. Then you take Dave here to a mosque to lead services. What's next?"

"I'm trying to make him a better person," he said.

"Do you think that's possible?" asked Kara grabbing my hand.

"Praise Allah. Miracles can always happen," said Mehmet as he watched me walk away into the street with Kara. "Even in a tough world like ours, miracles can always happen."

The End.

978-0-595-39128-8
0-595-39128-1

www.ingramcontent.com/pod-product-compliance
Lightning Source LLC
LaVergne TN
LVHW090432271224
799989LV00006B/64